SCOUNDREL
OF MY
HEART

By Lorraine Heath

SCOUNDREL OF MY HEART
BEAUTY TEMPTS THE BEAST
THE EARL TAKES A FANCY
THE DUCHESS IN HIS BED
THE SCOUNDREL IN HER BED
TEXAS LEGACY (novella)
WHEN A DUKE LOVES A WOMAN
BEYOND SCANDAL AND DESIRE
GENTLEMEN PREFER HEIRESSES (novella)
AN AFFAIR WITH A NOTORIOUS HEIRESS
WHEN THE MARQUESS FALLS (novella)
THE VISCOUNT AND THE VIXEN
THE EARL TAKES ALL
FALLING INTO BED WITH A DUKE
THE DUKE AND THE LADY IN RED
THE LAST WICKED SCOUNDREL (novella)
ONCE MORE, MY DARLING ROGUE
THE GUNSLINGER (novella)
WHEN THE DUKE WAS WICKED
DECK THE HALLS WITH LOVE (novella)
LORD OF WICKED INTENTIONS
LORD OF TEMPTATION
SHE TEMPTS THE DUKE
WAKING UP WITH THE DUKE
PLEASURES OF A NOTORIOUS GENTLEMAN
PASSIONS OF A WICKED EARL
MIDNIGHT PLEASURES WITH A SCOUNDREL
SURRENDER TO THE DEVIL • BETWEEN THE DEVIL AND DESIRE
IN BED WITH THE DEVIL • JUST WICKED ENOUGH
A DUKE OF HER OWN • PROMISE ME FOREVER
A MATTER OF TEMPTATION • AS AN EARL DESIRES
AN INVITATION TO SEDUCTION
LOVE WITH A SCANDALOUS LORD
TO MARRY AN HEIRESS
THE OUTLAW AND THE LADY
NEVER MARRY A COWBOY
NEVER LOVE A COWBOY
A ROGUE IN TEXAS
TEXAS SPLENDOR
TEXAS GLORY
TEXAS DESTINY
ALWAYS TO REMEMBER
PARTING GIFTS
SWEET LULLABY

SCOUNDREL
OF MY
HEART

A ONCE UPON A DUKEDOM NOVEL

LORRAINE HEATH

AVONBOOKS

An Imprint of HarperCollins*Publishers*

First Avon Books mass market printing: April 2021
First Avon Books hardcover printing: March 2021

Print Edition ISBN: 978-0-06-305933-7
Digital Edition ISBN: 978-0-06-295197-7

FIRST EDITION

21 22 23 24 25   LSC   10 9 8 7 6 5 4 3 2 1

With love to my dear friend, Nancy Haddock,
who taught me the joy to be found
in dancing on the beach

And in memory of Jerry Haddock,
a gentle giant among men,
who always made me feel welcome

Chapter 1

"*I* SAY, THIS IS a marvelous opportunity for one of us to snag herself a duke."

The raspy voice—like fine sandpaper massaged over velvet, a bit of roughness against tantalizing softness—forced Lord Griffith Stanwick to come awake with a jolt of pure physical want that nearly made him groan as his cock responded with a need that would go unsatisfied that morning. Not that he had a particular interest in bedding this particular woman.

On the best of days, he found Lady Kathryn Lambert's optimistic presence deuced irritating, but at this precise minute her wretched cheerfulness was particularly annoying because tiny hammers were bombarding his skull, his stomach was roiling, and he was striving to remember how he had come to be lying facedown in the dirt behind the hedgerows near the terrace where his sister was no doubt enjoying a morning repast with her dear friend, who had been residing with them for a fortnight now, while her parents toured Italy. Obviously too much scotch the night before was partially responsible for his unwelcomed state, but he was no stranger to inebriation and had never before ended up where he didn't want to be. What else had he gotten up to that had led him to a garden bed rather than a more enticing one with sheets?

"But surely the duke is in want of a debutante," a sterner voice suggested. Lady Jocelyn, another friend to his sister, was equally irritating. Apparently, she had decided to join them at this ungodly hour, whatever it was. When the trio was together, gossip flowed, and silence was not to be found. Right now, he dearly craved silence. "Closing in on four and twenty, we're nearly on the shelf. We'd be lucky to attract a spare."

"Not a spare. Never a spare," Lady Kathryn insisted. "That would not work for me at all."

It wasn't the first time he'd overheard her make such a claim in a tone that implied to find herself shackled with a spare would be the equivalent of encasing herself in horse manure. In spite of his foggy mind, the words stung. Capturing the heart of a second son was not the worst circumstance that could befall a woman. He knew dukes whose breath could knock a man over at twenty paces, marquesses whose laugh resembled a mule's bray, earls with hands as soft as porridge, and viscounts with boils. Although considering his present state, he had to acknowledge that he might not be the best one to cast stones.

Besides, he was well aware that Lady Kathryn was not alone in her distaste for those never destined to inherit. It was one of the reasons that at seven and twenty, he had yet to do any serious wooing. Another reason was that as the spare, he was not required to provide an heir. And he enjoyed bachelorhood. No responsibilities. A modest allowance. An abundance of spirits, wagering, and women of questionable moral character at his disposal. Every night was bursting with escapades, although the mornings were beginning to become quite tedious. It wasn't bad when he awoke next to a warm, willing adventuress, but of late, if he was honest, he was growing a bit bored with them as well. Not so bored, however, that he preferred awakening among the hedgerows.

How the bloody hell had he ended his night here?

"As Cupid's arrow has struck true in my case," Althea announced with calm determination and a bit of glee at her recent good fortune, "I cannot help but believe, dearest friends, that you both will join me in betrothal bliss before this Season's end."

"Chadbourne is one fortunate fellow," Lady Kathryn said. "All of London knows you've completely won him over, and he will make a marvelous husband. He is besotted with you. Absolutely besotted."

He imagined his sister, blushing and smiling at the mention of the earl. Althea was equally besotted with the gentleman she was to marry in January.

"As I said, like me, you will soon receive offers. I'm positively certain of it. And here is the perfect opportunity to put my prediction to the test."

"But is this the best way to go about it?" Lady Jocelyn asked. "To write a letter to the duke outlining why he should choose me over all others? It seems rather forward."

"The Duke of Kingsland is an extremely busy man, overseeing his vast estates and increasing his fortune, by all accounts," Lady Kathryn said. "He doesn't have time to court one woman after another until he finds one who might be suitable. I think he's brilliant to come up with this strategy."

The Duke of Kingsland, the most eligible and sought-after bachelor among the *ton*. The man avoided the social scene, stayed in London only long enough to see to his duties in the House of Lords, and never lost at games of chance. As far as Griffith knew, the duke had few close friends. He wielded wealth, power, and influence in equal measure thanks to a title that had carried weight for generations. Which might explain the advert he'd placed in the *Times* encouraging the daughters of peers to write him explaining why he should consider them as a potential duchess. Audition for him through the post. He would announce his selection at a ball he was hosting the last evening in June, would court her the remainder of the Season, and if he found her to be as appealing as her letter indicated, he would marry her before the end of the next Season.

Neat and tidy and so deuced boring. Griffith preferred to experience that first unexpected hint of allure, of interest, and then to explore the potential in a slow, seductive unraveling that revealed commonalities, differences, and secrets. He liked discovering how everything came together to make a woman intriguing. Some things he discovered before he bedded her, some things during, some things after. But always he enjoyed uncovering the various parts that created the whole. Even if, when the whole took shape, he lost interest, he still relished the journey. For him, it was always about savoring the discoveries, appreciating each nuance as though it was a fine wine he'd never before tasted.

"I'm not certain it's brilliant," Lady Jocelyn said. It wasn't. It was damned lazy. It was an injustice to the woman, reduced her to a list of attributes, as though she was no more important than cattle. Besides, could a woman even know herself well enough to understand what any particular man might fancy about her? "But I suppose there is no harm in writing him. It's not as though I have suitors falling at my feet."

"Jolly good! I've always found competition encourages us to call to our better selves," Lady Kathryn exclaimed heartily, causing insidious pain to travel through Griffith's ears and brain. He couldn't hold back his groan of discomfort.

"What the deuce was that?" his sister asked, and he wished he could curl into a minuscule ball or scooch his way around to the side of the house, but any movement at all was bound to elicit an objection from his aching head and increase the severity of the pounding in his skull. Best to merely lie still and hope the ladies simply went on about their business.

He heard the rustle of leaves and the snap of a twig. Apparently hope was not the best of strategies.

"Griff? What the devil are you doing sprawled out over the ground back there?"

Squinting—was the morning sun always this bright?—he peered up at Althea. "To be honest, I'm not quite sure, but it does appear I got turned about returning home last night." For some inexplicable reason he'd not used the front door. Perhaps he'd been unable, with clumsy fingers, to grasp the key nestled in his waistcoat pocket. Although, patting said pocket now, he found it empty. Had he misplaced the bit of brass?

"You were well in your cups again, weren't you?"

"I do seem to recall some celebrating going on." For a while the games had favored him . . . until they hadn't. What was a man supposed to do when fortune slipped away except seek solace in drink?

"Well, stir yourself and come out of there," she ordered briskly, as though she wasn't three years his junior but was instead his elder.

With a great deal of effort, he shoved himself to his feet, pressed his back to the brick, and crept out through the narrow space between wall and foliage, trying to avoid getting snagged by the sharp-edged leaves of the hedges. When he reached his sister, she scrunched up her entire face. "You smell like a distillery."

"How do you know how a distillery smells?" Looking past her to the two ladies sitting at the white linen-covered round table, he forced his most charming grin to form, a smile he didn't feel like granting, not only because of the increased ache in his head but because of what he'd overheard. "Ladies, how are you this fine morning?"

"I daresay better than you," Lady Kathryn retorted, using the tone she seemed to reserve only for him.

"Here," Althea said, reaching quickly for the teapot. "Have a spot of tea. You look as though you could use it."

Tea was nowhere on the list of things he could use. A hot bath—he did indeed smell like a distillery, along with a cheroot factory—a shave, and the blackest coffee would serve him better. If the other ladies hadn't been staring at him with twin expressions of disgust, he might have made his excuses and headed straight to his most urgent need: a soft bed. But knowing he'd take some perverse delight in irritating them by delaying his escape and joining them, he dragged back a chair, dropped into it, and took the offered cup and saucer. "You are indeed kind, dear sister."

It was so like her, looking out for others. He really didn't deserve to have a sister so generous of spirit. Peering through the steam rising from the brew, he took a long, slow swallow. She'd laced it with an abundance of sugar, and his body reacted with gratitude, the ache behind his eyes dissipating a fraction so the day seemed at least survivable.

Lady Kathryn looked on disapprovingly, a tightness to her mouth, and he wouldn't have been surprised if she'd announced, "You're better than this."

Only he wasn't. Precisely because of what she had voiced earlier. No one wanted the spare. Not the ladies of the *ton*. Not his father. Not his mother. Even the heir, two years older than he was, had little time for him. But scotch, cards, and actresses seldom turned him away.

"Perhaps your brother's presence here is fortuitous," Lady Jocelyn said. "You no doubt overheard what we were discussing."

"I apologize, ladies, as it was not my intention to eavesdrop, but you did manage to garner my undivided attention with your dulcet tones."

While Lady Kathryn fairly glowered, signaling she'd caught the sarcasm in his tone, Lady Jocelyn smiled as though he'd handed her one of the Crown Jewels. She'd never struck him as being particularly cognizant of subtleties. "Then perhaps you would be good enough to share with us how we might impress upon the duke that we are worth considering for courtship."

"How would he know what a duke wants?" Lady Kathryn asked.

He allowed a corner of his mouth to ease up provocatively, sensually. "A duke wants what any man wants. A woman who is a saint in society and a wild wanton in the bedchamber."

Her hazel eyes narrowed until they resembled the finely honed blade of a dagger. She riled so easily, and for some inexplicable reason, he'd always taken great delight in pricking her temper. "That is hardly helpful," she snapped.

"But 'tis true."

"We are genteel ladies of good breeding, and as such, we've hardly been bedded so can offer no insight into our capabilities beneath the sheets, as it were." He imagined her beneath the sheets, with him stirring her until she fully comprehended her capacity for pleasure. As his body began to respond to the images, he shoved them back. Whatever was wrong with him to even contemplate an intimacy with her? "Besides, it is for our husband to tell us what he wants regarding that particular aspect of our marriage."

"Why?" he asked, truly befuddled. "Why should he be the only one to have a say? Surely, Freckles, you've given some thought to what you might enjoy."

"I have not," she countered testily.

"'The lady doth protest too much, methinks.'"

"Don't be absurd. Ladies do not sully their minds by thinking carnal thoughts."

"If you've never thought them, how do you know they'd sully your mind?"

"You're being preposterously difficult."

"No, I'm actually curious as to what you envision happens between a man and a woman that would be so lurid as to tarnish an otherwise pristine brain if pondered or mulled over."

She looked as though she'd like to toss her tea on him. "You know well enough."

Her voice had gone lower, more gravelly, causing his belly to tighten. "Caresses along bare skin, the nip of a collarbone, a squeeze here, a rub there? Kisses along curves, hollows, and dips? How is any of that sordid?"

Her lips had slowly parted, and her cheeks had deepened from an enticing rose into a lovely crimson. He wondered if, like him, she was now imagining his bare hand, fingers splayed, on her bare thigh, slipping up toward that heavenly apex where paradise waited, previously untouched and unexplored. Christ. What the devil was wrong with him? She was the very last woman he had any interest in bedding. It didn't matter that her coppery hair turned the shade of fire when lit by the sun, and that he had, on occasion and much to his chagrin, wondered if it would be as hot to the touch, if it would spark pleasure. It didn't matter that her fragrance was more spicy than sweet, and he'd always enjoyed foods with a great deal of seasoning. It didn't matter that her lips were more pink than red, and on the rare occasion he painted, he preferred the subtle allure of pastels.

"Griff, I'm not quite certain this is an appropriate topic of discussion considering the company," Althea remarked hesitantly.

"But that is my point." He did hope they'd attribute the croak of his voice to his having recently been pulled from slumber and not the fact that his mouth had suddenly gone as arid as a desert. "It shouldn't be taboo. Men are allowed to think about it, discuss it, experience it—without benefit of marriage. Why shouldn't women?"

A series of gasps met that pronouncement. He shook his head. "Even if a woman is not to *experience* it without marriage"— although he didn't agree with that belief—"she should at least be able to think about it and discuss it without shame, without fearing she has mired her mind."

He gave his attention back to Lady Kathryn. "You *never* think about it?"

"I do not."

"Then, how can you know what you want, what you might enjoy?"

"As I stated earlier, it is for my husband to show me."

"You have never struck me as a woman without an opinion on any matter." He leaned forward. "I would wager a month's allowance that you have thought about it, and quite thoroughly."

That her nostrils flared and her breaths seemed to slow only served to tighten his belly more. What images did she conjure in that mind of hers?

"Griff, I do believe you have just called our guest a liar," Althea said, her upset evident in her tone.

Because she was. Not that he was going to call her on it again, but damned if he didn't want to uncover her fantasies. "My apologies. It seems I am not yet fit for company as my indulgences from last night are still having their way with me." He shoved back his chair and stood. Then he turned his attention to Lady Jocelyn, who had first posed the question, because studying Lady Kathryn was beginning to make him feel light-headed as blood wanted to rush where it shouldn't. "Write to the duke of your comely features, mastery of etiquette, interests, and accomplishments."

"Thank you, my lord."

He offered her a small smile. "And may the best lady win."

With that, he left them and strode into the residence, knowing the hot bath he'd craved earlier would have to wait. Lady Kathryn might not allow thoughts to sully her mind, but now his was filled with a sordid display of her body writhing against his that required he plunge into a bitingly cold tub of water first.

SITTING IN THE front parlor, the escritoire on her lap, almost forgotten, Kathryn cursed Lord Griffith Stanwick for the hundredth time. His words had put salacious thoughts in her head that she could not seem to be rid of. Hands gliding over her bared shoulders and lower, to places they ought not. Blast him!

Then, to insinuate that she'd been lying when she'd claimed not to have ever had improper musings—the cur. Of course, she had, but it had been bad form on his part to insist she confess it. A lady of genteel breeding should not harbor lurid reflections and most certainly should not admit to it, especially when they often involved her dearest friend's obnoxious brother doing terribly wicked things to her, running a finger over her décolletage where silk met flesh or kissing the inside of her wrist where she always put a dab of perfume just in case. She cursed him again.

To make matters worse, he'd used that awful moniker he'd bestowed upon her when she'd met him at the age of twelve, Freckles. Ghastly name, that. The brown spots had always been the bane of her existence. Wearing bonnets that she loathed and rubbing all sorts of magical creams on her face had caused the spots to fade, but the barest of shadows remained, which gave her a rather blotchy appearance when she blushed. Which for some reason Lord Griffith Stanwick caused to happen with regular frequency whenever he was near.

Since she was presently staying with her dearest friend, Lady Althea, crossing paths with Griff—as his sister called him and Kathryn secretly did as well—had become a regular part of her day . . . and sometimes her night.

She fought not to give in to guilt because she was the one responsible for his having awakened near the hedgerows. Having difficulty sleeping the evening before, she'd been on her way to the library to fetch a book and had just reached the foyer, when she spotted the front door opening. Then he had stumbled in, only a fraction, enough to press himself against the jamb without releasing his hold on the latch. His disheveled state had been appalling. His neckcloth was unknotted and his hat missing. His hair stood at odd angles as though a dozen women had run their fingers through it, which they no doubt had. When his gaze landed on her, one corner of his mouth had hitched up. "Hello, Freckles."

She'd hated seeing him in such disarray, behaving like her Uncle George—her father's brother. The man drank too much, played rather than worked, and constantly came to her father because he was in need of funds to support his gambling habits. He argued that he was owed because her father had inherited the titles and estates while he'd been left with nothing. Although, eventually he would inherit because her father had no son with whom to leave everything. It hadn't helped her opinion regarding Uncle George when his own mother was so disappointed in him. "Never marry a second son," her grandmother had advised her numerous times when he'd shown up at a family function three sheets to the wind. He cared about only himself, no one else. Not his wife or his own son, who had taken after him in every regard, even going so far as to hold out his hand to her father. "It'll all be mine eventually. Might as well give me a bit now."

And it seemed Lord Griffith Stanwick was cut of the same cloth. She shouldn't care, but she did, damn him. Although for the life of her, she couldn't figure out why. But she just wanted him to be better than he was. Therefore, last night when the opportunity had presented itself, she'd decided to bring him some misery and had hurried over to him.

"I hear your father coming. He mustn't see you in this state. Go round to the back. I'll let you in there." His father hadn't been coming. The duke wasn't even at home. He spent more nights away from the residence than he spent in it. It was a well-known secret that he had a mistress and preferred her company to that of his duchess.

But Griff, in his inebriated state, hadn't the presence of mind to question her lie, had steadfastly believed her, and had made haste to exit through the door he'd just entered. She'd pocketed his key from where he'd left it in the keyhole, shut the door, and locked it. After scurrying to the servants' entrance, she made certain that door was locked as well. In delight, she had stood there listening as the daft lord knocked and knocked and knocked.

Then he'd called for her. "Freckles! Come on, Freckles, open the door. Be a good girl."

Only she hadn't wanted to be a good girl. Had wanted him to stop calling her that ridiculous name, had wanted him to be different from the two men who were causing such heartache for her family.

Finally, all had gone quiet. After she'd gathered enough courage to open the door and peer out, the lord was nowhere to be seen. A momentary panic struck her until she heard him singing some ditty about a woman with bowlegs. She'd watched his silhouette weaving through the garden until he finally disappeared behind the hedgerows. All had gone silent for a couple of minutes before she'd heard the snores and decided he deserved the uncomfortable bed.

Although now, she felt badly about it because she had determined that afternoon to ask a favor of him. But finding any time alone with him in order to broach the subject of her request had proven impossible, which was part of the reason Kathryn had sought solitude in the front parlor while Althea and her mother had adjourned to the duchess's favorite drawing room for a bit of tea following dinner.

Kathryn had eaten numerous times with the family, but only tonight had she noticed that the duke, sitting at the head of the table, only addressed his elder son, Marcus, who sat to his right. Never the younger who sat to his left.

Although she had been on the other side of Griff, as only six of them were at the table—the duchess at its foot and Althea across from Kathryn—she'd hardly been able to carry on a quiet conversation with him. To look at him, no one would have guessed how he'd begun his morning. He smelled decadent, a combination of bay rum and a fragrance that was uniquely him, like the earthy scent of autumn when leaves turned. His hair was perfectly styled, not a single finger had gone through it yet. As though he was accustomed to being ignored, his focus seemed to center on one of two things: either his plate or his wineglass.

A couple of times the duke asked questions of Althea. Once he asked Kathryn if she'd heard from her parents since they'd arrived in Italy. She'd answered that she had and that they were well. The duke had then regaled them with an account of his last trip to Rome. He seemed to prefer speaking to listening.

Her parents would arrive at their London residence tomorrow evening, and Kathryn would return to them the following morning. Not that she would find dinners any more comfortable. Her parents were striving to rekindle their affection for each other, almost to the exclusion of anyone else. Hence the trip. Neither of them had ever been good at expressing their emotions. But Kathryn had received all the love she'd craved from her grandmother. Her best memories came from the days she'd spent with the dear woman at her cottage by the sea. She wondered if Griff had someplace that had brought him comfort, not that she was particularly happy about empathizing with him, felt a tad guilty about her desire to use him, but one must do what one must to gain what one wanted.

She was rather certain he'd be leaving again tonight, because he had every night since her arrival. Hence she was in the front parlor with her escritoire in her lap as she made a list of her best qualities. Or tried to. So far she'd written only *Skilled at whist*. Lady Jocelyn had the right of it. It seemed rather pompous to brag about oneself, although she had no doubt her friend would rise to the challenge of listing her own good qualities, suspected she'd take up sheaves and sheaves of foolscap, laying them all out. She'd never possessed Jocelyn's confidence, found it most irritating on occasion, which was part of the reason she'd always felt closer to Althea.

But it was imperative that she catch the duke's favor. She had a rather substantial dowry, and it included the cottage in which her grandmother had lived out her later years and died. It would be placed in a trust so it would remain in Kathryn's care to be used as her dower house, while the remainder of her dowry would transfer to her husband. But she didn't care about the remainder of her dowry. She cared only about the beloved cottage. However, in order to gain it, she must marry a peer. Because her wastrel uncle would inherit, and later her cousin, her grandmother had wanted to ensure she was well cared for, as she hadn't believed she could rely on the future earl to see to the needs of her beloved granddaughter. Her grandmother had believed only a man with a title could offer Kathryn the life she deserved. However, with each passing year since her first

Season, the prospect of meeting that marker and obtaining the one thing she treasured most had dimmed.

Kingsland was perfect. She'd met him once. She could do without his pompousness, but then, most dukes possessed that trait. They were dukes, after all. She would be a dutiful wife, provide him with an heir and a spare, and when he tired of her, she would find her solace in the cottage. With it and the memories of the love her grandmother had showered on her, she could weather anything.

She heard the heavy tread of footsteps on the marble stairs. Since the duke and his heir had left earlier, she knew it had to be Griff. Setting aside her writing desk, she rose to her feet, shook out her skirts, and glided over to the doorway.

He was wearing the fine dark blue coat and silver waistcoat he'd worn to dinner. In his hand, he held his tall beaver hat. The sight of him caused her heart to give a little stutter in her chest as it normally did when she first caught a glimpse of him. But it was only because they were always at odds and she was bracing for the encounter. It had nothing at all to do with the fact that over the years, he'd grown into quite the handsome specimen.

He'd obviously not spotted her because he'd almost reached the door. On the verge of missing her opportunity, a panic nearly set in. Quickly she held up the brass. "My lord, I believe I may have found your key."

He came to an abrupt halt, and his gaze slowly traveled the length of her. She was grateful the pale green gown flattered her and softened her coloring.

He took several steps toward her, and she didn't know why it felt as though her corset was being tugged tighter as he came nearer until she could see his eyes more clearly. She'd always thought them beautiful. A deep blue with the tiniest streaks of gray.

"Where did you find it?" he asked.

"On the front drive. I enjoyed a walk earlier in the afternoon and spotted it, just lying there."

"Interesting." As he had yet to put on his gloves, his fingers grazed over hers as he took her offering, and a strange sort of warmth traveled not only along her arm but through all her limbs. "I searched the drive after I left you in the garden and had no luck finding it."

Drat it. Her lie was on the cusp of being found out. "You must admit you were not in your finest form this morning. Perhaps your eyesight was affected."

His gaze captured hers. "Do you find that I have a fine form, Lady Kathryn?"

He'd lowered his voice and drawn out his words as though they were sharing a delicious secret. She wanted to give one of her usual retorts, although now she was noticing things about him that she hadn't before. When had his shoulders broadened so? When had he begun to fill out his clothing so nicely? From all appearances, he looked quite toned, and she wondered if he engaged in any sports. He was her dear friend's brother, and yet she knew so little about the specifics of him, really.

Still, she ignored his question, instead saying, "I assume you're on your way to a gaming hell or gentleman's club."

"As the *spare*, what else am I expected to do?"

She did not miss the sarcasm in his tone. He no doubt took exception to what he'd overheard that morning. She wasn't against all spares, merely the reprobate ones, the ones like her uncle and cousin—unfortunately a category into which Griff fell. "Join the army, become a vicar, seek a position as a member of Parliament."

"You can't truly see me engaged in any of those occupations, surely."

"Do you intend to be just a gentleman of leisure all of your life?" Why had she asked that? Why was she prolonging this encounter?

Something—almost a longing—flashed in his eyes before he stepped back. "More like a scoundrel, I should think. Thank you for the key." With a wink, he tucked it into the pocket of his waistcoat and turned to leave.

"You haven't a pocket watch or fob."

His attention was back on her, and she wondered why she'd only now noticed his lack of accessory and had bothered to ask about it. Why was he suddenly rousing her curiosity?

"No. When Marcus reached his majority, Father handed him the one that his father had passed on to him. I thought he might purchase one for me when I reached my majority, but as that is six years past, I suppose I should see about purchasing my own."

"What did he give you when you reached your majority?"

"Nothing, as I recall."

The words came out even and flat, as though he harbored no emotion regarding them, but how could he have not been disappointed? "I'm so terribly sorry."

An emotion now sparked in those blue-gray eyes. Anger, embarrassment, irritation. "I don't require your pity. If you'll excuse me, I must away. Lady Luck and other ladies await my arrival."

Once more he made to leave—

"Is it likely that you might cross paths with the Duke of Kingsland this evening?"

This time when he faced her, his eyes were narrowed and his jaw taut. "It's possible. We frequent the same club."

Licking her lips, she clasped her hands together and took a step toward him. "Would you do me the kind service of asking him precisely what he is looking for in a wife?"

He gave his head a quick shake. "The duke is an utter arse. He hasn't the ability to care for anyone save himself. You would be miserable married to him."

As though he would care about her misery. In truth, she suspected he'd wish it upon her. "Please, I have my reasons for wanting to be the one he seeks to court."

"To beat Lady Jocelyn?"

She offered a wan smile. "Partly. But I have other reasons that are more personal."

"Will you pen falsehoods in your letter or change yourself to be what he wants?"

"I will not lie when I write to him, but I can be certain to emphasize the qualities I might possess that he hopes to find."

He sighed deeply. "If I have occasion to do so, I will make inquiries of him. But I will not inconvenience myself or ruin my evening to help you with this ridiculous endeavor."

"Thank you, my lord. I appreciate your generosity of spirit."

"The day you appreciate anything about me, Lady Kathryn, will be the day hell freezes over."

Her smile turned a bit more teasing. "I suppose you have a point. And, pray tell, I do hope you won't drink so much that you are unable to remember what he conveys to you."

"Why would you think drinking to excess would cause me to forget something?"

Had he no recollection regarding where he'd awoken that morning? "I heard you tell Althea that you didn't recall how you came to be sleeping behind the hedgerows."

"Ah, that. The memory loss is only temporary. The details will eventually come back to me."

She couldn't have stiffened more if he'd dropped her into a vat of cold water. Dear God, she hoped he had the wrong of it there.

"Good night, Freckles." Settling his hat in place, he headed for the door.

Oh, the daft man. "Have you not noticed that I no longer have freckles?"

Opening the door, he stepped through it before turning back to her, his grin the sort that would cause a lady comprised of a weaker constitution to swoon. "But I can still recall where they once were."

Then he disappeared, making her regret that she'd returned his key to him, that she'd asked a favor of him . . . that she enjoyed their sparring perhaps a little too much.

CHAPTER 2

$\mathcal{A}$S THE CARRIAGE he'd called for earlier rumbled through the streets, Griff pulled from his waistcoat pocket the key she'd handed him and imagined he could still feel the warmth from her fingers being wrapped around it. It was quite possible that her taking a later stroll, when the afternoon sunlight might have glinted off it, had caused her to find it when he couldn't earlier. It was also possible something a bit more nefarious was afoot.

Flashing through his mind were images of her in a night wrapper at the door. Had she been responsible for sending him around to the back, for his ending up in the hedgerows? He wouldn't put it past the little vixen.

As for her freckles, of course he'd noticed they were no longer there. He noticed everything about her. He always had, and it had always been deuced irritating. The way the red in her hair looked almost brown in the shadows but competed for brilliance with bright sunlight. The way the end of her nose tipped up slightly as though it were straining toward a kiss. The manner in which her auburn brows would furrow when she was worried. The way her lips curling up into a smile would mesmerize. That her mouth was designed to provide the perfect haven for a man's, and he'd awoken too many times with an aching cock because it had dominated his dreams.

It was one of the reasons he chose to torment her and keep that mouth set in a mulish expression, although even then it taunted him. But his actions ensured she kept her distance. He'd always known he wasn't the sort she'd ever fancy nor was he the sort she deserved. He was an afterthought, the one held in reserve, hopefully never to be needed. She, on the other hand, was destined for a more prestigious lord, a peer. A duke.

But did she have to ask him to help her gain the blasted noble?

The carriage came to a stop, and he leapt out before a footman could appear to assist. "Thank you, James," he called up to the driver. "You can go on. I'll make my way home when I'm done." After making his way to his favorite club.

"Yes, m'lord."

When the carriage rattling over the cobblestones disappeared into the traffic, Griff leaned against a lamppost and studied the three story brick building across the street. Not a single light appeared within. It was completely shuttered, abandoned, and neglected. The affinity he felt for the place was ridiculous, but he wanted it with a desperation that sometimes caused him to make foolish decisions, to wager recklessly in his hurry to gain it. It was for sale, but he didn't yet have the funds to purchase it.

But he had plans for it. He wanted to restore it to its former grandeur and turn it into a club whose membership would be denied to the firstborn sons in line for a title. It would be for the spares and their younger brothers and the young men with wealth who were not welcomed among the *ton*. It would be for the wallflowers, the spinsters, and the young ladies who were overlooked because of family scandal. It would be a place for the misfits of Society—or those who *should* be in Society—to meet, visit, dine, drink, and engage in forbidden pleasures. But first he had to gain the means to make it all happen.

With purpose to his stride, he began walking, his destination Dodger's Drawing Room. He had money in his pocket, twenty-five pounds in gambling blunt, all that remained from this month's allowance. When it was gone, his wagering for the month would be over. He never borrowed, never asked for credit. Too easy to fall into the trap of thinking it could be paid back with the turn of a card or the spin of a wheel. He either won with what he had on hand or he lost. The night before, he'd won two hundred quid at the gaming tables, then promptly lost it when he'd gotten greedy and bet it all on one spin of the roulette wheel. He'd furthered his stupidity by then turning heavily to drink in an effort to ease the disappointment. Instead, he'd merely ensured a rather rough start to his day. But that was behind him, and it was time to begin anew. Tonight he needed to win.

Griff didn't favor four-card brag, but here he sat at the table because it was the blasted Duke of Kingsland's preferred game. He would rather have gathered some winnings elsewhere first, but as he'd spotted the duke shortly after coming into the club and a chair had been available at the table, he'd decided to get the unpleasant task done with.

At great inconvenience to himself. Perhaps he should insist on a favor from Lady Kathryn. He would have to give some thought to what she could possibly give him that would be comparable in value to this irritation.

The ante was called for, chips were tossed into the pot, and cards were dealt. After studying his, Griff discarded the one he didn't wish to keep. He cleared his throat. "So, Your Grace,"—as Kingsland was the only duke at the table, he didn't have to clarify—"I saw your advert in the *Times*. What precisely are you looking for in a wife?"

"Quiet."

The word was spoken brusquely, dismissively, and Griff decided he was going to remain in the game until he'd taken every farthing Kingsland had. He was not a child to be told how to behave, to be seen and not heard. When he was done with him, the duke was going to regret his insufferable attitude.

After casting aside a card, Kingsland turned his attention to Griff and practically skewered him with a pointed look designed to intimidate, which he had no doubt practiced since birth. But it had little impact on Griff because he'd weathered the same stare from his father more times than he could count.

"I want quiet in a wife. One who will not disturb me when I am concentrating on important matters. One who rarely speaks but knows when it is important to do so."

"You are familiar with women, are you not?" Griff's comment was quickly followed by several chuckles from the other four gents gathered at the table.

"I am intimately familiar with women," the duke said.

"Then you are aware that asking a woman not to talk is like asking the sun not to shine. Besides, why seek silence when you could have pleasant conversation?"

"It's not as though you have to actually listen to the words," one of the gents said, grinning broadly. "The softness of her voice is usually enough for me."

The duke's gaze landed on the viscount with an almost audible slap.

"Silence is good," the poor fellow sputtered. "I like silence."

"Perhaps you should practice it," Kingsland suggested in a silky voice.

"Yes, Your Grace." The lord began concentrating on his cards as though he feared they might fly away if not shackled by his attention.

The duke's focus returned to bear on Griff. "You're the Duke of Wolfford's spare, are you not?"

"I am."

"You have a sister, as I recall."

"I do."

"Is it her intent to send me a letter?"

Griff scoffed in a manner to imply he considered her fortunate to not have to seek the duke's attention and favorable regard via post. "Hardly. She has captured the attention of the Earl of Chad-bourne."

"Ah, yes, I saw an announcement about their betrothal in the *Times*. Why, then, do you care what qualities I am seeking in a wife?"

"Mere curiosity, I assure you. You've taken a novel approach to courtship, and I wondered why normal methods weren't to your liking. I thought perhaps you were searching for something rare."

"I find the accepted avenue of courtship tedious and a waste of precious time. Why spend hours in a ballroom, suffering through one introduction after another, one dance after another, when I can simply read the attributes as I might a business venture I am considering for investment? Quicker, tidier, more efficient."

"You view a wife as an investment?"

"Absolutely. Are *you* not familiar with women? They cost a bloody fortune. I'd rather not spend my coins wooing one who in the end is not going to pay dividends. Is it your intent to play or fold?"

Griff tossed his chips onto the pile, signaling he was playing. In the end, he won the hand and a good many of the hands afterward. Earned back the two hundred pounds he'd lost the night before. He didn't want to consider that he owed Lady Kathryn for keeping him away from the roulette wheel and inadvertently guiding him toward the card table, that he might have to attribute some of tonight's success to her.

CHAPTER 3

$\mathcal{K}$ATHRYN COULDN'T SLEEP. She shouldn't have asked Griff for the favor. He'd capitulated far too easily which meant he'd tease her unmercifully for making the request of him, whether or not he saw it through. If he did have success at gathering the information she sought, he would make her pay a price for it. But it would be worth it to gain what she wanted.

Why hadn't her grandmother simply left her the cottage out-right? Why had she put a stupid stipulation on it? Was it because Kathryn had enjoyed spending time playing with the children in the village? Had her grandmother been worried that she'd move to the quaint dwelling and marry the blacksmith's son or the baker's? Why was her family so obsessed with their place in Society? Had it brought any of them happiness?

If her uncle or cousin didn't see to her welfare, was she not per-fectly capable of seeing to it herself? She could hire out as a nanny, governess, or companion. She wasn't averse to work, considered that it might give her the freedom she longed for. Why among the aristocracy was marriage so highly valued? Shouldn't a woman be wanted for more than bedding, breeding, and beauty?

The gentle rap on the door had all her thoughts scattering. It was nearly two. A little late for Althea to join her for some twittering about the Season or Society. Too early for Griff to have returned from his night of certain decadence. Had someone received word from her parents? Had something happened to them?

Tossing back the covers, she scrambled out of bed, raced to the door, and opened it. Her heart nearly skidded to a stop. It *was* Griff. While his neckcloth was undone, he didn't look nearly as disheveled as he had the night before. Neither did he smell as ghastly. As a matter of fact, his fragrance was quite pleasant. She detected a bit of scotch on the air, but he wasn't reeking with it. She couldn't recall ever seeing him quite so relaxed. The tiniest of smiles reached up to make his eyes sparkle.

"I have what you requested," he said, his words clear and concise. Not a slur to be found. He actually sounded happy, triumphant. She didn't want to acknowledge how appealing a happy, triumphant Lord Griffith Stanwick was.

"You spoke with the duke?"

He leaned a shoulder against the doorjamb. "I did."

"What did he say?"

A corner of his mouth hitched up a little higher. "What are you willing to trade in order to learn of his preferences?"

Why couldn't he have disappointed her on this matter? Why couldn't she have been wrong that he would require something of her? "Why can't you merely tell me?"

"Because I was rather inconvenienced." He lowered his head slightly and arched a blond brow. "As I believe I mentioned I would be."

She sighed heavily. "What do you want?"

Reaching behind her, he took hold of her plaited hair and draped it over her shoulder, the one nearest to him. "Your hair unraveled, like Rapunzel."

Blinking, she stared at him. "So you can tease me about how hideous it is?"

"Why would you think it hideous?"

"Because the color is an unusual red, not a pretty shade. And I possess an abundance of unruly curls."

"The color is why I've always liked it. Because it is so bright, not drab or boring. Why I've always wondered how it might look spread out"—abruptly he stopped speaking and gave his head a small shake—"loose."

"You like something about me?"

"It's only a small thing. Don't let it go to your head."

His disgruntlement made her feel a little more settled. She lifted the tip of her plait and reached for the ribbon that held the woven strands secure.

"I'll do that."

She watched in fascination as his deft fingers pulled on the end of the ribbon until the bow her lady's maid had created earlier disappeared. Slowly, so very slowly, he loosened the satin until he could slide it free. Into the small pocket of his waistcoat it went.

"Carry on." His voice was low, soft, sensual almost.

She wondered why he didn't complete the task, wondered why she wished he had. He studied her with such intensity as she began unraveling the strands that it became difficult to draw in breath.

"Not so quickly," he murmured.

"I'd never realized you were a man of patience."

His gaze lifted to hers, stayed for a heartbeat before drifting back to her hands. "Only when it comes to certain things."

"Women?"

The grin he gave her was devilish. "Most assuredly."

She slowed her fingers even more, for her enjoyment as much as his. She liked the way his eyes darkened, his nostrils flared, his lips parted ever so slightly. It was doubtful she'd have noticed if she hadn't been scrutinizing him so closely. At balls, she'd held conversations with gentlemen, had danced with them, but not a single one had ever looked at her as though at any moment he might leap on her and devour her.

It was an odd thing that Lord Griffith Stanwick was looking at her thus. He was probably further in his cups than she realized, so far in fact that he'd forgotten who stood before him. And that they'd always been at odds.

When she unraveled the last bit of weave, she shook her head to scatter the tresses and give them absolute freedom. She heard his breath hitch, and her own responded in kind. She was not at all comfortable with the warmth and strange tingles traveling through her in a chaotic manner. She needed to be done with this. "So what does the duke want in a wife?"

"Quiet."

Balling up her fist, she smacked him hard enough on the shoulder that he reeled back two steps.

"What the devil?" He wasn't studying her hair now but was glaring at her as she was him in equal measure.

"I did what you asked, and you tell me to shush? You go back on your word?"

Rubbing his shoulder, he scowled. "Kingsland wants quiet in a wife. I daresay you're going to have a time of it fulfilling that requirement."

Oh. Well. She felt rather foolish. Brushing his hand aside, she began stroking his shoulder to ease the hurt she'd inflicted. She hadn't expected him to be so firm, so toned. Obviously, she'd misjudged how he spent his days. It seemed they encompassed very little idleness. "My apologies for misunderstanding, although a complete sentence issued on your part might have prevented the confusion. What else does he require?"

As the silence stretched out, she darted a quick glance up to see him staring at her hand as though he'd never seen one. She couldn't recall ever touching him with such purpose before that moment. A grazing of their fingers when he took the key hardly counted, even as it had caused her lungs to seize up momentarily. Self-conscious regarding the intimacy she was displaying, she gave him a little pat as she might a hound she wanted to send on its way. "There, that's better, isn't it?"

Nodding, he scanned the hallway as though searching for an escape from what was becoming an increasingly awkward encounter.

"You didn't answer. What else does he require?"

His attention was once more focused on her, but he seemed troubled now, his brow deeply furrowed. "Only silence."

She gave a brusque nod of reassurance. "I can manage that quite easily."

He barked out a laugh that seemed to circle the hallway before striking the center of her chest like a well-aimed arrow. "The devil you say."

Her irritation with this man knew no bounds, even when he was helping her. She planted her hands on her hips. "I am fully capable of holding my tongue when necessary."

"Why would you want to marry a man who has no interest in even hearing your captivating discourse?"

She couldn't discern if he was teasing or being sarcastic. Surely, he'd never found anything she had to say spellbinding. "Because it might be the only way to gain what I truly desire."

"Which is what? A husband? A duke? The title of duchess?"

If he didn't sound so disgusted, she might have closed the door in his face. Instead, she felt an awful need not to have him judge her poorly in this one regard.

"A cottage."

HE DIDN'T LIKE it when she surprised him, and it seemed of late she was doing it with increasing regularity. A few minutes earlier, her unexpectedly rubbing his shoulder had nearly robbed him of all good judgment, and he'd begun contemplating the merits of caressing her in return. What a mistake that would have been. "A cottage?"

She nodded. "By the sea. Windswept Cottage belonged to my grandmother. My fondest memories were made there, but she stipulated that it be placed in a trust for me only if I married a titled gentleman by my twenty-fifth birthday. Next year, in August, I shall see a quarter of a century. Kingsland might be my last chance to meet that deadline in a timely fashion."

He knew something about wanting a property with a desperation that defied all logic. "Kingsland mentioned something about not wanting to be disturbed when he was concentrating. Bloody hell, he didn't provide a lot of insight, did he?"

"Hardly worth the unraveling of my hair. I should make you brush it and replait it."

To comb his fingers through the glorious strands, to know if they felt as silky as they looked, to divide them into thirds—

It was hair, for God's sake. Every woman he'd ever been with had hair. He had hair. Why was it that he ached to know the texture of hers? "I'd probably just knot it all up."

She smiled, a soft, sweet smile as though they'd never had a harsh word, as though he wasn't a spare. "Yes, you probably would. You also make an awful spy. But you did inquire and have given me a bit more information than I had possessed, so thank you for that. Especially as it was so deuced inconvenient for you."

But he'd walked away with two hundred pounds. He owed her for that. "I'll keep an ear out and let you know if I discover anything else."

"I'd appreciate that, my lord."

"Lady Kathryn, you have been friends with my sister for a dozen years now. You are her dearest confidante. Perhaps we could dispense with the formalities."

"You know precisely how long Althea and I have been friends?"

He remembered the first moment he'd spied her. Her dress had been blue, her bonnet white. It had rested against her back, its ribbons tied around her neck keeping it tethered to her as she'd skipped over fields of clover, laughing—before her governess chastised her for behaving like a hoyden. Perhaps that was another reason that he worked to keep her at a distance. Because he'd been so drawn in by the siren of her laugh. Or maybe he knew that if he was to catch another glimpse of the hoyden, he'd be lost.

"Not precisely." He stepped back. "'Tis late. I should abed. My apologies for disturbing your slumber when I had so little to contribute."

"I wasn't asleep."

"Neither were you last night when I returned." Ah, there was the blush he enjoyed bringing forth, creeping up her neck and into her cheeks! He wondered if the pinkish tinge ran the length of her.

"I have no idea what you're talking about," she said sharply.

"What a liar you are, Kathryn. I told you I'd remember. So perhaps you owed me the unfurling of your hair, after all."

Her indignant expression had him chuckling all the way into his bedchamber, into his bed. He sobered only after he began stroking the ribbon that had held her hair in place. Damned stupid of him to be jealous of a bit of cloth for being so intimately involved with her.

Although he'd caught himself in time, he'd nearly mistakenly confessed that he wanted her tresses freed so he could imagine the bright copper mane spread out over his pristine white pillow. Or over his bared chest. Her hair was long enough that it would reach down to his groin. He groaned as that rebellious part of his anatomy reacted as though the soft strands were in fact brushing over it, teasing it, at that very minute.

He didn't know why he'd tormented himself by asking that particular favor of her. He should have asked for something simpler, something that would have brought him joy for more than three minutes—even if the memory of those three minutes might never fade. *Smile whenever you first glimpse sight of me. Laugh when I tell a joke, even if you don't think it's funny. Look at me as though I'm not an irritation. Welcome my company. Never again confine your hair with pins or ribbons.*

So many things he could have asked for, but following his usual habit, he'd chosen the most immediate and strongest of gratifications to which she wouldn't object. So now he was left aching without hope of acquiring more.

CHAPTER 4

*D*ISEMBARKING FROM THE hansom cab, Griff ambled up the drive toward the residence, feeling quite satisfied after spending an hour with his solicitor. A solicitor no one in his family was even aware he had retained.

It wasn't only the wagering and the thrill of winning at the tables that lured him to the clubs. It was the information about various investment opportunities the members shared that was also a draw. He knew he couldn't count on always coming out ahead each night if he wanted to save enough money to start his business. But if he wisely invested some of those winnings, then he might find himself in a better position financially. He was determined to supplement the inadequate allowance his father gave him. Then with considerable relish, he'd return to his father every farthing he'd ever given him.

He knew the greater the risk, the higher the return. Unfortunately, two investments had resulted in losses. One had yet to pay off, in spite of it showing earlier promise.

But last night, after taking a good bit of the duke's blunt, the man had invited him for a drink and mentioned that he was investing in model dwelling companies, which were building much-needed residences for the poor. While Griff had invested only half of the amount he had won the night before, with luck, he would eventually see himself with a small but steady income. As his finances allowed, he would follow with more investments.

He had a spring in his step as he strode into the residence and handed his hat to the butler. "Is my sister about?"

"She is enjoying her afternoon nap, my lord."

"As is Lady Kathryn, I assume."

"No, sir. She's presently in the garden."

He didn't particularly like the way his heart pounded a little harder at the thought of spending time with her alone. If he was wise, he'd retire to his bedchamber and read. But he'd spent the afternoon being wise and was in the mood to be a bit reckless.

She was sitting on a cast-iron bench beneath the shade of an elm, near the delphiniums blooming in pink, purple, and white. But she was far more colorful in her lilac frock with her hair down and held in place with a white ribbon. He suspected she'd unpinned it before taking the afternoon rest his mother insisted all ladies required. A wide-brimmed straw bonnet rested near her feet. He was glad she'd dispensed with it, so her face wasn't lost to shadows. She was staring into the distance, her delicate brow deeply furrowed, her bottom lip barely visible as she gnawed at what should only ever be kissed. On her lap sat her small writing desk, seemingly forgotten.

"Aren't you supposed to be napping?"

She jerked her head in his direction, and for a brief span of time, it looked as though she was pleased to see him. Then just as quickly, she shuttered whatever emotions she was feeling, but still her smile, if not her eyes, remained warm. "It's such a lovely afternoon that it seemed a shame to spend it indoors."

"You mustn't let my mother find out. You'll give her the vapors."

Her smile grew. "She does believe a lady must rest. I never nap at home and don't seem to suffer for it in the evenings." She tilted her head a fraction, like a puppy striving to figure out its master. "You didn't join us for breakfast or luncheon."

"I had some matters to attend to and dined at the club. May I?" He indicated the empty half of the bench.

"Please." Reaching out, she tucked her voluminous skirt against her thigh as much as possible while he lowered himself to the cool metal, not bothering to lean away from her.

The bench had been designed for lovers to take a rest while strolling through the gardens, so it placed him nearer to her than he'd ever been. The slight breeze caused her clean fragrance of delicious oranges—his favorite fruit—mixed with cinnamon to tease his nostrils. A few strands of her hair had escaped their bondage of ribbons in order to frame her delicate face. She didn't look at him directly but offered a little bit more than her profile. He wished he was skilled at sketching. Instead he was left to commit the lovely image of her to memory. "What are you writing?"

With a sigh, she gave him a sideways glance while her cheeks blossomed into a pinkish hue. "I've been striving to catalogue my good qualities."

"Ah, for your letter to the duke." The blasted duke, the man who would know what it was to have her thigh pressed against his with no tightly woven threads to keep her silken warmth from him.

She nodded, her cheeks brightening further, until they were possibly in danger of igniting. "It's a sobering experience. I believe I've identified the reason I find myself close to being on the shelf. I'm rather unaccomplished and boring."

I very much doubt that. But he was beginning to understand she was much more modest than he'd ever assumed, and he found her modesty somewhat endearing. He doubted any other lady was struggling to list her accomplishments, suspected a good many of them would take liberties listing what they considered their best qualities. A skill at dancing they might not possess. A tendency toward wit and humor when nothing they ever said caused even a hint of a smile. Perfect management of a household when they'd yet to take any reins. He held out his hand. "May I?"

She rolled her eyes with an exaggeration that would have had him taking his leave at any other time. "You'll only laugh or tease me about them."

For the life of him, he couldn't comprehend why he cared so much about what she'd written, why it was suddenly important that she gained what she desired. "I won't. I promise."

Shifting slightly, she faced him more squarely, the small pleat between her auburn brows once again forming. "Why are you being kind to me? I'm accustomed to us sparring, not actually conversing."

Devil take him if he knew, but he wasn't about to confess that. "Because the next time I return home after too much drink, I don't want you tempted to send me round to the back. I'd prefer you help me up the stairs."

"You remembered everything?"

"Everything." The mischief in her eyes, the slight smile indicating she thought she was getting away with something wicked. He rather liked how triumphant she'd appeared when she'd believed herself to have the upper hand.

Her sigh mingled with the whisper of the slight breeze, and a jolt of pure need traveled straight to his groin as he envisioned her sigh under a different circumstance, a carnal one where pleasure reigned. "I feel rather badly about my behavior toward you now."

"Only because you got caught."

A twitch of those pink lips. So much about her was fair. He wondered if the same applied to portions he couldn't see.

"Yes."

For a moment, he became disoriented, thinking she was confirming pale nipples and the pinkest of skin between her thighs. The next breath he released was not as steady as it should have been. "Well, for what it's worth, neither my parents nor Althea would have let me in, either."

"Do you often get that drunk?"

"Not often. I'd had a disappointing night at the gaming hell and was feeling both sorry for myself and cross with myself. Bad judgment on my part led to the disappointment. Last night went much better. Except for the spying bit." He snapped his fingers. "Show me what you've written."

With a slow, tentative movement, she handed him the sheaf of paper.

> *Skilled at whist.*
> *Mastered the pianoforte.*
> *Speak only when I have something important to say.*

The first two he couldn't judge because he'd never played cards with her or heard her perform. The last was debatable and no doubt her attempt to demonstrate that she could be quiet, although she often engaged him when what she had to say wasn't important at all—just a desire to needle, to elicit a reaction. He'd always been too quick to rise to the bait, mainly because any attention from her was better than none at all. But reading over her list again now, he knew no matter how she worded what she had identified as her strengths, the duke was going to toss her letter in the rubbish bin. Griff had guessed correctly. A woman couldn't identify what attributes she possessed that would appeal to a man. "He wants quiet in a wife. He's not going to play whist with you. He's not going to ask you to entertain him with the pianoforte."

He couldn't help but believe that in foregoing those pleasures with her, the duke would be poorer for it. "That you've written two qualities in which he'll have no interest makes him likely to question the veracity of the third."

"What would you suggest, then?"

"What are you willing to give me in exchange for my wisdom?"

"You blackguard." The teasing in her eyes caused a tightness in his chest. She'd known he'd want a favor. Contentment at her knowing him well enough to anticipate his move swept through him. "At the duke's ball, I shall save my first waltz for you."

"You expect me to wait a couple of weeks to claim what I am owed?"

"Anticipation will make it all the sweeter."

He attended few balls, had never danced with her. He imagined holding her in his arms, gliding her over the floor. Damned bloody hell, if it wasn't something he'd like to experience once. "Pay close attention to what I am about to reveal. It is a rare thing for any man to give away secrets that would see another shackled in marriage."

Her triumphant smile rocked him to his core. "You're accepting the trade?"

He gave a little shrug, as though the matter was of no consequence, as though he wasn't in fact looking forward to claiming his reward. "It'll give me an excuse to learn the waltz."

"You know how to waltz. I've seen you do so."

Taking satisfaction in knowing she had noticed him at a previous ball, he hoped he heard the tiniest bit of jealousy. "Have you?"

She plucked at her skirt as though she'd suddenly spotted an invisible thread unraveling. "You're the brother of my dearest friend. It's not as though I'm not going to notice you on the dance floor."

"But you never acknowledge me on the dance floor."

She looked at him then, remorse in the eyes that were almost blue today. He'd noticed before how the hazel shade seemed to alter slightly depending on what she wore. "I've found it sometimes easier to ignore when not certain of the welcome."

"I might tease you on occasion, Freckles, but I would never do anything to embarrass you in public. You must know that, surely."

"I do now."

For the longest time, they only looked at each other, as though they were weighing words, confessions, interest, vulnerabilities. She was the first to glance away, licking her lips as she did so, causing a tightness low in his belly that might have dropped him to his knees had he been standing. Had she always possessed this power over him, tantalized and seduced with so little effort? Or did knowing she was in pursuit of another serve to awaken him to the notion that he'd like her to be in pursuit of him?

But through marriage to him, she could not gain what she coveted. He cleared his throat. "Pay attention, sweetheart, and be astonished by my wisdom."

She bestowed upon him the most beautiful, unpretentious smile he'd ever received from her. Warm and generous, it was the sort for which men launched ships. "You are so frightfully conceited."

He heard no censure, only a bit of playful teasing, not the caustic tone fraught with disapproval that she'd always tossed his way in the past. "You shouldn't complain. You're about to benefit from my superior knowledge."

"Impress me, then. Tell me what I must write to win the duke's favor."

Angling himself in order to view the whole of her features, he stretched his arm out along the back of the bench. Without taking his eyes from hers, he skimmed a finger over a silken curl at her shoulder. If she minded, she gave no indication, so he touched another. "Tell him your hair is like fire, your eyes like forest moss, but changeable depending on your mood. The green of plants in the garden when you're happy, the brown of soil when you're melancholy, the blue of the sky at dawn when passion takes hold."

Those eyes that tipped up slightly at the corners widened. "I'm not going to say that about *passion*. You certainly have never seen them when passion takes hold."

He'd seen even more, had seen them when she was aroused. Last night as she'd unraveled her hair, a kaleidoscope of heat, hunger, and arousal had turned them a brilliant blue. "Why the offense? Are you not excited by a fine aria? A beautiful sunset? The arrival of dessert? Especially when it includes strawberries." He'd seen that as well. She favored strawberries. He'd feed her an entire bushel for one of her smiles.

She dipped her head. "I thought you were referring to something else."

"What sort of passion did you have in mind?"

Her head snapped up, and her hazel eyes in anger comprised all the shades. "I think you know precisely what sort of passion I assumed you were referring to."

Slipping a finger beneath the ringlets, he skimmed it lightly along the nape of her neck, felt the tiny hairs quiver. "Longing, yearning, craving."

"You shouldn't be touching me like that."

"Slap my hand away. Or leave it, so we can know for certain what color your eyes become when you are stirred by desire."

"You do not stir me."

"Then, where is the harm in the touch?" Other than the fact that it did stir him to yearn for what he shouldn't, and if he wasn't careful in holding himself in check, she was going to know exactly how much he yearned.

"Why would he care about my hair or my eyes?"

"Because he wants a woman he can set upon a shelf and take down occasionally to adorn his arm."

"All men want that. Don't you want a woman to adorn your arm?"

"Of course I want a woman on my arm, but my pride in having her there would have nothing to do with the shade of her hair or her eyes. Or the delicate cut of her cheekbones or the long sweep of her neck. It would be because of her intelligence, her compassion, her boldness. I would certainly never place her upon a shelf to gather dust as though she were naught but a doll to be appreciated for her appearance rather than her mind. I would want her to share her opinion on matters, to discuss things that are important to me, to her, to argue with me, and on the rare occasion when I am wrong to convince me that she is correct. I would want her beside me because I valued her judgment, because she wasn't afraid to be honest with me. And because she made me smile, made me laugh, made me glad to wake up with her in my arms."

Sometime during his ridiculous diatribe, his hand had closed around her nape as though he would guide her toward him. With her lips parted slightly, she stared at him as though she'd never heard such poppycock. Whatever had possessed him to blather on like that?

He'd never contemplated having a wife at his side, had never considered the qualities he would want in a woman he might marry. Yet suddenly he did know what he wanted, recognized that perhaps it—*she*—was what he'd always wanted. Someone with a bit of competitiveness in her, who could look at a situation realistically rather than romantically, who would stand up to him. Tease him, scoff at him, tell him honestly when he was being an arse or should be better. Who made him want to *be* better. Who called to his better nature. Who completed him, made him feel whole, instead of only partial.

"What sort of things would you want her opinion on?" she asked quietly. "What important matters would you want to discuss?"

She sounded truly interested. He wondered how she might respond if his answer came in the form of a kiss. Of late, a curiosity regarding what it might be like to press his lips against hers had risen in him. To urge her to part those luscious lips in invitation, to stroke his tongue over hers, to deepen the kiss until her fingers clutched his shoulders and her sighs wafted around him.

He watched the delicate muscles at her silky-smooth throat work as she swallowed. Had she ever pondered what a kiss between them might be like? Would she object if the hand he'd clasped around her nape drew her in closer? To ensure it didn't, he eased it away and clutched the back of the bench instead. "If you truly want to know, meet me on the front drive after everyone has gone to bed tonight. With no chaperone."

She blinked, studied him. "That would be scandalous."

"Only if you're caught."

She touched her tongue to her upper lip, before gnawing on the lower. God, she was considering it. A strange sense—he suspected it might be elation—coursed through him. He'd expected her to dismiss his challenge out of hand, not contemplate its merits. "If you meet me, you can write to Kingsland that you're an adventurous sort."

"You think I'm not normally?"

"Are you?"

Slowly, she shook her head, seemingly embarrassed by the confession. "I never do anything I ought not."

"Whereas I do everything I ought not."

"Is it more fun, I wonder?"

"It gives me stories to tell." He bent toward her. "Don't you want a story to tell, Lady Kathryn?"

He couldn't have felt her gaze traveling over his face more solidly if she'd used her fingers to trace every line, dip, and curve of his features. Why he suddenly yearned for a more intense scrutiny from her was beyond comprehension. He wasn't usually slow-witted, but he couldn't seem to think beyond her, beyond this moment, wondering what might be ruminating in that clever mind of hers. Would the duke appreciate a woman who could bring him to task? Would the duke want a woman who made him wonder what the devil she was thinking?

"Why are you being so accommodating, providing me with information on how I might snag Kingsland, especially when you seem to have such a low regard for him? Do you wish to see me miserable?"

It was the last thing he wanted for her. "Just because he selects you doesn't mean you will be forced to marry him if you decide he's not for you. Although, perhaps you'll be well suited."

She ran her finger along the edge of her escritoire. "But why are you offering advice? Why are you helping me to secure him? We were always at cross-purposes before."

"Perhaps I decided that it's time we weren't. Besides, I already explained that I'd rather you help me up the stairs if I'm drunk."

"But in the morning, I'll return to my parents' residence, so I won't be about to help you. What do you gain?"

Why was she being so suspicious? Why could she not simply accept his help and her good fortune? "A waltz."

Obviously displeased with that answer, she furrowed her brow and puckered her mouth. "But you could have had that by merely asking. Why have you never asked?"

"You always were quite clear regarding your aversion to second sons." And he'd always taken it personally, although now he understood her reasons. Didn't mean he liked them, but he understood them.

"Not an aversion, but it would do me no good to encourage one. I'm sorry if I gave the impression that you were somehow . . . less."

"I never took offense." Lie, but he saw no point in making her feel badly about it, when conditions over which she had no control had been placed on her.

She scrutinized him with a deliberation he'd never observed in her before, and he feared she was attempting to delve into his soul, wretched and mired as it was.

"Oh, there you are!" Althea called out as she rounded the curve in the path that allowed for some privacy for lovers who took advantage of the bench.

While he simply leaned back and crossed his ankles, Kathryn gave a guilty start and jumped to her feet as though being caught so near to him was a sin. Or maybe it was her musings that had bordered on the sinful. Maybe she hadn't been searching his soul but had been contemplating sending her fingers on a search over his person. "I was working on my letter to Kingsland."

"Then, I suspect you could use a bit of a respite. Shall we go for a ride in the park?"

"That would be lovely."

"Griff, would you care to join us?" Althea asked. "Your presence would save me having to bother a groom."

He shouldn't. He absolutely should not. He'd already spent too much time in Kathryn's company. That he'd shared such intimate thoughts and invited her to go on an outing with him was a prelude to disaster. What the devil had he been thinking? He needed to make himself scarce, but the words needed eluded him, and instead he heard himself say, "I believe I shall."

CHAPTER 5

$\mathcal{W}$HILE THEIR HORSES plodded along Rotten Row, Kathryn continually stole glances at Griff on the other side of Althea. Propriety dictated his sister serve as a barrier between the two of them, yet Kathryn was disappointed he wasn't nearer to her, that conversing with him here would not be the intimate encounter it had been in the garden, when for the briefest of moments, she'd thought perhaps he was contemplating kissing her. For the briefest of moments, she'd wanted him to.

He sat a horse well. Whenever a lady passed by, he tipped his hat while giving her a smile certain to leave her a little unsteady in the saddle. She'd never noticed he had such a charmingly wicked smile that promised fun and adventure. Might all the teasing she'd so abhorred be an innocuous sort of flirting? His nature was not to take anything seriously—or so she'd thought.

But based on what she'd observed since coming to spend several days with Althea, perhaps all his lightheartedness was merely like ivy that climbed ever higher to hide a wall behind which a person could feel safe.

In the garden, they'd spoken longer than they ever had before, and she'd enjoyed it. More than that, she'd been a little cross with Althea for interrupting, for bringing a halt to the conversation that had revealed a man who believed a woman should be more than an ornament.

She had sat there mesmerized as he'd laid out what he wanted in a wife as though he'd given it intense and thorough consideration, when she would have thought that he'd not given it a single minute of deliberation. He cared about a woman's heart and soul. He wanted her involved in his life, as a part of it. Not on the periphery. Not an afterthought.

While it was highly unlikely that he was doing so, Griff could have been describing her. She didn't want to examine why she hoped he had been, why she had thought *If only you would gain a title*. Why her heart had seemed to shrink and expand at the same time. For the span of their time in the garden she'd felt that he truly saw her. Understood her need not to be overlooked but to be valued not for her physical attributes but for her mind, her heart, her very soul.

Something inside her had twisted and turned, bunched up and unfurled, until she'd seen him in a very different light. He was far more complicated than she'd ever imagined, and she wanted to unravel the threads in order to more thoroughly examine all the various shades that made him who he was. She was beginning to think bits of silver and gold were woven through the tapestry that comprised Lord Griffith Stanwick.

"Look steady, Kat," Althea said. "I do believe that's the Duke of Kingsland headed our way."

She'd been giving so much examination to their time in the garden and watching Griff now that she'd hardly noticed her surroundings, but, yes, indeed that was in fact the duke trotting toward them with such smooth movements that he and the horse seemed as one. Shouldn't her heart speed up with the prospect of speaking with him? Shouldn't she care that the man she hoped to marry was approaching? Shouldn't she want to unravel his tapestry?

They brought their horses to a halt just before he reached them.

His gaze swept over them before landing on Griff. "Good afternoon, my lord."

Griff tipped his head slightly. "Your Grace. Allow me the honor of introducing my sister, Lady Althea, and her dear friend, Lady Kathryn Lambert."

He removed his silk hat, black as a raven's wing, from his head. "Ladies. I understand congratulations are in order, Lady Althea. Lord Chadbourne is indeed a fortunate man."

"Thank you, Your Grace."

Then he was studying Kathryn, as though she was a puzzle in need of deciphering. "Lady Kathryn, are you spoken for?"

"That's a rather impertinent question."

"But it gets to the heart of things, does it not?"

Out of the corner of her eye, she detected Griff stiffening, and she wondered exactly how he might have garnered the information about the duke's preferences in a wife. "I presently have no suitor."

He didn't need to know she'd never had a suitor. Oh, a few gentlemen had flirted now and then, but she'd encouraged none of them because she'd found none to her liking.

His gaze darted to Griff, then back to her, and she couldn't help but believe he was assessing both of them, striving to decipher a mystery. "Then I shall be receiving a letter from you, in the near future, sometime before my ball."

"To be honest, I haven't yet decided."

"Oh, I think you have."

Arrogant cad. "I do hope, Your Grace, that you do not intend to tell your wife what she thinks, what decisions she's made."

"If she is in need of being told, I shall do so. Have you not heard that a husband tells his wife her opinion on matters?"

Was he jesting? She couldn't be sure. "Why would you want a woman who is unable to think for herself?"

"Why would I want one who might prove to be contrary?"

"For the challenge of it," Griff interjected.

The duke's brow furrowed deeply as he glowered at Griff. "I have enough challenges without adding one more."

"But this one would be much more pleasant. You wouldn't be able to accuse her of being dull. Would you not experience an anticipated excitement in not knowing what she might say next?"

Was he talking about her? Did he find her challenging? Did he look forward to learning what she might say, do, next? She suddenly felt like her world had gone topsy-turvy. Was he complimenting her?

"You make an interesting point." The duke's attention swung back to her. His focus so intense, it appeared the man did nothing in half measures. "What say you, Lady Kathryn? Would you ensure my days were never dull?"

"Your days as well as your evenings."

Griff's gelding gave a little start, a snort, a sidestep—and he quickly brought the horse under control. The duke had gone completely still, except for those assessing eyes of his that ran the length of her, as though she'd been hiding in moonlight and had suddenly stepped into the sunlight, giving him a clearer view of her.

"I'm quite skilled at reading animatedly," she continued, "in order to bring the story to life. My father always compliments me on my dynamic delivery."

"Reading." He cleared his throat. "Of course, that is to what you were referring."

What else? Good Lord. Had he thought she was referring to the bedding? Had Griff as well? Had her words startled him, causing him to unsettle his horse?

"I can attest to the fact that Lady Kathryn would be a feather in any man's cap," Althea said cheerily.

"Indeed." The duke never took his gaze from her.

"Although, I daresay it remains to be seen if the duke will be a feather in any lady's cap," Kathryn challenged. "Perhaps, Your Grace, you should have described more about yourself in your announcement so a lady might be assured that she did indeed wish to pen a letter to you."

His gaze intensified. "I would not have thought a lady would care for anything other than the title."

"I'm certain that assessment would apply to some, but not all."

"It doesn't apply to Lady Kathryn," Griff said. "She is not so shallow as all that."

"Is she not?"

"No, Your Grace, she is not." A curtness in his tone had the duke darting a quick glance Griff's way before settling his gaze back on her.

"Tell me, Lady Kathryn, do you play chess?"

"I do, Your Grace. Would you prefer it to my reading aloud in the evening?"

"That is as yet to be determined. However, I am curious. Which piece do you deem most important?"

Was this some sort of maneuver to gauge her intelligence? "The queen."

"The pawn."

"But the queen can move in any direction."

"You would argue with me?"

"If I thought you wrong. But I also give you leave to make your case."

"I so appreciate your indulgence." His tone implied that perhaps he didn't. "I will give you that the queen is the most powerful, but not the most important. The pawn is key to any good strategy. However, because it is a small piece and there are so many of them, it is often ignored. Much like second sons, I find."

"Are you implying that your younger brother is more important than you?"

"Without doubt. My father would have sacrificed him in a heartbeat to keep me safe. Which made him critical to my well-being. Never overlook the pawn."

"Would you sacrifice your brother?"

"I pray I am never in a position to find out." He turned his attention to Griff. "I hope to see you at the tables in the near future, my lord. I owe you a drubbing." He tipped his hat. "Ladies."

As he began to ride past her, he stopped. "Lady Kathryn, be certain to put a note in your letter that you were the argumentative wench I met at the park, so I give your words a bit more weight."

"I didn't think you liked argumentative wenches but preferred quiet ones."

With a bit of triumph, he looked at Griff as though he now knew for whom he'd made inquiries. "Perhaps you'll convince me I've misjudged what I like."

After he'd loped away, was beyond hearing distance, Althea gave a small squeal that unsettled the horses and caused each to sidestep. "I do believe he was flirting with you."

"Was he?" She'd found him rather cantankerous. She was also bothered that her excitement at the prospect that he might have been flirting with her paled when compared with Althea's.

"Without question. What say you, Griff?"

"Most assuredly." He seemed no happier about it than she did.

"Oh, Kat, I think meeting him today is fortuitous and will give you a leg up in the competition." Althea reached across and squeezed her hand. "I do believe you are going to find yourself the next Duchess of Kingsland."

"I think you give too much credence to a few passing words. Why would he want a woman almost on the shelf rather than a girl who has just entered the ballroom?"

"He strikes me as someone who would prefer maturity over giddiness."

But he also preferred a woman who spoke his mind and not her own. Could she hold her tongue?

When they set their horses back into motion, Griff skirted around Althea until he was riding beside Kathryn. "Were you intentionally trying to ruin your chances with him?"

He sounded truly cross, as though she'd personally attacked him, more like the Griff before their conversation in the garden than the one during. "Why should you care?"

"Because I went to a great deal of inconvenience for you. His opinion of me is on the line."

"Did you tell him you were making inquiries on my behalf?"

"Of course not. I didn't even tell him I would be advising anyone on what to write him. I made it sound as though I was merely curious about his methods. But it appears he might have guessed. He had that arrogance about him, so cocksure that he'd figured it out."

"I noticed that. And you're correct. I owe you. I should have been more receptive to his overtures, but should I not be who I am?"

"You can show him who you are after you wed."

She laughed. "That is guaranteed to create misery for both the duke and me. We may never have a grand love, but we can at least have an honest relationship. I cannot go into a marriage with anything less."

"Sometimes sacrifices must be made in order to gain what we want."

What knew he of sacrifices? If she joined him tonight, perhaps she'd ask. While she was leaning very much toward meeting him after everyone retired, she hadn't made a definite decision. It required she place an awful lot of faith and trust in him.

"What are you two whispering about?" Althea asked.

"Just discussing her impression of the duke," Griff offered.

"I thought he seemed rather nice," Althea said. "What was your impression of him, Kat?"

She released a sigh. "A bit disappointed that he didn't remember meeting me."

"You've met him before?" Griff asked, sounding none too pleased with the information.

She glanced over at him. "Two years ago, at a ball. He even danced with me."

"You must be mistaken. He can't have forgotten you if he danced with you."

"Would you never forget me if you danced with me?"

"I suppose I'm going to find out," he grumbled, his tone reflecting a bit of resignation.

What if she never forgot what it was like to dance with him?

CHAPTER 6

$\mathcal{S}$TANDING AT THE bottom of the steps, Griff leaned against the stone base that supported the statue of a wolf with its head thrown back, its mouth opened slightly as though howling at the moon or some transgression or unfairness. He'd certainly felt like howling earlier in the park when Kathryn had been her usual quarrelsome self. If the duke wanted a quiet wife, he certainly didn't want one who responded with such tartness and self-assurance, as though her opinion carried as much weight as his. Even if it did, even if she'd made some valid points. Even if he'd wanted to applaud her, had taken a bit of pride in her not cowering before a man of such rank and prestige.

But she was going to ruin her chances of landing the duke if she wasn't careful. He wanted her to win this blasted contest. He wanted her to come with him tonight, even as he knew she probably wouldn't join him. She hadn't said with words she would, hadn't given the impression with actions she would, so he was probably out here, headed for disappointment.

He should be on his way. Change the plans he'd arranged earlier because he'd thought she might join him. She was no doubt at this very moment tucked up tightly in bed, dreaming of the duke slipping a hand beneath the hem of her nightdress and taking his fingers on a journey over the silken skin of her thigh.

That she had met the duke before, that Kingsland had seemingly failed to recognize her or remember he'd encountered her
previously, was beyond reasoning. How could any man, once he'd
been introduced to her—nay, an introduction wasn't necessary:
to catch sight of her would be enough—forget she existed in his
world? But to have held her in his arms, to have circled her over
the dance floor? It was beyond the pale to even consider that he'd
not remembered her. The unusual coppery tint of her hair, the fire
in her eyes, her sharp tongue. To have her attention for the length
of a dance, to have basked in her presence, and then not to store
the memory away—when Griff had so many memories of her that
he'd never forget. None of them truly his, certainly not granted to
him on purpose. The sight of her skipping through a flower-filled
field with Althea. Sitting on a blanket enjoying a picnic with his
sister, laughing so loudly that the birds in the boughs above had
taken flight. Ascending or descending stairs at a ball. Waltzing
with one lord after another.

Furrowing her brow at him. Glaring at him. Fighting not to
laugh at something he said. Those were his favorite, when he'd almost broken through the cool façade that characterized so many
of their encounters.

He'd never even thought about those memories before he'd heard
her say she was setting her cap for a duke. Now it seemed the
remembrances were inside a zoetrope, going around and around
in his mind, in a blur of actions, and he couldn't seem to make them
stop.

What was he doing waiting here? He knew everyone was
abed. He'd stayed in the library reading *Twenty Thousand Leagues
under the Sea* until they were. That she wasn't already out here
was an indication that she wasn't going to come. Why should
she? He'd told her what to write in her letter to the duke. She'd
become reacquainted with Kingsland that afternoon. No way in
hell would he forget her this time. She had a decisive edge over
the other ladies that would see her in good stead.

The rambling he'd done in the garden that afternoon was an

embarrassment. He'd never given any thought to what he wanted in a wife, never intended to marry, so why had he given the impression that he had, that he would? Why of a sudden was he finding her company so damned enjoyable?

Obviously, she didn't feel the same. He needed to stop mooning about. Altering his plans was easy enough. He could head to the gaming hell. The carriage was there in the drive waiting for him to climb aboard. The horses were snorting, ready to be off.

Yet, here he stood, unable to give up that last glimmer of hope, the frayed remnant of anticipation that tonight they might put aside whatever ill-conceived animosity had always been between them and instead enjoy each other's company. What was he thinking—

All his thoughts stuttered to a stop as he heard a door open and close. Moving away from the stone support, he glanced up the stairs to see her darting down them. She was wearing a pelisse against the cool of the night, and beneath it, he caught a glimpse of the emerald gown she'd worn to dinner.

"I apologize for my tardiness," she said in a rush, her breath coming in rapid gusts as though she'd fairly flown from her bedchamber. "Althea came to my chamber to talk once more about our encounter with Kingsland at the park. Thank you for waiting."

She'd come. He hadn't known for sure that she would, but now to see her gratitude because he'd waited, he didn't know why he'd ever doubted. "We're not on a schedule."

"Still, it occurred to me that I never actually responded to your invitation, didn't reassure you that I was indeed interested in learning about whatever it was you so mysteriously alluded to in the garden. Are you going to tell me?"

"I'm going to do better than that. I'm going to show you."

KATHRYN HAD NEVER done anything as bold—or scandalous—as climb into a carriage with a gentleman during the late hours of the evening, with no chaperone and no one knowing. But Griff was her dearest friend's brother. He would do nothing untoward. He was safe.

Or so she'd once thought. But at present her mind was a conglomeration of strange thoughts, her body a hodgepodge of strange sensations as the carriage rumbled through the faintly lit streets. Although he sat opposite her, a respectful distance, she was acutely aware of his presence looming. Not at all in a frightening sort of way, but more in a not-to-be-ignored sort of way. When had he become so . . . substantial? He smelled of bay rum and spice, of mystery and decadence. This boy grown into a man whom she'd never truly noticed suddenly occupied a good portion of her musings, unwilling to be disregarded.

A change in the tenor of their relationship had happened as well, and she wasn't quite certain what to make of it, how to adjust to it. As the glow from passing streetlamps washed quickly over his face, she found herself waiting in anticipation of seeing him more clearly for the span of a few hoofbeats hitting the street, was nearly envious of the light that could touch him so freely and not be reprimanded for it. A lady couldn't caress with such abandon. On the rare occasions that a touch was permitted, such as during a dance, gloves had to be worn.

If she did find herself to be the duke's choice, if he did propose marriage, it was unlikely she would graze her skin over his in any manner before they married, before he visited her bedchamber on their wedding night. What if his touch made her recoil?

"You're looking quite serious over there," Griff remarked, his voice a rasp in the darkness that made it seem so much more intimate.

Perhaps it was because of the shadows, or the late hour, or the fact they were alone, but she found herself confessing, "I was thinking of courting rituals. How staid they are. How they don't lend themselves well to people getting to know each other."

She saw the flash of his grin, had never noticed that he had a remarkable smile. It made her feel included, treasured, special.

"Why, Lady Kathryn, if I didn't know better, I'd think you could read my mind."

"Were you thinking the same?"

"I've thought the same for years now. It's part of the impetus for what I'm going to show you."

"Does Althea know about it?"

"Absolutely not. I've told no one." He gazed out the window. "I don't know why I decided to share it with you. Especially as I was sober at the time."

His disgruntlement made her want to laugh. Getting the better of him always made her light and giddy. In truth, she'd never minded his teasing. She had to stay on her toes with him. Would conversation with the duke be as invigorating?

"Is some woman not waiting for you somewhere tonight?"

His gaze landed back on her, exactly where she wanted it. What was wrong with her, to desire his attention?

"Here I was under the distinct impression you were of the feminine persuasion."

"I'm not waiting on you."

"Trying to determine if I have a paramour?"

Was she? Yes, she rather thought she was. "I would not want to be responsible for her being cross with you."

"You think I would tell her of you?"

"Only if you took after your father and didn't keep your trysts secret."

"First, I am nothing at all like my father." The harshly ground out words implied he spoke through clenched teeth. "Second, I believe we would be hard-pressed to call this a tryst, as we are hardly lovers, nor do my plans for this outing involve anything remotely romantic. Third, I wouldn't be here with you if I had a paramour. I would be with her. Why are you smiling?"

"It's reassuring to know you wouldn't be unfaithful to a lover." And that he didn't have one.

"Are you looking to be cast into the role of my lover?"

"No! The audacity, to ask such a thing. I'm a genteel lady—"

"There's nothing remotely genteel about you. You're bold as brass, and you speak your mind. That Kingsland wants a woman who doesn't is beyond my comprehension."

"I don't want to talk about him."

"Do you not like him?"

"I don't know how I feel about him—which is what led to my earlier musings. I don't want the sort of marriage that my parents had. My father chose my mother for monetary gain—"

"Kingsland has no need of money." Whereas Griff did.

"—political gain—"

"He has no need of political alliances."

"True. Which leaves him being in want of a broodmare."

"Every man with a title is."

"That doesn't make it acceptable to a woman's heart. My parents traveled to Italy in an attempt to strengthen their relationship and possibly fall in love. I don't want to live thirty years in a loveless marriage. I want to be like Althea and have love right out of the starting gate."

"You think Chadbourne loves her?"

"Well, of course he does. He adores her." Although doubts suddenly plagued her. She leaned forward. "Don't you think?"

"Matters of the heart are not my strong suit."

"Have you never been in love, then?"

"I was in love with a puppy once."

She furrowed her brow. "I don't recall ever seeing a dog at any of your residences when I visited Althea."

"I wasn't allowed to keep him."

Her stomach knotted as she discovered one more thing he was denied. He was the son of a duke. He should never have gone without anything he wanted. Her parents had always spoiled her, perhaps because the three sons to whom her mother had given birth had all died shortly after drawing their first breath. "No woman, though?"

"Never. Was there some swain in your youth who stole your heart and then tossed you over for a lady with a larger dowry?"

"If a cad had tossed me over, all of London would have known about it because I would have shoved the scoundrel into the Thames."

Another grin from him. She was becoming addicted to creating them. "You see? You're no whimpering miss. Brazen and bold. Kingsland would be lucky to have you."

She offered him a smile in exchange. "You are the last person I would have expected to be my champion."

"It does seem odd." He glanced out the window. "We're almost there."

THERE WAS A large brick building that took up a good portion of the block. That no light shown from within and it appeared forbidden was a bit ominous, and Kathryn's heart pounded a little bit harder, but she trusted Griff not to place her in harm's way.

He'd taken one of the lanterns hanging on the outside of the carriage before directing the driver to take the vehicle around to the mews. "What is this place?" she asked.

"Presently abandoned." He held up a key. "We'll go in, shall we?"

"Is it yours?"

"Not yet, as I'm still short on funds, but the agent handling the sale of this property knows I've an interest in it and obliged me by lending me the key for the night." His lips twisted into an ironic smile. "Sometimes it pays to be the son of a duke. People make allowances and trust you with things they might not otherwise."

"What sort of interest have you in it?"

"I have it in mind for a business."

As he escorted her up the steps, she could sense the eagerness fairly thrumming through him and reverberating toward her. Holding the lantern aloft to guide his way, he inserted the key, turned it, and swung open the door. The hinges squeaked slightly in protest, which made her think that maybe entering wasn't such a good idea.

But when he indicated she should go in, she wasn't about to admit cowardice to him, so she stepped over the threshold and watched spellbound as the light from the lantern danced eerily through the cavernous entryway revealing an open doorway on either side and wide stairs that swept up in an elaborate curve befitting any grand residence.

"Come." His voice echoed around them as he directed her into a large room that she would label a parlor if it were in a home. Huge chandeliers draped down from the ceiling. A massive fireplace took up the far wall.

"This would be the receiving room," he said.

"Receiving what exactly? Your clients? Your customers?"

"My members. Are you familiar with a cock and hen club?"

"Why in God's name would you think I was familiar with any sort of club that would reference a part of the male—oh, wait. You mean, like a rooster and a hen?"

He grinned broadly, and even knowing he was going to tease her unmercifully, she thought it the most devilishly appealing smile she'd ever been fortunate enough to have bestowed upon her. "Why, Lady Kathryn, did your mind just travel to naughty places?"

"You blackguard, you knew it would. I daresay it's the reason you gave it such a ridiculous name. Cock and hen club, indeed."

"It exists, although I think you're probably correct—it was named such as a double entendre."

"What is its purpose?"

"To provide a place for men and women to meet someone with similar interests. The clubs are, or were, to be found among the less affluent areas of society. They're a bit rare these days."

"Have you been to one?"

"About ten years ago, when I was younger and searching for some sort of entertaining sport because I'd squandered my allowance. I ran across it quite by accident but was intrigued. The ladies had no chaperones."

"Then, they weren't ladies, were they?"

"We can discuss what makes a woman a lady at another time. What they were was uninhibited, fun, and free to dance with whomever they wanted—even if the music played on a pianoforte lent itself to a jig more than a waltz. They imbibed. I saw a couple of them smoke. As the evening wore on, each woman paired up with a bloke and went off to enjoy more intimate entertainments. The club's relaxed atmosphere lent itself to creating a place where people could more easily become familiar with one another."

"It lends itself to sin more easily." She knew precisely what activity those couples were going to engage in when they wandered away. Her mother had warned her often enough of how a man would attempt to seduce a woman alone, how easy it was to fall into temptation when no chaperone was about to guard against the falling. Which begged the question: What was she doing here alone with Griffith Stanwick?

But she wasn't going to succumb to his charms. She was a lady, knew her own mind, and would stand firm in her conviction to remain above reproach. As long as no one discovered she was here. She fought against sighing because it was becoming harder not to glide her fingers through his hair and see if it was as silky as it looked, to run her hands over his shoulders, to wonder what he might look like with a little less clothing.

"Is that such a bad thing?" He walked over to the fireplace and set the lantern on the mantelpiece, so it threw light about to illuminate the room more clearly. Crossing his arms over his chest, he leaned against the wall. "You have friends who have married. How well did they know their husbands before their wedding night? How well do you think Althea truly knows Chadbourne?"

"Is something wrong with him?"

"No." He shook his head. "Not as far as I know anyway, but whenever I see them, no matter how closely they are standing together, they seem as near to one another as London is to Paris. I doubt she's even kissed him."

She knew Althea hadn't, but she wasn't about to betray that confidence. She did find herself wondering if her mother would have even married her father if she'd known him well. They had so little in common. Perhaps Griff had a point, although she wasn't yet ready to admit it. Instead, she wandered around the outskirts of the barren room and envisioned it furnished and displaying art, statuettes, and greenery. "So you want to turn this into a cock and hen club?"

"My vision is based on that sort of club, but I want it to be more. The club I visited was one room where people danced, drank, talked, and went off. I want to have a room where couples can dance, one where they can lounge about and talk. It will be more of a social club, a place for the unattached to explore possibilities."

She sensed an underlying current of excitement in him and decided he was trying to appear casual with one foot crossed over the other, but his hands looked tense gripping his arms. They both lived in a world where every action, word, and nuance was judged. That he'd brought her here to share his plans, dreams, and aspirations made her feel a great responsibility to be worthy of his trust. "Tell me everything."

He shoved himself away from the wall and was at her side in four long strides. "None of my members would be heir to a title. Those who are to inherit get enough attention at balls and dinners. The men here would be the other sons who are often overlooked as well as the sons of merchants and tradesmen who have accumulated wealth but aren't invited into ballrooms. The members will also be men who have made their fortunes but aren't accepted by Society for one reason or another. Take the Trewloves, for example. The circumstances of their births kept them from receiving invitations and yet they are wealthy beyond measure."

"They've been marrying into the aristocracy."

"Exactly. They should have been welcomed without marriage. There are others like them. Some legitimate, some not. White's won't give them a membership, but I will. Then, there are the ladies. The wallflowers, the spinsters, and those who have been overlooked. The daughters of those same wealthy tradesmen and merchants. All these women, knowing they can't have the first son of a noble, might be content with a second."

She wondered if he was hoping one might be content with him. She didn't much like the notion of him flirting with some lovely lady. Which wasn't at all fair on her part when she'd asked him to help her determine how best to appeal to the duke via a letter. She was seeking to make an acceptable match. Why shouldn't he? "So you're setting up some sort of matchmaking club."

"Marriage isn't the ultimate goal. Having fun is. This room will serve as a reception area where one can come if questions need answering and where memberships are confirmed before one is allowed to explore the other offerings." He grabbed the lantern from the mantel, and when he returned to her, he threaded his fingers through hers in a casual manner as though he'd given no real thought to it, as though it was the most natural thing in the world.

The quivering in her stomach, the fluttering in her chest, told her that for her it was more than that. It was a gladness, an exhilaration she probably shouldn't be feeling. Becoming involved with Griff would be ruinous to her chances with the duke, would certainly result in her never gaining ownership of the cottage. Therefore, as he led her into the hallway, she fought against harboring a deeper feeling toward him. She wanted only to have an interest in his venture.

"On this level, are other rooms very similar to the first," he said. "They'll be for wandering through, greeting people, and conversing."

He started up the stairs. With the length of his legs, he could have taken the steps two at a time, but instead he kept pace with her. She should have been paying greater attention to the elaborate scrollwork on the spindles and the balustrade they supported but was finding it difficult to focus on anything other than him. He was tall and slender, in fine form. His motions smooth and elegant. Why had she never noticed how he moved like poetry? Every word in her vocabulary seemed insufficient for describing him.

She'd never spent as much time with him as she had the past couple of days. He'd always simply darted into view, delivered a retort, sparred with her a bit, then departed. They'd never explored what the other liked, what dreams the other held. She'd dared to share hers with him, and now he was sharing his with her.

Her world was suddenly discombobulated. It was as though nothing that had come before was real or of any importance, but these minutes, this hour, were terribly significant.

When they reached the landing, he brought her around to an area where they could look down on the floor below and up to the one above.

"I was thinking the rooms on this level, which very much mirror the ones below, would be for entertainments. A room for dancing, one for card playing. Darts, perhaps. Reading."

While all had been said as a statement, she detected a measure of doubt, a possible inquiry as though he sought her opinion. "That all sounds marvelous. Had you considered the merits of having a room with a pianoforte? Sometimes a woman who is shy when it comes to talking is freer with her fingers."

As his tightened around hers, she realized he still held her hand. He released his hold, but his gaze heated. "Is she?"

His voice came out as a low rasp, and she suspected he was envisioning a shy woman—or perhaps even herself—doing something else with her fingers. She didn't mind that his thoughts traveled along a wicked path. This place seemed to call for it. He was correct. Their soirees required so much damned formality and proper behavior, how did someone ever discover another's true self? "What about chaperones?"

"What of them?"

"Will they follow their charge around, or will you have a special room where they will wait?"

"They won't be allowed through the door. The whole point of this place would be the freedom to do as you pleased, with no one to judge."

"Oh, people will judge. Some will come here merely to judge."

"You have a valid point." His eyes lightened as he began thinking it through, and while she regretted that she'd broken whatever spell had held his attention on her, she also liked knowing that he was giving such careful consideration to what she'd said, that she'd offered a viewpoint that was of value to him.

She couldn't recall a gentleman ever asking her opinion on an important matter. Well, a man had once sought her guidance regarding the weather and whether he should carry an umbrella about on the following day, but that hardly compared with offering advice on a business venture.

"To be considered for membership one must be recommended by another member," he murmured. "Or I could post names and other members could strike off those not fitting."

"You'd have some who would strike off a name just to be petty or get even for some slight that had nothing at all to do with them being judgmental."

"Who would do such a thing?"

"Women, most certainly. Probably men as well. Some people are awful and vindictive for the silliest of reasons. I once received a cut from a woman simply because my gown very much mirrored hers. Should I win the duke's favor . . . I will lose friends or receive cuts from others who had sought his attentions."

"Why would they not celebrate and take joy in your success?"

"Because they wanted it for their own."

"Will you be jealous if someone else wins?"

"I like to think not. Oh, I will suffer the sting of rejection, certainly, but I hope I have it within me to be glad for her."

"The fact that you hope it is an indication you will."

She'd never have thought he'd hold such faith in her. "I suppose we shall see."

Watching her steadily, he lifted a hand. She thought he might graze his fingers over her cheek or stroke her chin as he seemed to be headed in that direction but quickly changed course and began rubbing the back of his neck. "You think I should go with referrals, then?"

Was there anything as reaffirming—as sensual—as a man asking for her judgment on so important a matter? She felt as though she'd grown two inches taller, although the fact that she barely reached his shoulder confirmed that she had not. "I believe it would be your wisest course."

His smile was as warm as a summer day, as bright as the sun at noon. "That's what I'll do, then."

Again he was studying her in a way that caused her nerve endings to tingle with an anticipation she didn't quite understand, that made her want his hands gliding over her to calm and settle them back into place. "What of the floor above?"

Her breathlessness astounded her.

"Smaller rooms that would be reserved for couples who want a more intimate . . . dialogue."

A private place where one communicated with touches more than words. "You'll be encouraging carnality."

"Not necessarily."

"Will there be beds in these rooms?"

"In some of them. Pleasure is brought in all sorts of ways. Take tonight, for example. We've done nothing untoward, and yet I can say, in all honesty, that it has been a good long while since I've enjoyed the company of a woman as much as I have yours this evening. No chaperone. No one to interrupt. No one to overhear. No one to judge. How often, in our world, do we have the opportunity to explore the possibilities without the sense of being constantly on display?"

His voice had gone lower, softer with each word spoken. Once in the market, she'd seen a man sitting on the ground, swaying, playing a flute. A cobra in a woven basket had followed his motions, weaving back and forth. At the moment, she felt very much like that cobra, entranced, willing to travel in whichever direction Griff went. Up those stairs with the more private rooms, even though there was no need because they were alone here. He was as dangerous as that viper, perhaps more so, because he made her question the value of things she'd clung to for so long: her purity, her reputation, her respectability.

None of them had ever brought her as much joy as these few hours of doing what she ought not with a man she shouldn't—sneaking out, traveling alone, wandering through rooms, hallways, and up the stairs, speaking about scandalous behavior as though it wasn't so scandalous. "What will you call it?"

Perhaps she was the flute player and he the cobra, mesmerized by her, because it seemed to take him a moment to realize she'd asked a question, to understand what the question was. He blinked, as though he'd been lost in her eyes or her hair or her mere existence. He released a long, slow exhalation. "The Fair Ladies' and Spare Gentlemen's Club. The Fair and Spare for short."

"I like it."

"Do you?"

She nodded. "And the purpose of it. I'm looking forward to visiting it once you have it opened." She put force behind her words, belief, because she wanted—needed—him to understand that she had complete faith in his ability to make a go of this place.

His smile seemed somewhat melancholy. "By the time I have the means to purchase this building and everything required for all the rooms, you'll be married. Only the unmarried can have a membership here since the purpose of the club is to provide a safe atmosphere in which to arrange assignations."

"You don't know that he'll choose me."

"Did you write him what I told you to?"

"Not yet. I've been working on it."

His hand came very near to touching her cheek before he returned it to his side. "You made an impression on him today. Identify yourself in the letter, as he told you to, and describe yourself as I suggested—and he's yours."

He made it sound so easy. Unfortunately, she was no longer certain she wanted Kingsland, a man who believed a wife should take her opinions from her husband.

A short time later, she and Griff were traveling back to the residence, a comfortable silence resting easily between them, each lost in thought. In the morning she would return home. It was doubtful that she would see Griff again until the duke's ball. But she knew she would never forget this remarkable night or the man with whom she'd shared it.

CHAPTER 7

$\mathcal{A}$ LITTLE OVER TWO weeks later, the night of the most important ball of the Season, the one destined to change lives, arrived. Excitement thrummed through Kathryn as she stood with Althea and Jocelyn in the grand salon of the Duke of Kingsland's Belgravia mansion. Oddly, her anticipation had nothing at all to do with the announcement the duke would be making at the stroke of ten or the fact that anyone of any renown was presently taking flutes of champagne from the elegant footmen or that the largest orchestra she'd ever seen sat in one corner of the balcony that encompassed three sides of the room for easy viewing of the lower section of the ballroom by guests.

No. Her elation was due solely to the fact that she would have her waltz with Griff.

If he remembered. If he showed. She had yet to see him.

"Who are you searching for?" her dearest friend asked.

"I'm just looking at everyone. Can you believe how many people are here?"

They were packed in like sardines in a tin. Ladies with intricate coiffures, sparkling jewelry, and extravagant gowns. It didn't seem to matter if they were married, or if they were hoping to gain the duke's attention. All of London wanted Kingsland to know that his affairs warranted any expense in clothing, any trouble to display their elegance. No one wanted to be found lacking.

"There must be at least two hundred," Lady Jocelyn mused. "The duke has never held a ball. It has brought out everyone of any consequence. I wonder how many letters he received."

"No doubt one from every lady not spoken for. Perhaps even a few from those who are betrothed but hoping to acquire something better than what is promised," Althea said. "I'm grateful I'm not having to compete."

"My letter ran the length of eight pages," Jocelyn boasted. "How long was yours, Kat?"

"Everything I wrote about myself filled only a single page."

With a roll of her eyes, Jocelyn scoffed in a manner of superiority that suddenly irritated. "I was unable to limit all my fine qualities and attributes to only one piece of foolscap. My hand fairly cramped when I was done outlining all the reasons he should select me for his duchess."

"I've no doubt of that," Kathryn murmured. Jocelyn would probably win, and she would wish her friend naught but happiness. She glanced at her dance card. A quadrille. A polka. A waltz. She'd written *his* name beside the waltz. "Are your brothers here, Althea?"

"Marcus is. He accompanied Mother and myself. Father had *other business* which we all know is code for visiting with his mistress. I don't even know the woman, yet I abhor her, which makes me feel at once ashamed for my uncharitable thoughts and gratified that I refuse to forgive him for the pain he's caused my mother."

"Maybe your parents should travel to Italy together. It seems to have done wonders for my parents' relationship." Having caught them twice in a passionate embrace, kissing enthusiastically, she had adopted the habit of peering into chambers before entering them.

"I don't think it would make a difference. His excuses and absences are increasing by the day. On a couple of occasions, he's even taken to dining elsewhere."

"I'm truly sorry."

Althea shrugged. "It's not your fault, but I am so terribly disappointed in him. One expects one's father to be above reproach, not to be such a disgraceful cad."

"And Lord Griffith?"

"Well, he can be a cad as well, I suppose, but as he is not yet married, I see no harm in it."

She laughed lightly, only because she didn't want to give away that while she'd once thought the same, she no longer did. "No, I meant, is he here?"

"Oh, I see. He made no mention of attending and didn't accompany us, but I can't imagine that he's not here. I doubt anyone is visiting the clubs tonight. If he is about, he's probably in the cardroom."

She refused to hunt him down. He was here or he wasn't. Upon first entering the residence, he would have been given the gentleman's dance card, which he would have slipped into the inside pocket of his evening coat, so he would know when the first waltz was. He'd either claim it or he wouldn't. She wasn't going to be disappointed if he didn't. Or at least not very. Oh, devil take him, she would be very disappointed, indeed. Since the night he'd shared his dream with her, he and it were all she'd been able to think about.

Jocelyn leaned in slightly. "The duke gave me a very secretive smile when I greeted him and his mother." Her upper teeth pressed into her lower lip as though she dearly wanted to squeal with triumph and was taking precautions not to do so. "I think he might have been hinting that he chose me."

Kingsland had been very formal with Kathryn, hadn't even given the impression that he remembered their encounter in the park. Obviously, he was not taken with her, which was no doubt for the best because she wasn't certain he would make her happy. And if she wasn't happy, could he be?

"I shall be thrilled if he calls out either of your names," Althea said diplomatically.

"Well, as Lord Griffith cheered us on that long-ago morning, may the best lady win," Jocelyn said with glee, as though she had no doubt that the honor would fall to her, that her name would be announced.

Kathryn should care, should be beside herself with worry or nerves. If not this duke, then who? The one thing she yearned to possess seemed beyond reach, and yet at that moment, she knew no sadness, all because of what would happen in her future, in a very short time. A waltz she was rather certain she'd never forget.

When the orchestra filled the room with the strains of the first dance, she greeted her partner with a smile before he led her out onto the floor. She'd always loved dancing, not only the movements that were now popular but the ones from times past. Even if her partner was not particularly skilled, she had the means to make him look so. She seldom lacked for men willing to take her about the floor, but a woman's ability to dance well did not translate into a proposal of marriage.

Above her the crystal chandeliers glittered. But then chandeliers sparkled in every chamber she'd passed on the way to this one. They would become the chandeliers of whomever the duke chose. What a silly thing to contemplate when she had the attention of a man for a few minutes.

"The atmosphere at this ball is the strangest I've ever known," her dance partner lamented.

"How so?"

"So many furrowed brows among the unmarried ladies as they wait for the duke's pronouncement. I suspect afterward, a good many tears will be shed, and many of us gents will be willing to lend our shoulders to those in need of comfort."

Apparently not only the ladies had been preparing for this extraordinary night. "Do you think all the single ladies wrote him letters?"

"Absolutely. My mother insisted each of my sisters write him, and one of them is only four and ten."

Astonished, she hardly knew what to say. "My word. Surely not."

"Indeed. I find the entire arrangement rather sordid and disgusting."

"I cannot imagine he would select a child."

"I shall certainly hope not. Otherwise I might have to call him out."

"And your mother while you're at it."

He grinned broadly. "Why are women so desperate to marry?"

"Why are lords so desperate not to?"

His smile widened further; his eyes twinkled merrily. She'd danced with the viscount numerous times but couldn't recall discussing anything other than the weather.

"I don't know if I've ever realized how blunt you are, Lady Kathryn."

"It is a fault of mine, I suppose."

"I rather like it. Perhaps more forthright conversations would result if men and women were not always at such cross-purposes, the ladies willing to shackle us while we prefer to remain untethered."

"I'm beginning to believe, my lord, that perhaps the problem is that we have different notions as to what marriage entails. You make it sound decidedly unpleasant. I can see why you might want to avoid it if you view it as some sort of prison." Although for women it could become a disagreeable arrangement because they lost so many of their rights when they married.

She was as relaxed with her next partner as she'd ever been, and he with her. It was as though tonight no one felt that they were being judged as marriage material, that they had to put on a show or present themselves as anything other than they were. Everyone was simply waiting for the duke's edict. When their dance was finished, they'd taken a mere half a dozen steps toward the chalked edge of the dance floor before Griff was standing before her, holding out a gloved hand.

"I believe the first waltz is mine," he said quietly.

He looked spectacularly handsome in his black tailcoat, black trousers, silver waistcoat, and perfectly knotted black cravat. His blond locks were neatly styled, and she was tempted to muss them.

With a slight bow, her previous partner left her in Griff's care, and his fingers closed securely around hers before he led her back into the center of the salon.

"I wasn't certain you were here," she said as they waited for the tune to begin.

"I always collect on debts owed."

She refused to be disappointed that his reasons weren't more personal, that it wasn't a desire to have her in his arms that had spurred him to make an appearance.

He lowered his head slightly. "Besides," he said on a whispered rasp, "I would be a fool to miss the opportunity to dance with such a ravishing creature."

She was striving very hard not to take his words to heart, not to blush. That she'd had a light green gown made for the occasion, one that flattered her skin and her eyes, hardly signified. "You're teasing."

"Not this time." His voice was more solemn than she'd ever heard it, and for some reason the sense of having found something to only quickly lose it skittered through her mind.

The music began, and effortlessly, they came together as though they'd done so a thousand times, when in fact they'd never once danced together, had never been quite this close, scandalously close actually, the fingers of one hand splayed over her back, his legs brushing up against the satin of her skirts. "Did you have any luck in the cardroom?"

"What makes you think I've been playing cards?"

"Althea indicated that's where you were, or where she thought you were."

Slowly, he shook his head. "I was watching from the balcony."

Curtains draped here and there made it possible to look down from above without being seen or to find a little privacy from prying eyes—as long as no one sought the same spot. "Anything of interest catch your fancy?"

His gaze held hers for what seemed an eternity—leading her to wonder if he might be on the verge of confessing that she had— before he finally spoke. "Did your parents reconcile?"

She almost insisted he answer her question, but perhaps it was less hurtful not to know the truth, to be able to believe what she wished. "They did, and it's been rather strange, actually. I'm not accustomed to them looking at each other with longing or exchanging secretive smiles or carrying on pleasant conversations without snapping at each other. I've even on occasion caught them kissing."

"Oh dear God, not kissing, surely."

How was it possible to have missed the playful side to him, to want to smile, laugh, and smack him for it, all at the same time. He was so lighthearted, was actually quite fun. "Tease if you like, but it can be rather disconcerting to enter a room and find your mother up against a wall, your father fairly flattened against her as they seem intent on devouring each other. I've begun to walk about with bells on my slippers, so they know I'm coming."

He tossed his head back and laughed, the most wondrous sound she'd ever heard. "The devil you say."

"Well, I may not have gone that far, but I have considered it. My mother spends a good bit of time lately looking unkempt." She felt her cheeks warm with his perusal, with the joy reflected in his eyes. "Still, I'm glad for them. I suppose it's never too late to find love."

"Does it give you hope of possessing it?"

"I've never given up hope, not completely. But I do try to be realistic." Pragmatic, even, but were memories of a past happiness, the time spent with her grandmother, enough to warrant giving up the possibility of a present one, with a man who might appreciate and hold affection for her? It was unfair not to be able to have both.

"Kingsland will no doubt come to love you."

A small laugh bubbled out of her. "He would have to choose me first from among the myriad ladies who are bound to have written him."

"Are you nervous, waiting to hear who he has selected?"

"To be honest, I've given it very little thought. Do you hope for love, Griff?"

"To be honest, I've given it very little thought."

A month earlier, his mimicking her words would have frustrated her. Now, she suspected it was a sort of defense from revealing what he feared might expose him to hurt. "At first, I found it strange when it seemed we were starting to get along. But in retrospect, I find it strange that we didn't from the beginning. I don't think we're that different, you and I."

"We're very different, Freckles."

For the first time, she heard the moniker she'd always loathed as an endearment, spoken so softly, yet with such urgency, as though it needed to convey an entire universe of emotions that were as confusing to him as to her. His fingers tightened more securely around hers, dug more steadily into her lower back where his palm rested at the shallow dip.

Perhaps it was merely the way the gaslight from the chandeliers struck his eyes, but the manner in which they darkened, smoldered, left her with the impression that he was referring to something else entirely, physical aspects about them that were not at all alike. Firm contours that sought cushioned ones. Hard features that sank into soft ones.

If he was courting her, she'd think he was conveying that she should meet him somewhere away from the crowd, where they could explore those differences. When had she ceased to view him as an irritant? When had she begun to notice the possibilities of him as a lover? "Other than your club, what do you dream of acquiring?"

His smile was slow in coming and the higher each side went, the warmer she became, as though he was revealing something intimate, something he'd never shared with another. "My dreams aren't appropriate for a lady's ears."

Disappointment slammed into her. Just when she thought they were becoming confidants, just when she wanted them to. "I'm serious, Griff."

The music stopped, and she took an irrational and pointed dislike for every gentleman in the orchestra. Releasing his close hold on her, Griff took her hand and barely touched his lips to her silk glove, yet she felt the heat of his mouth as though it were a poker just removed from a fire. His gaze held hers, and she could have sworn she saw regret in the blue-gray depths. "Some dreams, Kathryn, aren't meant to be. But yours are. I believe that with all that I am."

Then he strode away, leaving her there, disoriented, wondering why they couldn't both realize their dreams. Her legs suddenly weak, she fairly staggered to a group of chairs mostly filled by matrons and dropped into an empty one. She could feel eyes boring into her and offered a weak smile to the ladies sitting nearby, then nearly jumped out of her skin when her mother suddenly appeared and floated elegantly down beside her.

"I don't believe I've ever seen you dance with Lord Griffith Stanwick before. I was under the impression you didn't even like each other."

"I came to know him a little better while I was staying with Althea."

"You make a handsome couple. Pity he's a second son."

She sighed. "I don't think it's fair that conditions were placed on my inheritance of the cottage."

"Life is seldom fair, dear. It's best to learn that while you're young. Allows for fewer disappointments."

"Your disappointments should be less of late, what with Papa doting on you the way he's been."

Her mother's smile was soft, gentle. "I'm certain whoever you wed will dote on you from the start."

"Should I ever wed."

A gong sounded.

Her mother sighed with great relief. "Finally. The hour everyone has been waiting for has arrived."

KATHRYN WOULD HAVE thought that once the signal was given that the duke was on the verge of making his announcement, the room would have gone completely still and quiet. Instead, the walls echoed squeals and single ladies scrambled—some shoving, many glaring—for a position near the bottom of the stairs, as though they all wanted to give Kingsland one last look at them, one final opportunity to change his mind, rethink his decision, from his place at the top of the stairs.

With far less enthusiasm than that exhibited by all the other unattached young women, Kathryn skirted around one person after another until she reached Althea, whose arm was wrapped around the Earl of Chadbourne's. They made a dashing couple. The lord acknowledged her with a nod. Her dear friend squeezed her hand with her free one. "Don't you want to be closer to the front, so you won't have so far to walk when he announces your name?"

She shook her head. "He's not going to call my name."

"Don't be so sure. He seemed to be taken with you at the park."

"He wants a quiet wife. I believe I demonstrated that is not I."

"A man doesn't always know what he wants until he acquires it," Althea whispered near her ear. "Chadbourne confided that to me when he proposed."

"The Duke of Kingsland doesn't strike me as a man who doesn't know precisely what he wants."

The gong once again sounded. Silence thick with anticipation descended heavily over the stately ballroom as the duke slowly strode down six steps, his penetrating gaze sweeping out over the crowd. Had she ever seen a man exude such confidence, such a commanding presence, such . . . cold detachment? His would not be a marriage filled with warmth, or teasing, or giggles. He wouldn't call his wife by a pet name. He wouldn't look at his wife and see the shadows of where her freckles had been. He wouldn't ask about her dreams or try to help her achieve them—even at great inconvenience to himself. He would never share secrets, never entice her into doing what she ought not . . . never be a friend. And she found the last saddest of all.

Glancing around, she wondered where Griff had gone. Searching the balcony, she wondered if she might spot him spying from up there. Only wherever he was, he was well hidden. Perhaps he'd gone to the cardroom after their dance. Perhaps he'd left.

Or might he have stayed to offer her unexpected comfort when her name wasn't called? For surely, he was as invested in the outcome as Jocelyn who had devoted so many pages of foolscap to describing herself. He had been Kathryn's spy, had offered advice, knew what was at stake. He was here somewhere, watching. She was rather certain of it. He would want to know the outcome of his efforts to aid her in her quest. While they waltzed, she should have told him—

"My esteemed guests." The Duke of Kingsland's commanding voice rang out, reached into every corner of the immense chamber, into every unmarried lady's hopeful heart that beat solely for him. Only her heart had begun to beat for another. "I am honored you have joined me this evening as I announce the name of my potential future wife. We shall have a period of courtship, naturally, to ensure I find her satisfactory. I have little doubt, however, after reading over all the letters I received that the lady I have chosen will endeavor to exceed my expectations. To that end, I bid you congratulate Lady Kathryn Lambert."

Frozen in place as blood rushed through her ears like the constant roar of the ocean, she was vaguely aware of Althea squealing and hugging her, the din of gasps and murmurs, the duke's gaze landing on her with a palpable force as though he'd always known exactly where to find her. It was impossible. He could not have chosen her.

Then he was descending the stairs with an elegance and power that had no doubt seen his ancestors in good stead on a battlefield.

"Can you believe your good fortune?" Althea asked.

No, she absolutely could not.

"He's coming. At least smile."

But her lips refused to move as the sea of people parted for him. Then he was standing before her, so damned cocksure of himself. Yet there was a coldness there, a brittleness that sent a chill through her. He held out his hand to her. "Lady Kathryn."

"Why me?"

"Why not you?"

Because through him, she would gain what she wanted but would have to give up what she desired, what she'd only just recognized she yearned to have.

He lifted an arm and music began filling the air. Like the tide rolling out to sea, the curious surrounding them eased back, and he led her through the parted throng and into the waltz as she expected he intended to lead her into every aspect of her remaining life. He would tell her what to think, what to say, how to behave.

"You need not look so shocked, Lady Kathryn. At the very least, you should appear giddy, overjoyed, and honored."

She had to admit he was a fine dancer, every step graceful and perfect, as though he would tolerate no less from his person, would not allow any aspect of himself to be found lacking. What would he not tolerate in a wife? How would he react if she failed to meet his expectations? "May I be honest, Your Grace?"

"I should hope there would always be honesty between us."

"I'm rather stunned you selected me."

"And why is that, pray tell?"

"Because I never sent you a letter."

Chapter 8

*H*ow was it that in a gigantic ballroom crammed with people, he found her so easily? He had the first time he'd watched from his perch in the balcony, and he'd located her more quickly the second time—just before Kingsland made his dramatic announcement, his tone implying that the honor came from being accepted by him rather than the reality of the situation. He would be damned fortunate to have Kathryn as his wife.

But why had she shown no excitement when her name was called? Why hadn't she hopped around like Althea, as though her joy was too grand to be contained, was bubbling out of her, would carry her to the moon and beyond? Perhaps she was simply dazed by her good fortune.

But even as Kingsland swept her over the dance floor, only the two of them allowed in the space, everyone else hovering at its edges, she seemed stiff, uncomfortable, unhappy. Within Griff's arms, she had moved as fluidly as poetry, graceful with undercurrents of meaning that could only be deciphered with the most discerning of attentions. Or perhaps only with the foolishness of a man who was just coming to realize he possessed a heart. She was like the sun coaxing a bud into opening.

While she held his gaze, the fact that he'd come second into the world had not mattered. For those few minutes while the music and her faint fragrance of oranges had wafted around him, he'd felt as though he'd come first.

When the present tune came to an end, a group of well-wishers swarmed toward the couple of the hour, of the evening, of the century. Or at least the more mature attendees did. The young ladies forced to confront their dashed hopes had quickly exited the grand salon after the announcement had been made, no doubt to shed their tears away from prying eyes and sympathetic glances. He noted a few gents had followed, no doubt to lend comforting shoulders to the disappointed.

It seemed Kathryn also needed some time away. After several minutes of nodding and smiling, she slipped from the gathering and drifted through the open doors that led onto the terrace.

He followed.

It was madness to do so, especially as she had been claimed by another, was now officially off the marriage market, and had the future she wanted stretching out before her. It was time he set about seeing his own come to fruition, that he put his own plans into action, and he'd already taken the crucial step necessary for him to meet with success. But he would find time later to bask in his cleverness. For now, he wanted only one more minute in her company, to witness her joy at acquiring that for which she longed.

He caught up with her deep into the gardens where the gaslights that lined the cobbled path sent out no glow. It didn't surprise him that she would stray from where the duke had deemed it acceptable to stroll, that her barely visible silhouette would stop, and her hands would go to her hips. How many times over the years had she sent some cutting barb his way while projecting that exact stance? Only she didn't know he was there. Not until he stepped on a twig and its snap sounded like a rifle report.

She swung around.

"It's me," he said quickly, quietly, not wanting to cause her alarm. "Griff."

"I know. Why did you do it?"

Every fiber of his being went still. While it was impossible, it felt as though his heart, lungs, and blood did as well. "I know not to what you are referring."

She stepped closer, and it didn't matter that an abundance of flowers was hidden in the shadows, that their fragrance should have permeated the air. All he could smell were oranges and cinnamon. "*A quick wit, a biting tongue, and a sharp mind.*"

"Kath—"

"*Her mere presence will cause a man to yearn to know the intimacy of her thoughts, her secret desires, her touch.*"

"The duke—"

"*Like the finest of wines, she is bold, full-bodied, and tantalizing. Never disappointing. Yet never the same, always offering another aspect to be discovered. A lifetime in her company will never be long enough.* You wrote those words to Kingsland. It seems he has the ability to remember anything when read once. Why? Why would you do such a thing?"

"Because a man doesn't give a bloody damn how well a woman plays whist. Because you failed to see yourself in a favorable light, as others see you. Because you are too modest by half." He hadn't meant for the words to come out so sharply, but he was angry that she wasn't grateful, angry that she'd been chosen—even as he'd sent the letter to ensure this outcome. He should be glad. Instead he wanted to howl out his frustration.

"But why would you bother? If asking him a question at the gaming hell was an inconvenience, I can't imagine why you would go to the immense trouble of actually penning a letter."

His voice came out softer this time, the anger retreating. "You want a cottage. I know what it is to want." To yearn for what could never be held.

She stepped nearer, and he didn't know if it was the moon, or the stars, or the distant lamps, but when she tilted up her face, he could see her perfectly, clearly. Her gaze roamed over his features, finally settling on his eyes, and he hoped she couldn't see the truth there, couldn't see the depths of his feelings for her, how this moment was destroying him.

"But you don't even like me," she whispered.

God, how he wished that was true. How he wished the lies he'd told himself over the years to protect his heart weren't mocking him now.

Tentatively, she lifted her hand and placed it against his jaw, and he cursed whoever long ago decided that women and men should wear gloves to these blasted affairs. He wanted the warmth of her skin seeping into his. He wanted to know the smoothness of her palm. There was that word again, and no matter its form—*want, wanted, wanting*—it caused him to have idiotic thoughts and do stupid things. Like ensure she spent the remainder of her life in the arms of another.

"You tease me unmercifully." The usual rasp in her voice had gone lower, and it sent tingles racing along his spine, and he fought against imagining how deep-throated her cries when lost to ecstasy would sound, how they might cause a man to lose control of himself, how his own gruff groans might complement the crescendo.

"Have you no defense, nothing to say for yourself?" she asked.

"I have no defense." Except to continue on with his foolishness and lower his mouth to hers.

Of course, it was a mistake, but then every aspect of this night was. He never should have waltzed with her because now his arms felt all the emptier when she wasn't in them. He would pay a price for the kiss as well. He just didn't know yet what the exact cost would be.

When he urged her to open to him, she didn't hesitate to part her lips, to welcome the thrust of his tongue, so he could explore the hidden contours, could taste her fully. With one hand, he braced the base of her skull while he pressed the other at her back so she was flattened against him so thoroughly that even if the moon descended into the garden, not a wisp of its light would filter between them.

Her fingers skimmed along to his nape, then eased up slightly to swirl through his hair, as her mouth moved provocatively over his. She was no shy miss, no whimpering maiden. Although, an occasional whimper sounded, followed by a moan or a sigh, as she feasted.

Christ, he'd known her for years. How had he failed to notice that the proper Lady Kathryn could turn into a feral cat when let loose? When there was no one to see. When it was only the two of them. When they were doing things they ought not, but neither would tell.

She trusted him not to tell, to hold this breach of etiquette secret. That trust was like the most precious of jewels, something he could take out and examine during the lonely nights ahead. And there would be lonely nights.

This kiss wasn't the first mistake he'd ever made in his life, but it was the one that would leave in its wake the deepest regret. It would have been better to have never known the taste of her—light as champagne, rich and sweet—and the swiftness with which she melted against him, fit so perfectly, as though their bodies had been designed with each other in mind.

He wished he could hold her in his embrace forever. But that honor would go to another man. And because it would, he could take no more liberties.

Sliding his mouth from hers, he trailed it along her throat, tucking it up just beneath her jaw where he could feel the erratic pulsing of her heart. Up a little higher to nibble on her lobe before outlining the delicate shell. "You'll find happiness with him."

Then Lord Griffith Stanwick, second son, who had never denied himself anything he wanted, strode away, denying himself the only thing he'd ever truly desired.

CHAPTER 9

*T*HE NEXT MORNING found Kathryn lying in bed, staring at the ceiling, much as she'd been ever since she'd retired the night before. She couldn't stop thinking about what had transpired in the garden.

As Griff had deepened the kiss, explored the confines previously untouched by any gentleman, he'd moaned, a low lament that reminded her of how she responded when she first bit into a delicious new chocolate confection. As though nothing before it had ever been as flavorful, as though nothing after it would ever usurp the exquisite satisfaction it wrought. All-encompassing, exhaustively intoxicating. More. She always wanted more, indulged her desires.

It seemed he had been of a like mind. While they'd once parried with words, last night they'd done so with their tongues in a much friendlier encounter. He advanced, withdrew. When she followed, he captured and suckled gently, provocatively. She'd never imagined a kiss would encompass so many different textures—rough, silky, smooth, grainy—or such a variety of moves—slow, fast, soft, forceful.

She'd never wanted it to end.

But it had. He'd simply walked away, leaving her alone in the darkened garden, wanting him back, calling after him, forever changed.

How was it that after delivering such a blistering kiss, he could carry on without even looking back? She'd been at once hurt and angry and confused. Emotions had rioted through her, and it had taken several minutes to reclaim her calm.

She'd returned to the ballroom where Kingsland had immediately greeted her and claimed another dance. As he'd swept her over the floor, her mind had been searching for some explanation regarding her swollen, still-tingling lips should he ask about their plumpness. She'd had a feeling her hair was not as tidy as it had been when she'd made her excuse of needing some fresh air, but the loose curls she could blame on the breeze. Her rapidly pounding, erratic heart on her rush to rejoin him. But he'd asked nothing of her, revealed none of his thoughts to her. Merely studied her with an astuteness that hinted he thought himself capable of deciphering her with his eyes alone. However, she'd kept her thoughts and feelings shuttered. Now she worried that she might do it for the remainder of her life. That he would never truly know her.

Her parents had been beside themselves with joy, had smiled brightly in the carriage on the journey home, and had reflected on how pleased her grandmother would have been to know that Kathryn had snagged herself a duke. She would be a duchess.

"I believe he has other tests I must pass," she'd remarked distractedly, hoping to assuage any disappointment they might feel if things went sour. She could hardly stand their enthusiasm over something she hadn't accomplished herself.

Why had Griff done it? Why had he written the duke? Why had he kissed her? She needed the answers, a better understanding of his motivations. What had been in it for him? Had he begun to care for her as she had for him? The kiss had certainly implied he was drawn to her, but if he wanted her, why give her to another? She'd never thought of him as being altruistic. While he'd claimed to know what it was to want, was that reason enough to place her into another's keeping? She had to see him, had to know exactly what his feelings regarding her were. Otherwise, how could she possibly ask her heart to accept the duke?

After tossing back the covers, she yanked on the bellpull to summon her maid. Within the hour, she was headed down to breakfast.

Walking into the small dining room, she didn't know if she'd ever grow accustomed to her parents tittering and giggling. Giggling like schoolchildren for goodness' sake. Her mother now sat to her father's right, rather than miles away from him, a place at the foot of the table she'd occupied for years.

"Hello, darling," her mother said, glancing up and catching sight of her. She looked so remarkably happy. Kathryn was glad of that. "Did you sleep well?"

"Not really, to be honest. Too much excitement, I suppose." A kiss that had left her wanting for more.

After filling a plate with a wide selection of meat, eggs, and cheeses from the sideboard, she joined her parents at the table, taking a seat opposite her mother.

"Kingsland is a jolly good sort," her father said. "He mentioned that he'll be calling on you this afternoon. Wants to take you on a carriage ride through the park, I believe."

She should be thrilled by the prospect of being properly courted, should be overjoyed by the prospect of *him*. Instead, Griff occupied every thought, every corner of her mind.

"Don't look so glum, dear," her mother said. "You are the toast of the *ton*, on everyone's tongue. I can't tell you how many congratulations on your behalf I received last night."

But she had no doubt her mother would try.

"I daresay not as many as Lord Griffith Stanwick," her father drawled with a bit of testiness.

Curiosity getting the better of her, she immediately perked up. "What has he accomplished to earn congratulations?"

"Made out like a highwayman on the wager he made at White's and quite possibly at other clubs as well."

A chill began forming along her spine, like frost at the edge of a window before it completely covered the pane. She licked her lips, swallowed. "What wager was that?"

"He predicted Kingsland would choose you over all others."

As THE CARRIAGE traveled through the streets, Kathryn's fury was simmering into a boil. It hadn't helped cool her temper when her father went on to explain that everyone had thought it a foolish wager, but then Wolfford's spare was known for wagering foolishly. Therefore, many had taken him up on it, no one believing she would be the one selected. Only she had been. What else precisely had he put in the letter that Kingsland might have omitted as he'd shared some of what Griff had written?

Was it guilt that had driven him to the garden? Was the kiss the result of a man overcome with joy because he'd managed to gain so much by doing so little? Now she saw his parting words as more of an attempt to convince himself rather than her, perhaps to ease his guilt, to reassure himself he'd not done her a disservice.

The scapegrace. The unmitigated swindler. The scoundrel who'd taken advantage of her good fortune. It no longer mattered that he was responsible for it. She'd thought he'd done it because he cared for her. As always he cared for only himself. And he'd found an easy way to put coins in his coffers.

He'd answer to her now.

The carriage came to a stop in front of the Duke of Wolfford's residence.

"You needn't accompany me inside," she said to the maid serving as her chaperone. "I shan't be long."

Her footman climbed down, opened the door, lowered the steps, and extended his hand. Her righteous indignation shimmered through her as she disembarked and then marched up the wide stone stairs. At the door, she gave one solid rap with her gloved knuckles, not using the knocker because she needed that physical contact and was preparing her fist for its encounter with Griff's nose.

The door opened, and the butler allowed her in. "Lady Kathryn, I'll alert Lady Althea that you're here." His tone was that of someone in mourning.

"I've actually come to see Lord Griffith."

"I'm afraid he's not at home."

Of course, he wasn't. He was no doubt off spending his ill-gotten gains, the rotter.

"Then, yes, please, Lady Althea." Her friend was going to be horrified by her brother's actions.

Scarcely a couple of minutes passed before Althea was rushing toward her with red, swollen eyes, her hair untidy, her face pale and drawn. She was wringing a silk handkerchief between her hands, her brow deeply furrowed. "You've come. How did you know to come? Where did you hear of it? Is it all over London already?"

Kathryn shook her head. "I'm sorry, I'm not certain what you're talking about. I came to speak with Griff about the damned wager he made regarding whom Kingsland would select."

"Then you haven't heard."

"Haven't heard what, precisely?"

"My father and brothers have been arrested for treason."

Chapter 10

April 20, 1874

His BREATHING HARSH, *heavy, and labored, his heart pounding, he was running, running, yet he didn't seem to be going anywhere. It was all an inky blackness, but beyond it . . . surely there was something beyond it—if he could only reach it. She was beyond it, if only he could reach* her.

Suddenly he was in a room, sitting in a hard chair, his hands tied behind him, surrounded by shadows. Light shone down on him, the brightness causing him to squint. Where was its origin? There were no lamps, no windows. Nothing. Only him, the chair, and the shadows.

"Give us the names."

"Of whom?"

"Who else is involved?"

"Involved in what, precisely?"

"How many are there?"

"I haven't the foggiest notion what the devil you're referring to."

"You expect us to believe you knew nothing of the plot?"

"What plot?"

The blackness returned, and he was running again. With Althea. He had to protect her. She became his duty, his responsibility. Only she didn't need him, had her own plans. Still, he reached for her—

But she faded away.

Marcus appeared. Secrets, deception, danger. The heir, no longer an heir, vanished.

Leaving him to face the consequences alone. Always alone. Always—

Griff jerked awake, shaking off the gossamer nightmare the way a dog did water after coming out of a stream. But the reality of it remained to haunt him as he scrubbed his hands up and down his face, struggling to bring himself back to the present and out of the past.

It had been ten months since he and Marcus had been hauled to the Tower because the authorities had believed them to be involved in a plot to assassinate Her Majesty, the Queen. A plot that, it turned out, the Duke of Wolfford had participated in. He hadn't been going to see his mistress every night. He'd been meeting with his fellow conspirators. While their father hadn't been acting alone, he'd been the only one caught. It had taken two weeks of daily interrogations before Griff and Marcus had managed to convince the Home Secretary of their innocence, their total ignorance regarding the treasonous undertaking that had consumed their father.

After all this time, Griff still found it difficult to believe their father had been capable of such machinations and had sought to place someone else on the throne. But apparently there had been a dark and dangerous aspect to their father that none of them had known anything about. After being found guilty of treason, the Duke of Wolfford had stood upon a scaffold while the noose had been placed around his neck. Thank God, the law no longer allowed for public hangings. It was ironic that in 1870 his father had voted against the bill that did away with drawing and quartering traitors. Its passage had spared him a more gruesome death. Shortly after his execution, the Crown had confiscated the duke's titles and properties and left Griff and his family with naught but the clothes on their backs and the few belongings they'd managed to gather before they were evicted from the residence. The truth of the duke had broken their mother's heart, and she'd passed away in ruin and despair. Family and friends had abandoned them, and they'd been left to their own devices. Even Chadbourne had turned his back on Althea and broken the engagement, which had resulted in Society shunning her completely.

Working in the shadows, Marcus was determined to regain the family honor by discovering who else had been involved in the plot to do away with Queen Victoria. For a few months Griff had joined in the quest but had recently lost patience with it and decided his efforts would be better spent striving to ensure he could provide funds when needed. Little money was to be earned in clandestine endeavors.

Rolling out of the bed, the only piece of furniture presently in this room, he snatched up his trousers and pulled them on. His investments had finally come to fruition, providing him with enough money to purchase the building he'd wanted, but more was needed to turn it into what he'd envisioned. And he knew just where to get the blunt.

His clubs had cancelled his memberships, refused him entry. But a well-placed sovereign in the palm of an otherwise-trusted employee had gotten him what he needed.

Reaching into his coat pocket, he removed the slip of paper on which was listed the name of every damned lord who had wagered against his prediction that the Duke of Kingsland would select Lady Kathryn Lambert as the woman he would court with the intention of marrying. While paying a debt from a wager was a matter of honor, it seemed gentlemen were not compelled to honor those debts when they were owed to the son of a traitor. The money would have come in handy when he and his siblings had found themselves with nothing.

Now those very same lords and gentlemen who'd turned their backs on him, who had refused to make good on their wagers, were going to learn that eventually the devil always got his due—with interest.

The following night

KATHRYN HAD ALWAYS loved the theater, and since last June, she'd become a regular fixture in Kingsland's box. Attending plays was one of the few things they did with any regularity, although sitting beside him now, with her maid serving as chaperone and settled in a chair behind her, she wondered if he brought her here because it removed the need for much conversation. She always became so absorbed in the performances that she easily maintained the quietness he claimed to prefer. On the rare occasion when she did glance over at him, it was to see a man who appeared distant, distracted, as though he was busily engaged in running sums through his mind.

They'd attended a few dinners together, and he'd carried on conversation with ease, but she suspected that after they married and it was only the two of them at the table, he would be occupied with ruminations on his business affairs rather than discourse revolving around her interests or how she might have spent her day. Not that she needed to be the center of his world or the focus of his attention. She had accepted that theirs wouldn't be a love match, but then love was not required among the aristocracy for a well-suited marriage.

"Is something amiss? You seem distracted."

With a start, she glanced over at the man she was to marry—if he ever got around to asking. If she ever insisted that he did. Since he'd called out her name, they'd had relatively little time together. He'd been in France, Belgium, and even America for a while and had only just returned from Scotland the day before. It seemed his business ventures took him all over the world. Although, whenever he was away, she received small tokens indicating he was thinking of her: flowers, chocolates, an invitation to use his box when a new play began. He sent nothing that would be inappropriate for her to accept. Still, she would have preferred a letter sharing the details of his travels. But having received none, it seemed they should have had a great deal to discuss each time he returned, and yet she was growing weary of having to ask how his journey had gone, especially when his answer was always "Simply filled with boring business."

Sometimes it made her wonder if he considered her boring business.

She was beginning to suspect that it wasn't so much that he wanted a quiet wife but rather an absent one. All he really required of her was an heir. She might have taken offense, but wasn't a hypocrite. She was using him as well to gain what she wanted. Certainly no mad passion would rise up between them. She would have to find passion elsewhere, with other endeavors. To that end, she'd become involved with several charitable activities, taking particular interest in bettering the lives of underprivileged women.

"I'm simply in a reflective mood this evening. You seem equally preoccupied."

"I apologize. I have the opportunity to purchase a coal mine in Yorkshire. I'm afraid I've been running the advantages and disadvantages through my mind."

"Which one is winning?"

He flashed a grin. "At the moment, they're equal, although I shall probably need to take a trip to Yorkshire in the near future to ensure I have all the information at hand to make my decision."

"When you have a wife, will you welcome her traveling with you?"

"I certainly wouldn't prevent you from going with me, although you might find it a lonely experience as much of my time would be taken up with the pressing matters that prompted the journey."

Her stomach clutched at his inferring she would be his wife. He often did that, implied that she would become his duchess, but they had no formal agreement. He'd not spoken with her father. "You don't really view a wife as part of your life, do you?"

"I will not view you as my life, but you most certainly will be part of it. That day in the park, you did not strike me as a woman who needs to be coddled."

"Still, a woman likes to feel she is wanted."

"I would not deign to marry a woman if she was not."

She wondered why his words brought her no comfort, why she couldn't imagine losing herself to his kiss in the garden or being wretchedly hurt if he disappointed her by making a wager that involved her.

She hadn't seen Griff since that night in Kingsland's garden. She'd barely seen Althea. Oh, she'd been there for her friend that fateful morning when she'd gone to confront Griff. She'd held Althea as she wept, rubbed her back as she trembled, and reassured her that it was all simply a horrendous mistake, would be quickly sorted, and everything would return to normal in short order.

However, by the time she'd returned home in the early afternoon, word of the duke's transgressions and the suspicions regarding his sons' involvement had spread throughout London. Her father had forbidden her to have any further association with Lady Althea Stanwick. When a daughter lives beneath her father's roof and has no means to acquire her own, she has little choice except to obey his dictates.

She'd managed to secretly visit with Althea a couple of times, but after her friend's father had been hanged for treason, Althea and her brothers had disappeared. It had been quite upsetting to have no word at all, to wonder how they fared. But then several weeks ago, her friend had come back into her life—after she'd become involved with Benedict Trewlove, the newly-anointed Earl of Tewksbury. They'd recently married and were presently in Scotland. Neither Marcus nor Griff had attended the wedding, and Althea was reluctant to share any news about them, other than to reassure her that they were fine, if not readily accessible.

"You have every right to be upset with my frequent absences," the duke said now.

But that was the crux of the issue. She wasn't bothered by them in the least. While he was away, she didn't miss him, didn't wonder what he was doing. It was ludicrous that her thoughts would often drift to Griff, and she would wonder if he was well, if he was wandering the streets or enjoying a pint at a pub. In spite of her upset with him regarding the wager, she couldn't seem to not worry about him, to wonder what sort of toll his father's actions had taken on him.

"Yet, I assure you," the duke continued, "that nothing will distract me—"

"King?"

Immediately he turned his attention away from her to the young man who had entered his box. "Lawrence, I didn't realize you had an interest in joining us this evening."

"I don't, but I'm in a spot of bother, and Pettypeace informed me I'd find you here."

"How much?"

She heard in his tone that this matter was a frequent conversation between him and his brother, the one he'd once told her he considered more important than himself.

Lord Lawrence crouched so he was on a more equal level with Kingsland. "A thousand."

"You lost a thousand quid after only a few hours at a gaming hell tonight? Good God, Lawrence, that's totally unacceptable."

"No, no, I've not even been to the gaming hell yet. It's that damned wager I made with Griffith Stanwick last Season."

Kathryn's heart gave a wild thump at the mention of Griff. And the mention of a wager from last Season. Could he be referring to any wager other than the awful one that involved her? Why was Griff only collecting on it now?

"He's come out of the shadows, has he?"

"To collect what is owed, yes."

"You haven't already settled with him? Paying on a lost wager is a matter of honor."

"No one paid him. His father was a traitor, and we all agreed it nullified the matter."

So all this time, Griff had not had access to the money he'd won? It didn't lessen her upset with him for making the blasted bet in the first place, but it did serve to make her angry at those who hadn't paid up. Based on what Althea had told her, she knew they'd all been in dire straits financially after they were ousted from Mayfair. They'd been relegated to living in the rookeries, to actually *working* in order to survive.

"Remorse seems rather late in coming, so what changed your mind about paying what was owed?" Kingsland asked.

"He's threatening bodily harm or the spilling of secrets that some don't want spilled."

That did not sound at all like the teasing Griffith Stanwick she knew, a man who smiled and laughed easily.

"Which applies to you?"

"Does it matter?"

She watched as Kingsland scrutinized his younger brother, another example of a spare who was always holding out his hand. Little wonder her grandmother had warned her against marrying one.

The duke released a long sigh. "Tell Pettypeace to give you what you need."

"Your secretary isn't going to give over any blunt unless I know the secret word the two of you use to indicate you're willing to open your coffers to me. Or have a note with your signature signifying you approve of my having the funds."

The duke removed a small notebook and tiny pencil from inside his jacket, scrawled something, tore the paper free of its mooring, and held it out to his brother.

"Thank you," Lawrence offered quietly before straightening. It was only then that he acknowledged her. "Lady Kathryn, I apologize for disturbing your evening. Enjoy the performance."

With that, the young lord took his leave, giving her no time to ask if he knew where she might find Griff and if he looked well. Not that she would have given so much of her thoughts and feelings away, especially as she didn't want Kingsland to doubt her devotion to him—even if she doubted it herself.

The lights in the theater began to dim until only those illuminating the stage provided a meaningful glow. The curtains drew back to reveal several actors in a forest.

"Have you had any word from Mr. Griffith Stanwick?"

She jerked her attention to Kingsland. "I haven't, no. He'd have no reason to pay me a visit or correspond. I certainly didn't make a wager with him."

"I assumed as his sister's friend, you might know how he's weathered his father's betrayal to the Crown."

"I'm not even certain she knows what he's involved in these days. I can't believe he threatened your brother."

"We gents take our wagers damned seriously. Some have fought duels over the honor associated with them."

"It wasn't very sporting of you not to let your brother know whom you'd selected so that he wouldn't lose money in that ridiculous wager." She felt the anger and hurt bubbling back to the surface as she was reminded of the reason Griff had assisted her.

The duke leaned toward her. "You know the details of the wager to which he was referring?"

His voice was low, but she heard no intimacy in it and didn't know if he'd gone quiet out of respect for her or so as not to disturb those sitting in nearby balconies. "I'm assuming he's referring to the one that predicted you would select me. My father told me of it. Did you make a bet on the matter?"

"It would be unethical for me to do so when I was the one who would determine the outcome. It would have also been unfair for me to tell my brother. Knowing what was written in the betting book at White's, I kept my decision to myself, told no one, not even my best mates."

"Oh yes, of course." She knotted her hands in her lap. "I didn't know he hadn't collected on it. Would you have paid him if no one else did?"

"I always honor my debts. I wonder where he's been."

She wondered as well, then cursed her blasted curiosity. She was spending the evening with a man who had never taken advantage of what he knew about her to benefit himself. Mr. Griffith Stanwick shouldn't occupy her thoughts. Yet, she seemed unable not to think about him.

After their brief discourse regarding the wager, they watched the play in silence, and then journeyed home with nary a word spoken. When they reached the manor, he asked her to wait with him a moment for a quiet word while her maid carried on into the residence. But he didn't give her a quiet word. He gave her a kiss. A brief one to be sure, a mere passing of his lips over hers, but it was the first time he'd taken such liberties. She couldn't deny that her heart had certainly sped up, but there was no fluttering in her stomach, no weakening of her knees, no curling of her toes—none of the visceral sensations she'd experienced when Griff had kissed her, but then his had been the kiss of a scoundrel, not a gentleman.

If she was wise, she'd toss out every memory of Griffith Stanwick she possessed. She certainly shouldn't make any effort to compare the duke to him.

Chapter 11

June 1, 1874

Six weeks later, with no ball or soiree scheduled for the evening, Kingsland in Yorkshire as he'd predicted, and her parents visiting Paris, Kathryn went to the Elysium Club, a gaming hell for ladies—or at least the ladies assumed it was close to being one that rivaled those the men in their lives frequented. Kathryn suspected it was a bit posher than its counterpart for men because it didn't resemble her idea of hell in the least. But Aiden Trewlove had certainly taken great pains to ensure his establishment reflected women's fantasies.

The gaming room was softly lit. Handsome gents in evening attire wandered through offering advice on strategy, a light touch on a shoulder, or just a smile. Other rooms provided different entertainments—food, dancing, foot rubs—but Kathryn preferred this one because while they might occasionally flirt, the gentlemen weren't delivering so much attention as to be distracting, and within these walls, it was never completely quiet. Clacking dice, spinning wheels, and the shuffling of cards created a cacophony that served as a backdrop for the gossip that was often shared during play.

Her favorite game was *vingt-et-un*. The rules were simple: accumulating cards, striving to reach a value of twenty-one or as near to it as possible without going over. She'd acquired her membership here shortly after that fateful night when Kingsland had announced her name. She'd heard of the club, had been curious about it, and had decided that if she was to soon marry, she should do everything she'd ever wanted to before she exchanged vows in case her husband had objections to his wife being entertained in such a scandalous manner. Now, however, she suspected she could continue to come here, and he wouldn't care one whit. Her marriage would very likely resemble the one her parents had before they fell in love. She couldn't quite envision Kingsland plastering her against walls and devouring her. He had yet to strike her as a man who would lose control of himself or a situation.

"Lady Kathryn?"

She glanced up at the dealer, studied her cards, nodded. "Yes, I'll have another."

Then she smiled as the card he dealt her left her two shy of twenty-one. "I'll stop here."

He moved on to the lady beside her, one who wore a domino mask. Some of the members preferred a disguise because for various reasons they wanted to keep their identity secret, but Kathryn didn't care who knew she was here. She wasn't going to slink about as though ashamed of her behavior when she wasn't. The one thing she could claim with certainty regarding her relationship with Kingsland was that it reflected an honesty that ensured she never had to pretend to be other than as she was.

"Have you found someone to recommend you?" Lady Prudence, sitting beside Kathryn said sotto voce to Lady Caroline, who sat on the other side of Lady Prudence.

"I have, yes."

"Would she recommend me, do you think?"

"I'll recommend you if I gain membership."

"What's this then?" Kathryn asked, knowing it was rude to eavesdrop, but having her attention snagged by the *recommend* portion of their conversation.

Both ladies gave a start and looked rather guilty. They studied each other for a minute before finally nodding. Lady Prudence leaned toward Kathryn and whispered so low that she almost didn't hear her. "There's a new club."

Her heart gave a lurch as suspicion took hold. Griff should be flush with funds after collecting on his wager. He might have obtained enough to purchase the building he wanted. "What sort of club?"

Lady Prudence glanced around as though fearful of being spied upon, of being caught doing what she ought not. "It's a place where men and women meet for . . . companionship. But the membership is very exclusive, and you're admitted only upon someone else's recommendation." Once more her gaze darted around the room. Seemingly satisfied with her observations, she inched her mouth ever closer to Kathryn's ear. "And you must swear an oath not to divulge what happens within or whom you see there. More importantly whom you see together. I heard one lady didn't honor the oath, began whispering about a gent in the company of a lady another was courting—and the offender awoke to find the club owner in her bedchamber threatening to see her reputation ruined if she didn't cease with the gossiping."

Kathryn seemed unable to stop herself from staring, to come up with a proper response. All of this sounded far, far too familiar, except for the notion of Griff breaking into a woman's bedchamber to threaten reprisals. First of all, he wouldn't have the skills needed for gaining entry into a residence locked up for the night, and secondly, he wasn't one to threaten. Not seriously. If anything, he would be teasing.

"Scandalous, I know, for such a place to exist," Lady Prudence murmured in the wake of her silence. "Not to mention the sneaking into a lady's bedchamber."

However, it wasn't the scandal of the place but rather the fact that she knew owning such a business had been Griff's dream. She even knew the building he'd wanted to purchase, had driven by it a few times after their nighttime visit to it. The last time she did so, it still appeared to be for sale. But that was a couple of months ago. "Who is the owner?"

Lady Prudence's eyes widened with glee. "That's just it. Only the members know, and they aren't tattling. It's just all so delightfully mysterious and deliciously disreputable."

"Ladies, are you going to continue to play?"

Kathryn jerked her attention to the dealer, noting as she did so that he'd revealed his cards, the sum he'd reached greater than twenty-one. Her winnings already sat in front of her. She shook her head. "I believe I'll call it a night."

After gathering up her chips, she stood, started to move aside, halted, and lowered herself to Lady Prudence's ear so she could make a discreet inquiry. "Has this establishment a name?"

"The Fair and Spare. But you shan't be allowed in if your name isn't on the list. And its membership is so secret that it's deuced difficult to figure out who you can ask to sponsor you."

"I shan't require a sponsor." Or a recommendation or her name on a list.

As she headed for the door, she knew nothing on God's green earth was going to stop her from gaining entry.

FROM THE TOP of the stairs, Griff looked over the railing and down onto the crowded foyer where the new arrivals mingled, waiting for the woman he'd hired to search for their name on a list and verify their membership before allowing them access to the main portion of the building. The Fair and Spare had officially opened a fortnight earlier, and word had spread more quickly than he'd anticipated. Everyone he'd invited to the first night's celebration had come. He'd not put his name on the invitation, but neither had he hidden his identity from those who had walked through the door out of curiosity. As a matter of fact, he'd taken perverse delight in their shock when they'd realized they'd answered the summons of the traitor's son. He'd debated operating in secret but had decided to hell with it. He was no longer going to let his father's legacy define him.

Even though he couldn't deny that, in many ways, it had made him the man he was now, barely clinging to the few frayed remnants of who he'd once been.

Besides, he liked being visible, moving about. His presence ensured people behaved. The hands that had bled and scarred provided an ominous signal that he was no longer a proper gentleman, and he kept them on display by never wearing gloves. When he walked through the rooms, people gave him a wide berth. He didn't mind that, either. Their membership was putting coins into his coffers. He didn't need them as friends, acquaintances, or mates, preferred they were a bit wary of him.

He no longer belonged in their world, wasn't going to pretend that he did.

Weary of his idleness, the boredom settling in because of his inaction, he decided it was time to strut through the various rooms, had just started to turn when he caught sight of *her.*

She marched in with confidence and the bearing of a queen, an empress, the ruler of a dominion spread out before her, resting at her feet. His gut shouldn't have tightened. His heart shouldn't have started galloping wildly. He shouldn't have been grateful for her arrival.

And yet he'd known she would come if she ever heard of the place. After all this time, the sight of her was a balm to his tattered soul. Not that by word, deed, or expression he was going to give any indication that was the case.

She wore a gown of emerald green, one he'd never before seen, but he knew her eyes would reflect the shade. Gloriously dark, gloriously rich.

As though she were special—Lord help him if he didn't consider her so—she waltzed past the line of people having their membership confirmed, strolled farther into the hallway until her path was blocked by a big brute of a fellow, whom he'd hired to maintain order. He'd seen several men noticeably pale when Billy stepped in front of them, but she merely arched a brow at him as though his presence was a nuisance. God, he loved that she wasn't intimidated by a man who could snap her in half, but then there were so many things he'd come to admire about her, far too late for any of his realizations to do any good.

If he was smart, he'd go to his office and lock the door. Instead, he started down.

KATHRYN WOULD NOT have been surprised to learn the man standing before her had descended from giants. However, having just come from the Elysium Club, she was impatient to learn if what she suspected was accurate and didn't intend for anyone—giant or no—to stop her. "Let me pass."

"Ye gots to get yer membership vereefied first."

"I'm not a member, and I don't require membership to enter."

He blinked several times, and she thought perhaps he was striving to translate her words into something that made sense to him—or perhaps he simply wasn't accustomed to anyone challenging him. She noted a couple of gents nearly hugging the wall to avoid getting too close to the fellow as they made their way into what she was fairly certain were the more interesting sections of the building.

"Everyone requires membership," he finally said, although his tone lacked any real conviction. "'Ems the rules."

"I don't. Move out of my way."

"Can't do it. Lose me job."

"I assure you that you won't. Now step aside."

"Look 'ere, miss—"

"It's all right, Billy. Let her through."

She hated the way that voice could leave her breathless. Still, the brawny giant did as ordered, and then her vision was filled with Griff, standing there in formal evening attire that fit him to perfection. It had to have recently been tailored for him because his shoulders were broader, his arms thicker than they'd been the last time she'd seen him. Shoulders and arms that she knew the firmness of because she'd trailed her fingers over them when he'd kissed her in Kingsland's garden. That she wanted to do so again was inconvenient. She hadn't come here to do any trailing, kissing, or touching. She'd come to give him a piece of her mind.

As though he were king of the realm, he tipped his head slightly to the side as though granting her permission to come forward—when she didn't need his permission to do anything. Still, she took four steps toward him until she caught his fragrance of bay rum mingled with the aroma of freshly dug earth and inhaled his scent deeply as though she'd just emerged from years of living beneath the ocean and was finally free of it to take air into her lungs, filling them to near bursting.

His hair was lighter in shade, longer, curling against those massive shoulders. His jaw was shadowed by bristles as though it had been several hours since he'd shaved. Although, maybe he kept it that length on purpose. It made him appear tougher, more dangerous, someone to be reckoned with. However, his eyes served the same purpose. They no longer reflected a light-hearted, teasing mien. As a matter of fact, she was left with the impression that he might not ever laugh at all any longer. She'd never realized before how well she knew each detail of him. How it gratified and angered her at the same time.

"This establishment isn't open to those who are claimed," he said in a flat, curt tone.

"Then, I suppose it is fortunate that I am not claimed."

She noted a fissure of anger in those blue-gray eyes before he narrowed them. "You turned him down?"

"He has yet to ask."

"Then, you had better bloody well get yourself out of here. He won't take kindly to your being in a place that encourages scandalous behavior."

"Why should you care?" She took a step nearer. "You reaped the rewards of his selecting me for courtship. I heard you made a bloody fortune with your damned wager."

His jaw tautened. Good. Let him be angry. She was furious. Days, weeks, months of frustrated fury building to near exploding. Fury because of the wager. Fury because she often found herself worrying about him. Fury because he'd probably never given her another thought, had never deemed her important enough to send word to in order to let her know he was well. Sparking the fury further was the bitter disappointment that he might, in fact, have the skills necessary to slip undetected into another's bedchamber, but couldn't be bothered to steal into hers and reassure her that he was still alive.

"I believe I have a right to see how your ill-gotten gains have benefited you. I think I have a right to see if it is worth what it has cost me."

He looked as though she'd punched him. "What has it cost you, Lady Kathryn?"

"Do you want to discuss this here, *Mr.* Stanwick?"

An even harder punch, perhaps two or three. Her address indicated that she recognized he was no longer a lord, but also acknowledged it was the first time she'd seen him since he wasn't.

"Come with me to someplace more private. We'll discuss your membership there."

She supposed he added the last for the benefit of those who appeared to be straining to hear what they were saying between clenched teeth or perhaps to give some legitimacy to her following him up the stairs. And she did follow, more fool she. She wanted to notice all the changes he'd made to the building since he'd shown it to her, but she seemed unable to concentrate on anything other than the breadth of his shoulders, the manner in which his back narrowed down to his waist. He was lean and sinewy, and yet there was strength mirrored in his graceful movements.

She wasn't quite certain what his expression revealed, but those coming down the stairs paused to flatten themselves against the wall. She suspected it was the stomping of his feet that caused those ascending ahead of them to pick up their pace and hasten to their destination.

At the landing, he waited until she reached him before continuing down the hallway. She nodded at the few people she recognized and was relatively certain Kingsland would hear of her visit, in spite of the fact that nothing that happened within these walls was supposed to be whispered about beyond them. Some gossip was simply too tantalizing not to be shared. To be honest, she wouldn't mind seeing the duke exhibit a spark of jealousy.

At the end of the hallway, he opened a door and stepped back to allow her to precede him into the small room. It contained an intimate sitting area designed for seduction with two sofas. Even if a lady and gent started out sitting opposite each other, eventually they would no doubt share a sofa. Or the fainting couch that rested a short distance away. It appeared far more comfortable. In the corner was a table housing various decanters. She could use a splash of something from one of those at that very minute.

She turned to find him with his arms crossed, leaning against the wall near the open door. "I thought this was an establishment that prided itself on closing doors for privacy."

"Not when a lady needs to maintain her reputation. Why did you come here?"

She began wandering through the room, even though there was very little else to see. A few provocative paintings of women lounging about hung on the walls. They did nothing to ease her temper. "Why no men lounging about?"

"I beg your pardon?"

She faced him. "The paintings. Why the scantily clad women? Do you think ladies wouldn't like to see an exposed male buttock here and there?"

He squeezed his eyes shut, pressed his lips together tightly, and she thought perhaps he was striving not to laugh at her ludicrous observation, but it was warranted.

Clearing his throat, he opened his eyes, his irritation obvious. "What do you want?"

"I thought I deserved to see the fruits of your betrayal."

"How is it a betrayal when I ensured you gained what you wanted?"

"You gained as well. I thought—" She shook her head, not willing to give voice to her naivete. She thought he'd done it because he cared for her, fancied her, wanted to see her happy. But his actions had very little, if anything, to do with her. "You wrote that letter to ensure you won."

"I did."

"I only know bits of it. What exactly did you say?"

He lifted a shoulder, dropped it. "I can't see that it matters. It served its purpose."

"Made you a fortune."

"Not until recently. Those who owed me refused to pay. They didn't think it necessary to honor a debt made to the son of a traitor. I imagine you agree."

She didn't. As upset as she was about the wager, it should have been honored. "You terrified Lord Lawrence into paying you."

Another shrug, as though he could hardly be bothered to care about another's worries. "He had nothing to fear as long as he paid what was owed. He did. They all did."

"Why collect now and not before?" If he'd let it go, if he'd felt guilty for taking advantage, it might have eased her hurt and anger somewhat. Although better still, if he'd never made the wager at all.

"I thought my father's shame was mine as well. It wasn't. And I didn't have the . . . temerity to threaten harm."

She considered the journey they'd taken to this room, how no one spoke to him, barely acknowledged him, seemed intent on avoiding him. Plastering themselves against walls, moving quickly out of his way. "And now you do?"

"Do you know what it's like, Lady Kathryn, to be without? Without anything? Without friends, family, or refuge? When we left Mayfair, we had a few quid between us. We went hungry. Althea and I shared a hovel. Winter came, and there was no warmth to be found. If these blighters had paid what they owed when they owed, our situation might have been very different, more tolerable. When I was cold, bleeding, aching, and hungry, I grew to hate them. So, yes, I was willing to threaten harm to gain what I was owed."

Balling up her hands, she took three steps toward him. "Should I not be equally angry? You took advantage of what you knew about me for gain. It's the reason you were helping me."

"And you were mucking it up. Whist, for God's sake. What gentleman in his right mind would care about whist? I don't understand your upset. You got what you wanted. Why shouldn't I?"

"I felt ill-used. I told you things I'd never shared with another. You left me feeling . . . vulnerable, revealed for all the world to see." How did she explain how she had come to trust him—only to be tossed aside like so much rubbish? "You needed money, and you gained it through me. You should have at least sent me an invitation to this place. You wouldn't have it without me."

"As I mentioned earlier, you do not qualify for membership. Even if he hasn't asked for your hand, it is known you are his."

"You could have given me a private viewing. Just as you did before." When he'd taken her hand and shared his dream, his vision, his plans. When he'd made her feel privileged because he'd confided in her. When she'd seen a different side to him.

"I saw no point in it."

She wanted to smack him for standing there unmoving, tolerating her presence, obviously desperate for her to take her leave—

But then she noticed his knuckles, so very white, as though his grip was straining to shackle him there, against the wall, away from her. As she studied him more thoroughly, she realized it wasn't a casual stance. No, absolutely nothing about him was relaxed. As a matter of fact, he appeared quite brittle, nearly as stone-faced as a statue, as though every aspect of him required absolute concentration in order to remain as stoically unmoving as he was. But one good swipe with a hammer, and he would crumble.

She took a step toward him and detected a nearly imperceptible flinch. Was he threatened by her nearness? Was he not nearly as unaffected by her presence as he appeared?

She was still upset about the damned wager, about the steps he'd taken to ensure he won—that he'd taken the liberty of matching her with the duke when she hadn't been certain Kingsland was who she wanted. She'd not achieved the end on her own, and she didn't like the notion that she needed others to assist her in reaching her goals.

She was of a mind to torment him, and based on what she'd just discovered about his posture, she was fairly certain she knew how to do it with unerring accuracy.

Another step. This time his head moved back slightly as though he wanted to press it right through the wall.

"Did you never worry that you might have thrown me to a wolf in order to make a few quid?"

"I trusted that you're strong enough to walk away if you found him not to your liking. As it's been nearly a year since the courtship began and he recently took you to the theater—"

"How did you know that?"

"I know a good many things."

He'd never struck her as caring one whit about gossip or giving much credence to it. "His brother told you. Perhaps you were waiting outside the theater for Lord Lawrence to deliver the money to you."

Another shrug. A slight tightening of those fingers.

"Did you see us go in? I was wearing a new gown, a dark auburn sort of thing."

"It matched your hair." His jaw clenched, and she suspected he wished he'd bitten back the words.

She moved closer until she was standing in front of him. "You *were* there."

"Only because Lawrence asked me to meet him so he could make good on his debt. I wasn't there to spy on you."

But to have seen her, he would have needed to have arrived much earlier than the duke's brother. Had he wanted to catch a glimpse of her? "Did you like the way I looked that night? How I went to such pains to dress becomingly for him?"

"I really think it's time you took your leave."

"I'm not yet done with you."

Reaching out, she took hold of the door and pushed it shut.

HE HATED THAT she'd gone to pains to look lovely for Kingsland. Hated that the man had the right to touch her, to escort her with her hand resting on his arm. Hated that she was here now tormenting Griff with her presence.

During the past few months, he'd been forced to deal with footpads and cutthroats and had become quite skilled at defending himself, but facing a woman scorned—no, she wasn't scorned, merely severely put out with him—was a much more terrifying prospect. Or it might have been for a fellow who hadn't faced the dangers he had. So he wasn't particularly frightened, but he was wary. She had changed since he'd last seen her. If she wrote a letter to the duke now, he suspected it would be worded very differently from the one she'd written last summer, that it wouldn't make any mention of whist. She possessed a determination to gain retribution and believed she was owed. He could read in her eyes that she fully intended to ensure that he paid dearly for what she considered a betrayal.

If only she knew how much he was already suffering. To prevent himself from reaching for her, he was gripping his arms so forcefully he was fairly certain he'd see bruises there in the morning. His hands hadn't ached this badly since he'd torn them up working the docks for a few pence a day. And his jaw—with the pain periodically shooting through it because of how tightly it was clenched, he was surprised he could speak when words were called for.

"I wouldn't be as upset about the wager if you'd been honest, if I'd known what you were up to."

He hadn't wanted to increase her hopes of being selected. But that was only a small part of the truth. He hadn't wanted her to know that he'd taken advantage of the situation for gain. But still, she'd found out about it. He didn't blame her for the upset. He had felt guilty about it, and that guilt had resulted in his delay in collecting what was owed. And that delay had resulted in those who owed him banding together to form a united front in not paying him. But he'd been soft then, easily deterred. He wasn't now. After months of hardship, he'd learned to take what was owed. "I didn't think you'd mind since I sent Kingsland the letter without asking for something from you in exchange for my efforts."

Her gaze was steady. And green. The shade of clover that he wanted to lie in without care, but he suspected his life would never again be without care.

He'd been so lost in the depths of her eyes that it took him a moment to realize she'd closed the short distance between them. Her bodice was brushing up against his crossed arms, and his fingers dug more deeply into his muscle.

"It seems I should properly thank you for all the effort you went to on my behalf to see me married to a peer."

"It was no bother." Nothing he'd ever done for her was truly a bother.

"It inconvenienced you, surely."

"Yes, of course—" Before he stupidly confessed that he'd never minded inconveniencing himself for her, her fingers skimmed along his nape, eased up slightly to his skull, and tipped his head down so her lips could fasten themselves onto his. *Give me a list of ways to inconvenience myself for you.*

It was wrong to take the kiss further when she was going to marry another, but she wasn't yet wed, she wasn't yet a duchess. Where was the harm in simply taking what she was offering and no more?

Giving in to the temptation of her, he released his hold on himself and wrapped his arms around her, drawing her up against him until all her softness was flattened against all his hardness. Her bold and wicked mouth invited him into doing all the things he ought not, and he guided his hands over her back, gripping her hips and pressing her against him until she knew exactly how much he desired her.

She was delicious, a confection to be savored. One that he had delivered into another's keeping. Regret slammed into him. Regret that he'd written the damned letter. Regret that he'd made the damned wager. Regret that he cared too damned much for her to see her ruined here and now—regardless of how badly his entire body ached to possess her. The ache in his hands was nothing compared to the ache of his cock.

She trailed her mouth along his jaw, along the edge of his neck-cloth, her tongue dipping beneath the linen so provocatively that he couldn't hold back the deep growl. Her teeth nipped at the tender flesh, then took hold of his earlobe. She bit him, not hard, but not soft.

"You owe me," she whispered harshly in his ear. Drawing back, she held his gaze. "See that I get a membership."

With that, she opened the door and strode out, leaving him aching with the need to possess.

CHAPTER 12

$\mathcal{K}$ATHRYN HAD ALWAYS enjoyed the company of Lady Wilhelmina March. She'd helped fill the void after Althea had disappeared and Jocelyn's visits had become strained after her betrothal and subsequent marriage to Chadbourne. Kathryn found it difficult to forgive Chadbourne for turning his back on her dearest friend and had often wondered how much more favorably Society might have treated Althea if he had chosen instead to stand beside her. His so quickly asking Jocelyn to marry him had been wrong on several levels. And Jocelyn immediately accepting had seemed incredibly disloyal. Even if she had been concerned with ending up on the shelf, it was difficult to view her actions in a positive light.

And so Lady Wilhelmina March had become an integral part of Kathryn's friendships, one she treasured as they strolled arm in arm through Hyde Park during the fashionable hour when so many others were about.

"I've not encountered you at any of the balls this Season," Kathryn said.

"I can take them or leave them," Wilhelmina replied, her soft voice almost a sigh. Two years older than Kathryn, she considered herself permanently on the shelf.

"You don't miss the social interaction they provide?"

"Not particularly. Besides, I've acquired a new activity of late that I'm rather enjoying."

"Being pampered at the Elysium Club?" She knew her friend frequented the establishment. They sometimes went together.

"A different club, one you have an interest in as well, if your presence there last night was any indication."

Kathryn came to an abrupt halt and faced Wilhelmina. "You were at the Fair and Spare? I didn't see you."

The lady arched a brow. "I don't think you saw anyone other than Mr. Griffith Stanwick. He seemed to be your entire focus. And you his."

As the burgeoning heat of embarrassment warmed her cheeks, she glanced around, grateful no one was near to overhear. She'd been battling her guilt ever since she'd arrived home after her trip to the club. She hadn't intended to kiss Griff, certainly hadn't planned to do anything except confront him, but a bit of wickedness had taken hold when she'd realized he was struggling not to touch her. It made her feel powerful, powerful in a way she didn't experience when she was with Kingsland. It had also made her feel wanted and desired. The kiss he'd given her in the duke's garden had haunted her, and she'd wanted to know if what had once been devastating to her senses would once again be so.

It had been so much more. Hungry and needy and ravenous. She hadn't wanted it to end but had also known that it couldn't continue. Yet, still, she craved another.

"He is the brother of my dear friend, Althea. I merely wanted to see how he was getting on. What were you doing there?"

A bit of devilry edged Wilhelmina's smile. "Being naughty. I am all of seven and twenty, a spinster destined to never marry. While you may think less of me for admitting it, I see no harm at my age in taking a lover, and I'd heard rumors about a newly opened establishment that provided the perfect opportunity for the unwanted to be wanted."

"You're not unwanted." Her voice was firm, filled with conviction. She hated for Wilhelmina, for any woman, to feel as though she'd been discarded. Unfortunately, most lords in need of a wife favored the debutants, not those with some seasoning to them.

"I'm not saddened by my predicament. Quite the opposite, in fact. I can go where I want, do as I want, without needing to gain a husband's permission. My father set up a trust for me. I receive two thousand per annum, so I need not concern myself with monetary woes. I do not need a man, but sometimes I think it would be nice to have a gentleman look at me the way Mr. Griffith Stanwick did you last night."

"Angrily? He was rather put out with me for showing up in his dominion."

Wilhelmina shook her head. "You did not see him when he first caught sight of you. He looked as though the only person who mattered in the world had just walked in."

"You have the wrong of it there." Because it was easier not to face her friend directly, not to gaze into her eyes, when speaking of something so very personal, she hooked her arm around Wilhelmina's and urged her to continue with their turn about the park.

"It was only for a second or two. Then he shuttered his expression. But I know what I saw."

"You have always had a romantic bent." It was easier to believe Wilhelmina had shaded his expression with her own biases rather than to consider that he held deep affection for her. Or to acknowledge that she might have developed a fondness for him last Season, when her life had seemed so simple.

"I'm surprised he admitted you. A lady has to be five and twenty to gain a membership."

Kathryn wouldn't be twenty-five until August. "I wonder why he has that rule." To prevent any encounters between them?

"I suspect it's because he doesn't want to see any lady ruined who still has the prospect of marriage available to her. And, make no mistake, it is a place for ruination. It's the reason the membership is so closely guarded and only the most trusted to keep secrets are allowed access. People only learn of it when it's whispered to them."

Not true. It hadn't been whispered to her. She'd overheard. She wondered if she should mention he had a flaw in his system. If she returned. *When* she returned.

She glanced around at the ladies walking about or riding in carriages. Some with beaux, most without. It would change as the Season progressed, as matches were made. "What other rules has he put into place?"

"Only spinsters and bachelors are allowed entry. No firstborn sons who will inherit titles. The firstborn sons of commoners are welcomed. It's actually a very interesting mix. People of different backgrounds and social status. I've spent time in the company of some very intriguing gentlemen. They've had some success, or they wouldn't be able to afford the membership. It doesn't come cheaply."

She wondered if Griff would ask her to pay for hers. He could certainly ask, but she wasn't going to hand over any funds. As far as she was concerned, he owed her for that deuced wager. "Has anyone in particular taken your fancy?"

"No, I'm still on the hunt." She tapped her shoulder against Kathryn's. "But I find I rather enjoy the hunt."

"Are you going tonight?"

"I am indeed. I would offer to pick you up in my carriage, if you've a mind to return, but I fear it might become inconvenient if one of us wishes to stay later than the other. But I could meet you there, show you around. Last night, I don't think you saw much of what the place offers in the form of entertainments."

"I shouldn't go." She knew she shouldn't.

"Are you seeing Kingsland this evening?"

"No, he is in Yorkshire until next week." And her parents weren't a hindrance. They were in Paris for another sennight.

"I wouldn't get in the habit of putting my life on hold for him, for any man, truth be told."

She hadn't. She was involved with her charitable endeavors and attended social functions, even if he wasn't about to escort her. Then, there was the Elysium Club. "I might see you there."

"We should have a signal. If I'm holding a glass of white wine, then I am available to escort you about. A glass of red indicates that my attention is otherwise occupied, and I might not be quite as welcoming of an interruption."

"Why, Wilhelmina! A secret code? I do believe there is a side to you with which I am not familiar. I also believe you are implying that you intend to indulge in a bit of wickedness."

"Unlike you, Kathryn, should a gentleman catch my fancy and I catch his, if we explore our interest in each other, I have nothing to lose."

SHE HAD EVERYTHING to lose. A duke, respectability, an inheritance.

She should have taken up her needlework in the parlor. She should have gone to the Elysium for a bit of gambling or a waltz or dinner. She should have sat in her bedchamber and penned a letter to Althea to see how she was enjoying her time in Scotland with her new husband.

She should have done anything other than slip into the gown that matched the shade of her hair, the gown he'd seen her in when she went to the theater with Kingsland—but she thought it might serve as a reminder that the duke was her future, even as she traveled in the coach to see a man who should remain in her past.

Perhaps he wouldn't give her any attention this evening, and that would be all for the good, even as she knew she wouldn't tolerate his ignoring her. Not completely. If Wilhelmina was holding a glass of red wine, which Kathryn dearly hoped she was, then she would insist that he give her the grand tour.

She did want to see the place, every nook and cranny. Since the night he'd shown her the vacant building, she'd imagined countless times how it might have looked if he ever acquired it. Wilhelmina had the right of it. She'd noticed little save him once she'd heard his voice, once the giant barring her way had moved aside and Griff had stood before her. So she would go tonight, see what she wanted to see, and be done with it all. Be done with him.

Before rumors reached the duke.

No closed doors. No whispered words. No kisses. No touches. No moans.

GRIFF HAD KNOWN she'd come. It was the reason he'd been standing at the curve of the stairs, halfway up them, so he had a good view of the door. Every other night since he'd first opened, he'd gloried in the abundance of people streaming in. The curious, the extras, the ones who caught no one's attention when moving about Society, or those who stood at the edge of it peering in. But here the ladies were not outshone by seventeen- and eighteen-year-old girls who had recently curtsied before the Queen. Nor were the men outranked by dukes, marquesses, and earls.

They were equals. In search of a bit of fun. They were filling his coffers with the drinks they purchased, the food upon which they dined, the coins they passed over to his dealers. And the membership they paid for the privilege of doing all that.

But at the moment, unlike previous nights, he wasn't striving to estimate this evening's tally. He was concentrating on her, dressed in copper, crowned in copper, as she gracefully skirted around people, acknowledging with a slight nod those she knew. Second and third sons. Fourth and fifth. A couple of widows. A widower. Lonely people who sought companionship. Not always sex. He'd learned that quickly enough. The rooms he'd designated on the top floor for intimate encounters were seldom used. To his surprise, even when the opportunity presented itself, his members weren't quite as free as those he'd seen at the cock and hen club he'd visited. Reputations were still guarded. But he saw a lot more smiles here, heard a good deal more laughter, than he had experienced at fancy balls held by the elite. Perhaps eventually his club would become something else other than what he'd originally envisioned, but that was all for dissecting later.

For now, he descended the stairs and met her before she could disappear into one of the rooms beyond. "Lady Kathryn."

"Mr. Stanwick."

Last night she'd made a point of emphasizing the form of address that should have made him less than what he'd once been, and he'd detested her use of it, but it created a chasm between him and the man who had sired him, and for that he was grateful. "We require members register in the front room and have their membership verified."

"It's an inefficient system. I haven't the patience for it. You should give your members a card or a medallion that they can show to your lumbering giant and move on."

"So they can hand it to a friend who hasn't paid for the privilege to enter?"

She shrugged. "Hire someone to sketch their likeness onto the card."

He stared at her in astonishment, at the easy solution she'd suggested. "That's not a half-bad idea." It would get people in quicker. They would have more time to drink, to spend. "Not half-bad at all. What else would you change?"

"Well, I don't know. I haven't seen everything yet."

He fought not to smile. He wasn't going to give her a smile, give her reason to believe he was glad she'd returned. "Would you like to?"

"It seems only fair."

"You're still miffed at me."

"Not as much." It appeared she was striving not to smile as well, and it did strange things to his gut, causing it to tighten and expand at the same time.

"Allow me the honor, then, of escorting you through."

He didn't offer his arm, didn't give any indication at all that she meant more to him than any other member. Instead, after signaling with a wave of his arm the direction in which they should go—down the hallway just past the stairs—he placed his hands behind his back and clutched them in order to stop himself from touching her lightly on her upper arm or shoulder or back.

But he'd imagined this, showing her what he'd accomplished since he'd slept in missions until his investments earned enough that he could purchase this building and move into a room on the top floor. Collecting on the wagers had allowed him to furnish it. He'd often worked from dawn until midnight, assisting the carpenters, or moving furniture about, or interviewing and hiring staff, or having invitations printed. He wondered if she would notice that the shade of each room was a reflection of her in some manner. The coppery tint of her hair, the green of her eyes, the blue. The burnished brown of the freckles that were no longer there.

He led her into the parlor with its pale blue walls. A few dark blue sofas rested at the edge of the room, but here people mostly stood, mingled, visited, made new acquaintances, rekindled old. They purchased their libations at a mahogany counter and nibbled on tiny cucumber sandwiches.

A woman talking with a tall, dark-haired man looked toward them and lifted her glass of red wine in a slight salute. With a soft smile, Kathryn gave a little nod.

"You know Lady Wilhelmina March?" he asked.

"She is a friend, yes."

"Is she the one who told you of this place?"

She turned to him. "No, actually. I overheard two ladies discussing it while I was playing cards at the Elysium Club. I'm not convinced your members are as discreet as you want them to be."

Yet here she was, risking Kingsland discovering that she'd visited. "I don't mind them discussing the club. As a matter of fact, I very much rely on them talking about it for word to get around. It's the private business of the individual members and whom they see here that they are not to divulge. Which you'd know if you'd gone through the proper process and sat for an interview."

He wished he didn't enjoy seeing her look so victorious.

"So, it's official. I do have a membership."

"Until he goes down on a knee for you, until I see the announcement of your betrothal in the *Times*. Although I can't see that after tonight, once your curiosity is satisfied, that you'll have much use for the place. Those who are here are announcing they are in search of companionship . . . or something more intimate."

He didn't much like how quickly her triumph dissipated into something that seemed rather sad. "Is that what you're announcing when you're standing at the top of the stairs, or halfway down them"—so she'd seen him, and he wondered if she understood he'd been waiting for her, would have stood there all night, until they closed at two, waiting for her—"or wandering through?"

He should answer in the affirmative and let the knowledge affect her as it would, marking him as either cruel or kind or indifferent, depending on the direction in which her hopes led her. Instead, he told her the truth. "The members are not for me."

Because he couldn't have whom he wanted, he wouldn't take what he needed from someone who wasn't her.

She seemed relieved, perhaps guilty, maybe even a little embarrassed. Her cheeks turned that lovely pinkish hue before she glanced around. "What else do you offer?"

"Come. I'll show you."

SHE SHOULD NOT have been fairly giddy by his response, should not have been glad that all her imaginings—of him taking women to the room he'd taken her last night and closing the door—had turned to dust.

Perhaps he'd wanted her to focus on the lovely walls covered in blue silk or the elegant crystal chandelier or the gorgeous shiny mahogany counter that people sidled up to in order to purchase a drink. But what she had mostly noticed was the way the women devoured him with their eyes, the hope and the want she saw reflected in some.

He had changed after his family had lost everything. He possessed a strength now that he hadn't before, a confidence that clung to him like the finest of cloaks, tailor-made and perfectly stitched. He effectively communicated, *I am giving you this. Make good use of it.*

He fascinated her in ways different than he had before. When he looked at her, it was with a determined concentration that made her grow warm and long for that room with the barred door.

Unlike the night before when he'd led the way up the stairs, tonight he followed, and she could not have been more aware of him if he was brushing up against her spine. She wished she'd chosen a gown that revealed more of her back. Why was it that she gave so much thought to what she wore for him and so little regarding what she wore for Kingsland?

Even though she'd told him that she'd dressed for Kingsland the night of the theater, she hadn't actually gone to any extra effort for him. Unlike last night and tonight when she'd wanted to look perfect.

When they reached the landing, he took the lead, managing to escort her, guide her, without touching her, his hands still held securely behind his back. He wasn't nearly as relaxed with her as he'd been that long-ago night when he'd brought her here, before Kingsland made his announcement, before she knew about the wager, before his family was ruined because of his father's actions.

The first room was a cardroom, but the tables were small, only two chairs at each. Fewer than a dozen couples were playing. As cards were dealt, ladies blushed and gentlemen grinned. "Not very original."

"Look more closely." He'd lowered his head, and his breath fanned along her ear, stirring her curls, causing a delicious shiver to race along her spine. "What do you see? What do you *not* see?"

The game she recognized. It was the one she played at the Elysium. "There are no chips. No token, no coins. No wagers being made."

"Wagers are being made, but not for anything that can be stuffed into pockets."

She lifted her gaze to him and found he was closer than she'd realized, and everything about him seemed more focused. The blue in his eyes was richer, the silver brighter. His golden lashes were a darker hue than she remembered—but then she couldn't recall if she'd ever truly noticed them. They were long. Would rest on his cheeks when he slept, or when he closed his eyes as his lips met hers. "What are they wagering?"

"A touch . . . a whisper . . . a kiss. Perhaps more. Something that can't be given in this room, in front of others." His voice was raspy, raw, and sensual. What would he whisper in her ear, along her skin?

"Glance slyly at the couple in the far corner," he continued. "I would say at some point he wagered his neckcloth, and she the pins in her hair."

Doing as he bade, she saw the gentleman shrugging out of his coat while the lady opposite him smiled in triumph. "How far will they go?"

"As far as they're comfortable. Then perhaps they'll move to a private room to finish the game."

She jerked her attention back to him. "Is it a game?"

"Only they know."

"What if he misreads her intent?" It seemed a dangerous gamble. "What if he takes advantage? Or hurts her?"

"Then he'll answer to me—and it will not be a pleasant experience for him."

"Did you tell him that during the interview?"

"I showed him. I have a little wrestling match with prospective male members."

She was rather confident he was attempting to be subtle in his boasting. "And you won."

"I always win."

She didn't know why she suddenly felt an immense amount of pride. "I wasn't aware you wrestled."

"I didn't until recently." He backed out of the doorway. "There are other rooms."

A small ballroom. She was tempted to ask him to take her on a turn about the floor, but she refrained. He seemed intent on ensuring no portion of him touched any portion of her. Not so much as his small finger gliding along her elbow.

A dining room in which only candles provided the light that created an intimate setting. Perhaps some of the couples at the linen-covered tables had wagered in the cardroom on having dinner together.

A billiards room. A dart room.

Then he led her into a smoking room, where men and women had gathered. Some stood, some sat, but it was obvious they were enjoying each other's company. In the finest of houses, ladies were never allowed into the smoking room. How often had her father taken their male dinner guests to his private domain so they could puff on cheroots while the ladies sipped tea elsewhere?

"You're putting women on equal footing with men, giving them access to what they are usually denied."

"Don't give me too much credit. The choice was between having smoking in here or embroidery."

She laughed lightly. "Did you think the men might not enjoy spending their time as we do?"

"There is a library farther down the hallway. On the floor below is a recital room. I would have shown it to you, but the door was closed, indicating a private performance."

Pride caused her chest to swell. "You adopted my suggestion regarding a pianoforte."

"I favor a woman being comfortable enough to do as she will with her fingers."

Her eyes widened at that. "You do encourage naughtiness."

He shrugged. "No one is forced to come here. Those who do are old enough to know the risks and to be responsible for themselves."

"The women have to be twenty-five. I'm not."

"I know. Not until August fifteenth. I made an exception for you."

"You know precisely when my birthday is?"

He didn't say anything, simply studied her with that intense way he had developed, as though he now possessed the ability to mine souls. What path had he traveled since that fateful night when his family's world had come undone?

But this room, with its rich tobacco scent was not the place to make inquiries, to delve for answers, no matter how badly she wanted to know all his life had entailed since she'd last seen him. She doubted he would tell her anyway. So instead, she asked, "May I try a cheroot?"

One corner of his mouth hitched up. "What a wicked woman you are, Lady Kathryn."

She did feel a trifle naughty. Because she shouldn't be here, and yet she was. Because she shouldn't enjoy his company, and yet she did.

Without touching her, he guided her to a table where a large dark intricately carved wooden box rested. He opened it and removed a long cylinder of pressed tobacco leaves. "I'll prepare it for you."

"It has to be prepared?"

"What? Did you think you just lit and smoked it?" He picked up a silver device, placed it over the rounded tip of the cheroot, and snipped it off.

"I did rather."

He met and held her gaze. "The most pleasurable aspects of life require preparation."

She was left with the impression he was speaking about more than cheroots, was referring to something a bit more personal, an aspect of life that required closed doors.

Using a nearby burning candle, he lit a small paper taper and held it to the end he hadn't cut, running the flame slowly over it. Mesmerized, she watched as he placed the cheroot in his mouth, turning it as he applied the taper again. When he was apparently satisfied with the results, he inhaled, removed the cheroot from his mouth, and exhaled the smoke.

After extinguishing the flame, he set the taper aside and studied the end of the cheroot. "You don't want to inhale."

"You did."

He shook his head. "I drew the smoke into my mouth. You don't want it going into your lungs. A nasty bit of work there. The first time I wouldn't let it fill more than half your mouth. Just draw in the smoke, savor it, release it."

"Savor it?"

"Hmm. Afterward you can tell me what you tasted." He held it out to her.

She was going to place her mouth where his had been. At the prospect of it, she shouldn't be quivering with warm sensations and forbidden thoughts. She certainly shouldn't take delight at the intensity with which he watched her. Even as she told herself he was merely interested in gauging her initial reaction to this novel experience, she couldn't seem to dismiss the thought that she wanted a husband who would always look at her thusly, who wanted more from his wife than convenience and quiet.

Placing the collection of tobacco between her lips, she drew the smoke in—

Too far, too fast. It hit the back of her throat, and she thought she might be ill. She gave a little gag before coughing in the most unladylike manner. The smoke was hotter, thicker than she'd expected.

"Easy, easy. Blow it all out. Get some fresh air in there. Come on."

He'd placed his hand on her back, near her nape, his fingers kneading and massaging the space on either side of her spine, and she focused on the roughness of his skin against the silkiness of hers. She blinked back the tears that had filled her eyes, studied the concern in his.

"I handled that . . . rather poorly," she croaked, before taking another cleansing breath. "There was so much more of it than I was anticipating."

"It's all right. It takes practice to achieve a proper puff. Did you get any taste at all?"

She shook her head, held her hand to her mouth as she coughed again. "Somewhat of a chocolate flavor, perhaps?"

"It does dominate, but there are other subtle aspects. Did you want to try again?"

"I don't think so. I fear I've gone a bit green."

"Only a bit. I'm impressed, though. I cast up my accounts the first time I tried a cigar. But then I was only twelve. Snuck one from . . . the duke's study. Gave it a go behind the stables. The coachman caught me. Taught me how to do it correctly."

She didn't miss how he referred to his sire, so formally, and she wondered at the emotions that might be roiling through him with the thought of his father. He had yet to move his hand away from her back, and he seemed as lost in the sensations as she.

"What happened to your hands? How did they get so scarred?" She'd noticed them last night, the faint white lines on the back of his hands, the result of cuts or scrapes, but it was his palms that concerned her most. Ropy bits of raised flesh and calluses. Strange that he didn't wear gloves, didn't try to hide them. Perhaps he wanted them seen, perhaps they delivered a message, and she wanted to know it. Although, now she wished she hadn't asked because he was no longer touching her. He took the cheroot from her, gave it a little puff, and scrutinized the glowing end of it.

"After the Crown seized the titles and properties and left us with nothing, I began working on the docks, carting crates and sacks of goods. The hauling caused blisters and welts. Ropes and wood bit into my flesh. Until my hands toughened from scars and calluses, they were raw a good bit of the time."

She could only imagine how painful it must have been as his skin bled and oozed. "And you toughened up along with them."

Another puff, a slow release of the smoke. "Some of that had happened before, when they took us to the Tower. Some happened later, after the docks. But don't ask me for details, because I won't tell you about any of that." Looking past her, he gave a small nod of acknowledgment. "Gertie."

A woman she judged to be at least a decade older than herself held a folded bit of paper toward him. "This was just delivered."

He took the offering. "Lady Kathryn Lambert, allow me the honor of introducing Mrs. Ward, who manages things here."

"It's a pleasure, Mrs. Ward," she said.

The woman's nose went up ever so slightly. "You're the exception to all the rules."

Kathryn glanced over at Griff, who was grinning slightly as he unsealed and unfolded the missive. "Yes, I suppose I am."

Because she was watching him, she noted all the humor disappearing from his features, the alertness that suddenly seemed to dominate. He placed the cheroot on a glass dish. "I have an urgent matter I need to attend to. Gertie, if I've not returned by closing, see that all is done up tightly. Lady Kathryn, feel free to continue exploring at your leisure. Ladies."

He strode from the room, not in a rush, but definitely with some resolve. Surprised by his abrupt departure, she followed into the hallway and watched as he darted up some stairs at the far end of it. Mrs. Ward had stayed close as though fearing Kathryn would make off with the silver candlesticks. "Where is he going?"

"To his rooms, probably," Mrs. Ward responded. "Is there anything you require of me before I return to my duties?"

"No, thank you." As someone who no longer had anyone to accompany her, she would be wise to take her leave but couldn't shake off the sensation that something was terribly wrong. Acknowledging a couple of people she knew who were mingling about, she casually wandered along the hallway until she reached the stairs. She was tempted to go up them but didn't wish to intrude or become a bother when he'd seemed anxious to be rid of her.

Then he was coming down them, hat and walking stick in hand, purpose in his stride. When he reached the last step, she glided in front of him.

Impatience marred his features. "Lady Kathryn, I haven't time—"

"What is it? What's happened? Is it Althea?" As far as she knew, her friend was still in Scotland, but if some tragedy had befallen her, surely he would have been told.

His eyes reflected sympathy and understanding. "No." He hesitated before continuing. "I must meet with Marcus. Now, if you'll excuse me—"

"You mentioned it was urgent." His actions certainly reinforced that notion. "Even if you've a carriage, you'll need to have it readied. Mine is waiting in the mews. Allow me to provide you with transport to wherever you need to go."

"I'll hire a cab."

"My carriage will be quicker. I've seen all I wanted to see, anyway." Because all she'd truly wanted to see was him. "My driver could drop you off before taking me home."

He gave a quick nod. "All right, then. I appreciate it."

This time when he escorted her toward the other stairs, the red-carpeted wider ones that led down to the main floor, his hand rested lightly on the small of her back, the heat from his fingers pronounced, burning through the silk of her gown so strongly it was like it had been when they were near her neck, flesh on flesh. She welcomed the surety of them, the familiarity, the intimacy. As though he'd touched her without thinking, as though doing so was as natural as breathing. As though they were in this together, whatever this was.

She suspected it involved an element of danger and dearly wanted to instruct her driver to go in the opposite direction of wherever Griff indicated they should travel. To keep him safe, to protect him from harm.

She'd offered her carriage not out of benevolence but out of crushing curiosity, desperate for a little more time with him, to learn the secrets of what had transpired to make him the man he was now, one who hardly resembled the gentleman who had kissed her in the duke's garden.

HE SHOULD HAVE refused and have found his own transportation to meet with Marcus. But here he was, within the close confines of her carriage, with her faint orange fragrance wafting around him. When he should be nowhere near her.

"Why did you leave your cheroot to burn as though you intended to come back for it?" she asked. "It seemed a waste."

"It leaves a more pleasant aroma if left to burn out on its own. I prefer the pleasant to the unpleasant. And it will be wasted. A young man will come through and toss it in the rubbish bin."

"So many things to consider."

More than she'd ever know.

"Before Althea left for Scotland, we had a few occasions to visit, but she wasn't able to enlighten me as to what you and Marcus were doing."

So now she wanted to get to the heart of his urgent matter. It shouldn't please him that she'd asked after him, and he was no doubt reading too much into her inquiry. People asked after their friends' families as a show of politeness. It had probably been no more than that—or perhaps she'd wanted to find him to express her upset over the wager. "Marcus is striving to determine who organized the plot for which our father hanged. I helped him for a while but grew weary of the hunt."

"Is he in danger?"

Possibly. Probably. "His letter indicated only that he needed to meet."

"Yet you didn't hesitate."

"He's my brother. I am always there for him."

"What of Althea, being there for her? You didn't attend her wedding."

He detected a bit of censure in her tone. "It wouldn't do for those with whom Marcus associates to catch wind of him having any connection to the aristocracy, and there is evidence that he is often secretly followed. At the time, it seemed best for me to keep away as well."

"Considering how the lords and ladies turned their backs on your family, I'm surprised to see so many of them at your club."

He grinned. "I kept my involvement secret at first. By the time they realized I was the owner, they'd decided they enjoyed the place too much to avoid it on principle." They seldom acknowledged him, merely tolerated him. But he didn't mind. He was making a bloody fortune off them. He glanced out the window. "We're near enough to where I need to be."

Using his walking stick, he knocked twice on the ceiling. The horses began to slow. "Thank you for the use of your carriage." When the vehicle stopped, he opened the door, leapt out, and looked back at her. While she was naught but shadows, still he saw her clearly in his mind. "Safe journey home."

Suddenly her fingers were clutching the lapels of his coat. "You will be careful."

He wanted to cradle her face between his hands and take possession of her perfect mouth, to have a final kiss, a final taste, rather certain Marcus's reasons for sending for him did not lend themselves well to his being careful. But Griff was on his way to meet with a man for whom he'd taken unforgiveable actions, and he wasn't going to sully her with a touch when he was so near to the reminder. "Always."

"We'll wait for you."

"No. Go home now, Lady Kathryn. I can find my own way back to the club."

Her fingers loosened their hold. He stepped back, closed the door, and called up to the driver. "Carry on."

Without waiting to see them off, he began running toward one of the bridges that crossed the Thames, striving to calm his racing heart because Marcus's note had said simply, "Life and death."

CHAPTER 13

$\mathcal{H}$E SLOWED HIS steps as he neared the water that reflected moonlight. It created the sort of tapestry that evoked romantic overtures, but nothing about his present mission would lend itself to taking advantage of the beauty. He and his brother had used this spot repeatedly for their clandestine encounters, when one or the other of them had news to share or information to impart. So the missive hadn't needed to tell him where to go. He'd known where his brother would be waiting.

"Marcus?" It wasn't a shout, but it carried just the same, over the grass toward the shoreline where the water lapped with the incoming tide.

From behind a pylon stepped a familiar shadowy figure, and Griff drew comfort from seeing Marcus moving toward him with no hindrances. He'd feared the worst, feared seeing his brother hovering at death's door. Wishing he'd brought a lantern, he met him beyond the shadows of the bridge so the moon and stars could grace them with enough light to make out features. "Are you all right?"

His brother scoffed. "Have any of us been all right since Father was hanged?"

"I suppose not." Although, the interest in his club and its increasing membership were a salve allowing him to sometimes go hours without reflecting on the past. He'd always considered Marcus the fortunate one, the one who would inherit titles, properties, position, and wealth. While he'd never expected to have anything of value unless he'd earned it himself. Althea had recently found her place through love. Griff was finding his through hard work. But what did a man trained to be duke do when he was placed in the position of never becoming duke? "Are you injured?"

"No, but I have been found out. They've discovered my true identity, suspect it is my intent to betray them, see them arrested and hanged."

Marcus had adopted the moniker of Wolf, using part of the title he would have inherited if everything hadn't gone awry. None of the men with whom he presently associated knew him by any other name. "How did they learn all that?"

"That's the question, isn't it? I haven't a bloody clue. But I have to go away for a while, until things settle down and I can get it sorted."

He'd anticipated that his brother might be in need of funds. Reaching inside his jacket, he removed a package and held it toward him. "I brought you some blunt."

"I'm not going to take your money. I just wanted you to know I'd be scarce and the reason behind my absence so you wouldn't come looking for me and endanger yourself."

"Take it. I have more. Besides, one of the reasons I opened the club was to ensure we had funds at our disposal when they were needed."

Marcus flashed a grin. "So you were correct. There is interest in a club for the unwed who are not in high demand."

"Quite a bit of interest, actually. And more each day. To be honest, I'm astounded by the number of membership inquiries I receive."

"Good for you. Too bad Father isn't around to see your success."

"He wouldn't have cared." The duke had never seen his second son as anything other than someone to be held in reserve in case he was ever needed. "And I never cared enough to impress him."

"Just as well. As it turns out, he wasn't worthy of any of us." He took the packet. "I shall put this to good use. Thank you."

"Do you know where you'll go?"

"No. I just want—"

"Well, well, well, if it ain't the son of a duke seeking his revenge. And who'd that be with ye, Wolf? Yer assassin, mayhap?"

As soon as the stranger's voice had reached his ears, Griff had spun about. There were four of them, fanned out. But he paid scant attention to three of them. Only one was of interest to him. He was holding Kathryn against his chest, a knife to her throat. Touching her, threatening her, frightening her.

The footpad didn't know it yet, but he was already dead.

"BRUISE HER, HARM one hair on her head, and you'll be begging for death by the time I'm done with you."

The words spoken with such calm certainty sent icy fingers skittering down Kathryn's spine. She suspected they'd done the same to the man holding her, if the slight jerking she'd felt in him, as though his body dearly wanted to retreat but was being forced to remain, was any indication.

It took her a heartbeat to accept that it was Griff who'd uttered them, Griff who gave the impression he possessed the ability to carry out the threat and would do so without remorse or regret.

He'd told her to go home, and she should have followed his directive, but when she'd seen him running, she'd called up to the driver to halt. She'd sat there in the carriage wringing her hands, striving to determine if she should send the coachman and footman to offer assistance, afraid he'd lied to her about remaining safe, that so much more was at stake than she had even a hint of. Working the docks may have scarred his hands, but she was beginning to suspect he had earned other scars that weren't visible. He was no longer the sort of man who awoke among hedgerows or teased about freckles.

While she'd been wondering what kind of man he was, she'd heard grunts and muffled curses. The door had suddenly swung open, and she'd been dragged out by this blighter and watched in horror as his mates had bound her coachman and footman.

Now she stood, a figure in this strange tableau, a captive in an untenable situation for which she could envision no escape.

"Won't hurt her at all, mate, if the two of ye go to yer knees and don't fight the killing what's to come."

"No!" she cried out, as the ominous words chilled her to the bone and horrible images of what they foreshadowed rushed through her mind.

"Rest easy, Kathryn. Cowards who shield themselves with women never win."

How could Griff sound so composed, so unbothered, as though he'd just announced that it was going to rain? While her heart was pounding so hard she was surprised it didn't knock the man away from her.

Good Lord. Griff went to his knees without hesitation, and she wanted to scream. Marcus—she assumed that the silhouette standing a short distance away was Marcus—followed suit, lowering himself in the same manner that his brother had. Panic sought to take hold, but she fought it off, concentrating on her situation, what she could detect of it that might give her an edge.

"Whatever you do, Kathryn," Griff said in that steady, conversational tone, "don't stomp on his foot."

"Why the bloody hell would she—"

Before he could finish, she did exactly what Griff had ordered not to do because she realized it was exactly what he wanted her to do. He'd served up a distraction. As the man who'd held her within his grasp had been speaking, his grip had slackened until his clothing barely whispered against hers, and the knife was nowhere near her skin where he could easily mark her. So she struck. Hard and with purpose. As he yelled and jerked back in reaction to the onslaught of her heel digging into his instep, she twisted away, escaping him completely.

A growl, fierce enough to shake the heavens, like that of a feral beast, echoed through the air. She turned back in time to see Griff

smoothly lunging to his feet before charging forward, brandish-
ing a sword—where the devil had he gotten that?

The odious man who had threatened her gave a little squeak
like a frightened dormouse just before he was run through.

One of the other men was making a mad dash for her, and she
skittered back but needn't have bothered because Griff cut him off
before he got close. A second fellow joined the brawl. With a quick
glance around, she saw that Marcus was dealing with the fourth
fellow, and she returned her attention to Griff battling the two.
He'd not had time to reclaim his sword, but it appeared he had
a knife, as did those he fought. Every now and then, moonlight
glinted off steel. She wanted to rush into the middle of it and help
him, but she stayed where she was, knowing it was wrong of her
to find beauty in his feints and parries, in the skills he exhibited
with such grace. While she was terrified for him, she recalled the
confidence with which he'd spoken the night before about collecting what was owed to him. He knew how to carry out a threat,
how to deliver a blow, how to be victorious—and she fought
against creating any sound of alarm or any movement that might
distract him from his purpose.

Swinging a leg up and around, he knocked one of the fellows
to the ground, then took the other down by slamming into him.
They rolled. She could barely see their movements in the darkness, but heard the slap of flesh hitting flesh, a moan, a cry, and
silence.

Griff bounded up and turned his attention to the man he'd
earlier kicked. The villain had regained his footing. Knives were
clearly evident as they slowly circled each other.

"Drop the knife and run," Griff ordered, his voice flat, without sentiment, as though he'd tightly bound all his emotions so
they couldn't interfere and prevent him from doing the unpleasant tasks that needed to be done in order to survive the ordeal. "I
won't give chase. You have my word."

She sensed the fellow measuring the truth of his vow. How
could he not hear the veracity in his opponent's tone? Griff had

felled two of his mates, and looking to the side, she saw that Marcus had taken down the third. Did this man think he stood a chance of beating Griff?

Griff who had gone to his knees in surrender, but in the end hadn't surrendered at all? Who had never intended to surrender? Who had told her that he'd become quite skilled at effectively delivering a blow? He'd become skilled at more than that. He'd acquired a talent for surviving, and she was left to wonder what else he might have faced over the months since she'd last seen him.

"No knife in the back, then?" the man asked, and she heard the shrill of fear edging his voice.

"No." And no fear whatsoever in Griff's voice. He knew this battle was his to win. But he was showing mercy.

The footpad or assassin or whatever he was dropped his knife, spun on his heel, and took off at a run, loping past her as though the hounds of hell nipped at his ankles.

It was over. Her legs began to shake. Somehow, she'd misplaced her knees, because they didn't seem to be there to support her, but still she managed to remain upright when she wanted to sink to the ground.

"Kathryn?"

Perhaps she wasn't standing on her own as much as she'd thought, because Griff's arm had come around her, and he'd drawn her up against his right side, holding her tightly, his face lowered so his lips brushed over her cheek when he spoke, his voice strained but gentle. "Brave, brave girl. Are you hurt?"

Only then did she realize that the edges of her vision had begun to darken, that she might actually have been in danger of swooning—*danger, danger* of swooning, she would never use that word *danger* so lightly again. But now that he was here, everything was becoming clearer. Tears threatened, but she forced them back. "No, no, I'm unharmed."

She felt a shudder race through him. "I'm sorry to have placed you in danger."

"I feared he was going to kill me," she rasped.

"I'd have never let that happen." The absolute conviction with which he spoke was a soothing balm. Besides, how could she doubt it when she'd witnessed how deadly he could be?

"You . . . you had a sword."

"I carry it inside my walking stick."

And a knife. She could feel it digging into her side, no doubt now housed in a scabbard hidden beneath his coat.

At the sound of grass being crushed by heavy feet, he turned slightly without relinquishing his hold on her. "Marcus, are you hurt?"

"No. You?"

"No."

"Good." He tipped his head slightly. "Lady Kathryn, not the most favorable circumstance upon which to see you again. How did you come to be here?"

"She gave me a ride in her carriage," Griff said. "She was at the club. It was reckless of me to accept her offer."

"You can't blame yourself for what happened," she assured him. "It was reckless of me not to leave as you ordered."

"Your driver and footman?"

"They bound them up, but I think they're unharmed." They'd been mumbling and grumbling before they'd been gagged, so surely they were unhurt as well.

"I need to see them unbound then and ensure you get home safely." He gave his attention back to his brother. "Marcus, can we take you somewhere?"

"I have a boat waiting for me up the river. You two should leave. I'll take care of these three before I go."

"Send word if you need anything."

"I will. They shouldn't come after you. It's me they want. They don't even know who you are. They certainly won't know where to find you. You were simply in the wrong place at the wrong time, and I regret that. I was convinced I wasn't being followed."

"Do you think you can avoid them in the future?"

"I shall certainly try. Once I leave London, they shouldn't come searching for me. They'll think I've turned tail and run."

"I hope you're right about that."

"It's not your problem. You got out. Stay out."

"If you need me—"

"I know, but I won't."

Griff gave a nod. "Excuse me for just a minute." He strode over to the man he'd skewered and pulled free his sword.

"He had no choice, you know."

She looked at Marcus. "Did either of you?"

"They were all a nasty bit of work. I suspect eventually each would have been introduced to the hangman. I wouldn't have let the last fellow go, but then I'm not the one who would have had to live with him on my conscience."

She was glad Griff had given the man a choice. He returned to her side, no evidence of the sword in sight, merely his walking stick. The man traveled with weapons. She was having a difficult time reconciling that fact, although perhaps she shouldn't have been surprised. She'd a sense that life had changed him, that he was more dangerous than he'd been.

The brothers said their farewells and clapped each other on the shoulder. Then she and Griff began walking back toward the carriage.

"Why did they want to kill Marcus?" she finally asked.

"Because he intends to expose those who were working with Father, once he learns the name of the person who organized it all."

"You were expecting trouble."

"I always expect trouble when Marcus is involved. You were a clever girl to catch the meaning of what I was telling you to do."

She shouldn't have been so pleased by his praise. "At least I handled it better than I did the cheroot."

He chuckled low. "You did indeed."

At the carriage, his knife came out once again, and he cut the bindings on the coachman and footman, apologizing for the inconvenience, making it sound as though it had been ordinary footpads who'd come after them. She didn't like this world he'd once inhabited and was glad he was free of it. She hoped Marcus was correct, and he would never again be bothered by the likes of those who'd wished them harm.

When she was tucked inside the conveyance, traveling toward her residence, with him sitting opposite her because he'd insisted that he would see her safely there and make his own way back to the club, she studied his silhouette and longed to have brought a lantern inside to see him more clearly. She'd sensed subtle changes in him at the club. A confidence and bearing that was as attractive as his features. But he was so much more complicated than she'd realized.

She wished he hadn't released her, that when he'd climbed inside after her he'd settled on the squabs beside her, that his arm was once again around her and she was snuggled against his side. Standing on the banks of the Thames, with a knife at her throat, she'd thought of inconsequential things, things she would miss, things she wished she'd done. Things she wished she'd done with him. Another kiss. Another conversation. A laugh. A smile. A tease. God, even a tease would have been welcomed.

Odd thing that every thought had involved Griff. Poor Kingsland would have been left with the task of searching for another woman to woo into marriage, and yet she'd given him no thought. Perhaps because Griff had been there, and he hadn't.

"It would be best if you didn't tell anyone about tonight's adventure," he said quietly.

"I don't think anyone would believe me." She was having a difficult time believing it herself.

Glancing out the window, she fought to regain a sense of normalcy, to put what had happened earlier behind her, but it clung to her like the sea did when she first came up out of the water after going swimming at her grandmother's cottage, threatening to suck her and her soaked clothing back down, to reclaim her. "When I kissed you last night, I did it in anger."

It was one of the regrets that had bombarded her as she'd waited for the death she'd expected to come.

"I know."

She'd done it to torment him, to punish him, and instead, she'd punished herself. It had tarnished the memory of the kiss he'd given her in the garden. She no longer wanted their final kiss to be one of anger. Once she married Kingsland, Griff's lips would be forbidden to her, but tonight she'd been given an opportunity to replace their last kiss with another.

Pushing herself off the bench, balancing herself with the swaying of the carriage, she closed the short distance between them. He grunted as she settled on his lap, straddling him, her legs nestled on either side of his thighs. His hands bracketed her waist, steadying her as she cradled his face between her palms, enjoying the texture of his bristled jaw against her soft skin. It somehow made this moment more intimate. He remained still, waiting, and she wondered how his breathing could remain so steady when hers was frightfully erratic, when being so near to him caused rioting sensations to course through her. To be here when she knew she shouldn't, to be here because she desired it. Because she'd faced death tonight—they'd both faced death—and they'd been victorious and to the victors belonged the spoils. And for her, that involved a kiss. From him.

"I want to kiss you. No anger this time. Only gratitude that it's still a choice I have." His lips parted before she reached them, before she angled his head to give her easier access to that which she sought. She recalled his earlier lesson about how some things were better when met with preparation, and so she teased, licking the corner of his mouth, the side that curled up whenever he wasn't of a mind to give her a full smile, when he didn't want her to know that he'd taken delight in her words or actions. With her tongue, she painted his lower lip, so full, so enticing, a cushion to hers that promised pleasure.

Groaning low, cupping the back of her head, holding her in place, he thrust his tongue into her mouth, ending her taunting, thrilling her with his impatience. She wasn't the only one who wanted—needed—an affirmation that life, precious and dear, shouldn't be wasted with regrets for moments lost. They had here, they had now, when they might have had nothing else at all.

Where was the harm in taking advantage of the parrying in which neither sought the defeat of the other but gloried in each stroke, each sweep, each suckle? She caught the barest hint of chocolate and spice, imagined it was the lingering remnants of the cheroot he'd smoked earlier. Did she reflect the same flavor?

She hoped he wasn't tasting the fear that had brought a metallic tinge to her mouth. Not so much a fear for herself but for him. When he'd gone to his knees—

With deliberation, she pushed the recollection aside. She wanted this moment to wipe out the other memory, to give her moments to savor, to reflect on, to carry with her into slumber so she would dream of passion and desire. And when she awoke, it would be because her body yearned and craved.

She did yearn, did crave. The scent of him, the feel of him, the sound of him as he growled, taking the kiss deeper.

Skimming her hand over his neckcloth, she noted it was no longer perfectly knotted. Perhaps she'd remove it. Would he object? Or would he welcome her mouth nibbling along his neck? Gliding her fingers along his waistcoat, she considered loosening the buttons, reducing the amount of cloth separating his heat from hers. Lower—

She stilled at the warm dampness. Stiffening, he grabbed her wrist.

"What is that?" she insisted.

Only he didn't answer. His breathing was harsh, and she suspected perhaps it wasn't the kiss causing it. Wrenching her wrist free of him, she brought her fingers nearer to her face. There wasn't enough light with which to see, but she could smell the coppery tang. "You're bleeding. You told Marcus you weren't hurt."

"He wouldn't have left if he knew I was."

Oh dear God. And he was going to see her home and then take himself off to his club? To a surgeon? To suffer alone? To possibly . . . die? Horrified, she scrambled off his lap, sitting beside him, wanting to touch him, afraid of hurting him. "How bad is it?"

"Not so bad."

He'd lied to Marcus. Why wouldn't he be lying to her at that precise moment? She saw everything differently now. The strain in his voice when he'd first approached her. The manner in which he'd held her, tucked in against his right side, the rest of his body angled away from her. The wound was on the left. In the darkness, with only the moon and stars, he'd been able to hide so much from his brother, from her. It flayed her heart, scored her soul that he'd kept this from her, had not trusted her with it.

In the dark, she ran her hands across the bench until she located his unique walking stick, used it to bang on the ceiling, and immediately felt the coach slowing.

"What are you doing?" he asked.

"I'm going to instruct them to take you to hospital."

"No hospital."

"A surgeon then."

"No."

Infuriating man. "I will at least see how bad it is."

"Lady Kathryn, it's not your concern."

She did not miss the fact that he was using a formal address to put distance between them. "The devil it isn't."

Did he not understand that she cared for him? Did he think she went around kissing any gent who caught her fancy? Although even if she did, only one had ever come close. This one. This stubborn man who didn't seem to have it within him to ask for help of any kind—not from her, not from his family, not from anyone. While she admired his independence, it also frustrated her. He was alone, so alone.

The carriage came to a full stop. Without waiting for the foot-man to assist her, she opened the door before he reached it. "I need a lantern."

He removed one from a hook at the front of the carriage and handed it to her.

"Wait for my orders."

"Yes, milady."

Ducking back inside, she hung the lantern on a peg above the window, grateful the glow allowed her to see Griff more clearly—or perhaps not clearly enough. He appeared wan and pale, with tight lines about his mouth, and his brow furrowed. He was in pain, excruciating pain if his expression was any in-dication, and yet he'd kissed her, pretending all was as it should be, when it was anything but. "Show me."

"Lady Kathryn—"

"Show me."

He scowled. "When did you become such a termagant?"

"About the same time you became such an idiot. The coach cushions are probably going to have to be replaced, with your bleeding all over them."

That corner of his mouth, the one she'd licked only moments ago, curled up. "I don't think it's that bad."

Gingerly she helped him tug his blood-soaked shirt free of his trousers and lifted the hem up. Grabbing the lantern, she lowered it in order to direct most of the light on the glistening, gap-ing wound. "Oh God, Griff, it is that bad. It's a long, deep gash. I wouldn't know where to begin to stitch it up."

"I don't think it's deep enough to have pierced anything."

She shook her head. "No. It looks like he just sliced into you." But he'd done damage, horrible damage. She didn't think the bleeding was going to stop on its own. She lifted her gaze to his. "Please let me take you to a physician."

"Your parents are going to worry about you if you're not home soon."

"They're in Paris. I'm quite on my own. No one is going to know."

He studied her for what seemed an eternity before averting his gaze toward the window and nodding, as though he viewed himself as weak for allowing her to help. She cursed his father, the Society that had turned its back on him, and everyone else who had led him to believe that he stood alone in all his battles.

CHAPTER 14

$\mathcal{H}$E AWOKE TO faint sunlight drifting lazily into the bedchamber and the salt-scented air stirring the curtains at the open window. Aching and unsteady, he cursed the grogginess that was a result of the laudanum the surgeon had given him before he'd begun stitching him up. The medication had also been responsible for his inability to think clearly after the physician had finished his work. So when Kathryn had told Griff she needed to come to her grandmother's cottage in order to put the ugliness of the night behind her, he'd agreed to accompany her, not yet ready to let her out of his sight, still shaken by how close he'd come to losing her.

But before she had told him what she needed, she had held his hand, the one farther away from where the doctor worked, clutched it hard enough that he feared the bones might crack. Although her head had been bent and her gaze averted so she didn't have to view the torn flesh and muscle, the blood seeping out, he'd seen the solitary tear fall, landing silently on her hand where it clasped his, and he'd known an agony greater than anything he was enduring from the doctor's ministrations. That single tear had seemed far worse than a torrent. She'd been so courageous, so stoic—and he in so much pain, praying she wouldn't discover how badly he was hurt—that he had failed to comprehend fully how she was struggling to come to grips with all that had transpired.

As a result he'd been unable to refuse her request, to let her go on her own, to not be there for her after she had insisted on seeing him cared for when it would have been so much easier to simply send him on his way to tend to himself.

And so here he was where he shouldn't be, with a woman he shouldn't be with. A woman who belonged to another, even if they'd not yet come to terms. A woman he'd given to another.

He didn't want to think about that monstrous regret.

With a groan, he shoved himself out of the bed and glanced around at the pale blue room. Her grandmother's room, she'd told him. His gaze stopped at the plush chair with the small stack of clothes folded neatly on it. Not the things he'd been wearing last night because they needed a good washing and some mending. Through the fog of his mind, he remembered her saying something about a housemaid who saw to the place.

Kathryn had brought him to this room and helped him remove his clothes. All of his clothes. He'd never been particularly modest and wondered now if she'd liked what she'd seen. He grimaced at the inappropriate thought spawned by lust. She was deserving of nothing except his respect. Without her insistence, he might not have gone to a doctor, might have attempted to tend to his own wound.

He picked up the shirt and trousers. Coarse material, a simple style. Perhaps they'd belonged to her grandfather. Or perhaps she'd sent the footman out to borrow something from a villager. It didn't matter. They were clean. They'd be a tight fit, but they'd do for the short amount of time they were going to be here. He walked to the washstand and splashed the cold water on his face. He stilled, the droplets plopping back into the bowl as another image came to him, another memory.

Her washing him. Removing the blood, and the dirt, and the grime. Slowly, gently, tenderly. Him, gripping the edge of the bed, so he didn't reach for her, didn't carry her down to the mattress.

Her courage out on the banks of the Thames had undone him. He'd never wanted anyone more. When she'd crossed the expanse of the coach to straddle his lap and kiss him, he'd been unable to hold his desire in check. He'd forgotten about the wound and his intention to keep it hidden from her. All that had mattered was Kathryn and giving her what she needed, what she wanted.

He'd managed not to tumble her onto the bed during her sweet ministrations, but once he was in it and she'd brought the sheet and blankets over him, she'd joined him anyway, the covers separating them.

"Just for a little while," she'd whispered.

Slipping his arm around her, he'd brought her in against his uninjured side and held her close as the laudanum finished its work and took him under. How long had she stayed? Where was she now?

He shook off the memories, the unsteadiness, and the cobwebs that blurred so much of what had happened after his time with the physician: the journey here, the settling in, the falling into slumber. He tossed water on his face several more times, reached for the towel, and dried himself off. The clothes came next, and as he'd judged, they were intended for a somewhat smaller man.

After walking to the window, he looked out. Not another building or rooftop to be seen. Trees, flowers, and green eventually gave way to blue that stretched to the horizon. Not only sky, but water. The sea.

He'd heard it last night, crashing against the shore, but had been too weary to go to the bother of seeing it. But he had a memory of her standing there, gazing out. Had he awakened and seen her? Or only dreamed it?

They were in Kent, only a few hours from London. They could return to the city easily enough, sometime today if she was of a mind to. He would leave the decision to her. But he had to find her first.

He wandered down a small hallway, past a set of stairs, to the front of the house. On one side was a dining room with a circular table. Across from it was a cozy parlor.

"Ah, sir. Good morning to ye."

Turning back toward the dining room, he offered a polite smile to the woman dressed in a black frock, with a white apron and mobcap. "Good morning."

"I'll have breakfast ready by the time her ladyship returns from her walk."

"Very good. Think I'll stretch my legs as well." He carried on. Beyond the door, the cool breeze wafted over him. He took it deeply into his lungs, feeling revitalized by the scent of salty sea air. In the distance seagulls circled about, their cries mingling with the rush of the waves. Glancing around, he wondered in which direction Kathryn might have gone.

He began wandering toward what appeared to be a cliff's ledge, relishing the silk of grass against his soles. His boots had seemed like too much trouble to tug on. As a lad, he'd raced across meadows in bare feet whenever he was able to escape the watchful eye of a nanny or governess. His father had caught him once and taken a switch to his backside, while lecturing him about the importance of always being perceived as a gentleman. The irony of his traitorous father lecturing him about anything was not lost on him now.

When he reached the land's edge, he looked down, and his breath caught. Not because of the dizzying height but because she was there with her skirt hiked up over her knees as she waded about in the blue water. She gave a little screech, hopped back, and the wind carried her laughter up to him. He wondered if some sea creature had pinched her toe.

Gingerly he eased himself down to the ground and simply watched, feeling at peace for the first time in months. It was as though cares couldn't reside here. He understood why she'd wanted to come.

She began walking away from the waves rolling onto the shore, her movements light yet sinewy, not displaying the stiff posture, the erect spine, the calculated actions of a well-tutored lady. Instead he caught glimpses of the girl she'd been when she'd visited her grandmother here, more relaxed, more at home, more herself.

A woman the Duke of Kingsland would never see, would never explore, would never understand.

Abruptly she stopped, lowered herself to the ground, drew her knees against her chest, and wrapped her arms around her legs. Even from this distance, he could detect her shoulders heaving. Issuing a harsh curse, he shot to his feet, grinding out a slew of profanities as his wound protested his sudden actions. Glancing around, he noticed a spot where the grass looked to have been recently trampled. Heading for it, he discovered a path leading down to the shore and carefully navigated it until his feet hit the sand. With a purpose to his stride, he crossed over to where she sat with her brow pressed against her knees and crouched beside her, near enough that the fragrance of oranges mixed with salt wafted around him. "Kathryn?"

Giving a little sniff, she turned her head to the side, away from him, for all of two breaths. When she looked at him, he realized she'd been swiping at her tears, as unobtrusively as possible, but some still clung to her long auburn lashes. She gave him a tremulous smile. "How is your side this morning?"

"Aching like the devil." Little, if any, laudanum remained to course through his blood and dull the pain. He didn't know how many stitches had been needed to close the gaping wound. If she hadn't distracted him with her presence, he might have counted them. He'd felt every blasted one going in. Reaching out with his thumb, he captured a tear glistening at the corner of her eye. "How are *you* this morning?"

She released a shuddering breath. "I thought I was all right. And then suddenly I wasn't. All the emotions of last night just hit before I could prepare for them."

Lowering himself so he was sitting on the sand, better able to balance himself, he nestled her face against his shoulder. "There's no shame in weeping."

"It makes me feel weak."

"You're far from being weak, Kathryn. Your strength was clearly evident only a few hours ago."

"As was yours." Pulling away, she studied him as though she hadn't known him for years, had never really seen him before. "Where did you learn to fight like that?"

"While I was working the docks."

Her brow furrowed. "A lot of brawling goes on there?"

"No, but a lot of bruisers haul cargo. Like Billy, the fellow who stopped you at the door the first night. Althea and I lived in White-chapel for a while, and I wanted to ensure I had the wherewithal to protect her, if need be. On those streets they hardly follow the Queensberry Rules. So I hired Billy and a couple of other blokes to teach me how to fight in a manner no gentleman ever would."

"Did Althea know?"

He shook his head. "I didn't want her worrying that we were in dangerous environs or that I might get hurt. If the lessons went long and she asked where I'd been, I told her I was with a woman. She seemed to accept that easily enough." Without giving it much thought, he took hold of Kathryn's plait and brushed his thumb over the loose strands at the end of it, all the while watching the myriad emotions coursing over her features. "Go ahead and ask."

He saw the delicate muscles at her throat roll as she swallowed, part of her lower lip disappearing as she bit into it. "He referred to you as an assassin."

She left it there, but in the barest hint of a quiver in her voice, he heard what she didn't dare put into words, say aloud, as though doing so would taint this idyllic spot: *Are you?*

"These men Marcus was associating with . . . they're ruthless. You witnessed it. They didn't trust him, so they had their spies watching him. I spied on the spies. One night, one of them"—he shook his head, still baffled by it—"for some reason that we have yet to decipher, tried to kill him. I stopped him. Permanently."

He looked to the water, to the sea, wondering if he waded into it, if it would wash away his sins and regrets. "I'm not proud of it,

Kathryn. To be honest, I hadn't meant to kill him, just to wound him, to send a message that Marcus had a protector. I was aiming for his thigh, but he came in lower, quicker than I expected, and the knife went into his gut . . . deep. It was not a pretty death. But the message was sent." He dared to glance over at her. Her eyes were wide, the color of the sea in the distance, beyond this little alcove. Her face was pale.

"He killed himself, then, really."

He'd used the same argument many a night in order to find even a few minutes of sleep, but the truth wasn't so easily glossed over. He'd been the one holding the knife. He'd been the one who struck. "Shortly afterward, I decided I wanted no further part in Marcus's quest. I was tired of my father, even in death, determining my fate. He did what he did. I don't care why or with whom. But then, I didn't lose as much as Marcus."

"I would argue you all lost the same, but I think you were right to find your own path. Now you have a business that looks as though it's likely to succeed."

Her voice still carried a hesitancy, a slight tremor. She was willing to move on when questions remained to be answered, and he realized she feared the truth of them. He'd been too distracted by his own pain to truly recognize hers. "I didn't kill those men last night."

Her hand coming up to cover her mouth, she gave a little gasp. "You didn't?"

"The first one I wanted to, desperately, but I didn't want you to have his death on your conscience. I delivered a devastating wound, but it shouldn't kill him, although I suspect he'll have a slow recovery, might even wish it had." After he'd discovered the sword-hidden-in-a-cane in a pawnshop and purchased it, he'd visited with a physician to learn how and where to strike with maximum damage without causing death, as well as where to strike to cause it. "The other fellow I merely knocked out with a hard punch—after he got the better of me." He was the one who'd slid his knife across Griff's side.

Another gasp. And then she was weeping. "I kept seeing them dead. Marcus said they were."

"It was too dark for him to know for certain. He assumed." Perhaps because he'd had to kill the fellow he was fighting.

"I'm glad. Glad you didn't kill them."

Causing a man's death, even if it wasn't intentional, was not an easy thing with which to live. He had a feeling neither man was long for this world, would end their lives on a scaffold, but had seen no point in shortening their time. Although, the first fellow was going to require a long period of healing. In addition to the sword wound he'd given him, he'd broken his nose and jaw. Not that she needed to know all that. Once more, he gathered a tear. "So now you can dance on the beach without any guilt."

Her eyes stopped filling with water. "Did you see me?"

He nodded.

She scoffed a little laugh. "I only do that when I don't think anyone's watching."

"Do you always dance on the beach before breakfast?"

"My grandmother taught me that it was the best way to begin the day, because then no matter what trials or tribulations or disappointments might come my way, I would always have the joy of the morning to see me through. She used to skip about with me, so now it's as though she's still here with me."

"You appeared carefree for a while."

"Some of my happiest moments have been spent here. Thank you for coming."

"I was at the mercy of the laudanum." At the mercy of her. "Although Kingsland isn't going to be happy if he learns we're here."

"He won't. My servants are very loyal."

"The question, Lady Kathryn, is how loyal are we? Increased proximity sometimes breeds a more intimate familiarity. After all, you did kiss me in the carriage last night."

"Do you think he's being loyal? Do you think he has no mistress? That he's being celibate, doing without pleasure?"

"He would expect you to."

"Then, he should have gone to a knee before traipsing off to Yorkshire."

"He's not in London?"

"Not until Wednesday next. He travels quite a bit, actually. I think it's part of the reason that we've not formally come to terms. But I think he likes me well enough. I suspect he will ask soon."

"And you'll say yes."

She gazed past him. "If those dark clouds on the horizon are rolling this way, we should probably have our breakfast and begin the journey back to London. The road away from here gets boggy when it rains." Her gaze came back to him. "I should change your bandage as well. The doctor said at least once a day."

He didn't remember that, but then he'd been striving to block out the pain and everything surrounding it, everything except the feel of her hand clinging to his, as though the discomfort he experienced she experienced as well. "We should head in, then."

After gingerly rising to his feet, he fought against drawing her into his arms and claiming her mouth as his. But it never had been, never would be. Not permanently, not forever.

And now that she knew the truth of him, it was possible she wouldn't welcome him taking any liberties.

ON THE WAY to the cottage, they had decided to eat first, then see to his wound. They were halfway through breakfast when the storm arrived. Kathryn shouldn't have been grateful for the rapid pattering against the roof and windows that would delay their leaving. But she was glad the rain fell in heavy sheets and brought with it the crash of thunder and shattering lightning.

It was an aspect of the cottage that she loved best. The way it welcomed the rain and made her feel tucked in and safe. Her father's residences were too large. She could stand in the middle of one and never even know it was raining, but here it was all noise, wind, and purpose.

Relishing the calm inside the cottage while the thrashing outside created havoc, she carried the bowl of warm water into the bedchamber where Griff waited for her. She came up short at the unexpected sight of his bared torso as he stood at the window gazing out. Every inch she could see was lean muscle and corded sinew. From working the docks, from learning to brawl, from striving to protect those he loved. And last night he'd protected her.

"We waited too long," he said quietly, not taking his attention from the gloom beyond, and she wondered if he'd heard her arrival or sensed it. "It's too late to leave."

"Yes. I spoke with the coachman. He said we're likely to get stuck, probably more than once. With your wound, you won't be able to help them roll us out of the muck."

He released a long, drawn-out sigh that echoed his disappointment. She wasn't going to take offense that he didn't want to be here with her any longer, that he was anxious to return to his life. "Surely your club will survive a day without you. Mrs. Ward must be capable of handling things, or you'd not have put her in charge."

"The club is not my worry."

"What is, then?"

With a shake of his head, he turned away from the view. "Set the bowl on the bedside table. I can see to changing the dressing myself."

"You're less likely to pull any stitches if I do it." After placing the bowl and linens on the table, she held up a small jar. "I have some salve the doctor gave me to aid in the healing. It'll be easier for me to apply."

She waited as the debate he waged with himself was evident in the tightening of that luscious mouth of his, the narrowing of those beautiful eyes. Did he worry that this time he might initiate a kiss, one that shouldn't happen? Did he recognize that knowing what *shouldn't* happen didn't necessarily stop it from happening?

"I'll behave," she offered.

He laughed, only a quick burst of sound, but it was enough to warm her to her core, enough to let her know that she was on the right track regarding his concerns. Kingsland never made her feel as though he struggled not to touch her, not to have a taste of her. Since their last night at the theater, he'd kissed her a few more times, but they had all been polite, gentlemanly sorts of encounters. She was discovering she preferred the kiss of a scoundrel.

A smile was still playing over his lips as he approached. "Where do you want me? The chair?"

"The bed." He went still, his eyes heating with passion and promise that had her rushing to explain. "The chair is too small." Too bulky with its thickly upholstered back and arms. "I won't be able to work around you as I need to."

He eased onto the bed, sitting at its edge. "Be quick about it."

His hands clutched his thighs in the same manner they'd gripped his arms the first night she'd gone to his club. She shouldn't have taken satisfaction in the knowledge that he wanted her. Or perhaps she had the wrong of it, and he was simply preparing to deal with the pain that might result from her tending to his wound. But she intended to be gentle, careful. She couldn't bear the thought of causing him any agony.

Using the scissors, she cut off the knot the doctor had made to secure the bandage that he'd wrapped around Griff's torso. She unwound the linen, passing it off from hand to hand as she circled him, aware of his not breathing, of his holding so still he might as well have been a statue. Occasionally she misjudged and her knuckles skimmed over flesh she'd washed the night before. Grooves along his ribs she'd outlined after he'd gone to sleep, muscles roped along his arms that she'd explored. The laudanum had taken him under, and she'd touched him in ways she shouldn't, curiosity getting the better of her, as she investigated this man who had filled out during the months he'd been in exile.

The sheet had been gathered at his waist, and she'd used it as a barrier to the forbidden, hadn't investigated what she'd averted her gaze from seeing as she'd helped him disrobe. But his arms and chest had been as mysterious and wondrous to her questing fingers. She'd continued to trail them over him after she'd crawled onto the bed and nestled up against him, because she couldn't stand the notion of facing the demons who would surely haunt her. But they'd not come. Instinctually, he'd held her tight and kept them at bay.

Finished with her chore, she set the old linens aside and appreciated the flatness of his stomach, the broadness of his chest. His wound was long, red, and angry, the stitches making it look even more ghastly. He would be left with a scar. Kneeling, she pressed her fingers to it. He took in a sharp breath.

"I'm sorry. I know it hurts, but I have to check for putrefaction. The doctor showed me how."

"Good thing you were there. I don't recall any of that."

With the warm water, she cleaned around the wound, gently removing any blood that remained. After reaching for the salve, she dipped some out and smoothed it over the line of stitches. He sucked in his breath, his gut, and she didn't think it was because she'd hurt him. She didn't want to stop touching him, wanted to touch more of him. She needed to distract them both. "May I ask you a question?"

"That never bodes well," he said. "When someone asks if they can ask a question. You can ask all the questions you like. Whether or not I'll answer them is another thing entirely."

"What happened when you were arrested?"

His jaw clenched, but he stared straight ahead, as though the memories were playing out before him on a stage. "At first, we were confused, disoriented, frightened. I was asleep when they arrived and dragged me from my bed. Marcus insisted they at least allow us to dress. Carrying a courtesy title as an earl, his words held more weight than my protests. So we were at least allowed to make ourselves presentable. Still, they carted us away with no explanation.

"They put us together in a room in the Tower. They came for me first, and I thought, *They're going to chop off my head*. Ridiculous thought, really. But it seemed the place for it. As they marched me down the corridor, terror gripped me. I didn't want to continue to put one foot in front of the other. I wanted to rail, and scream, and run. How had Anne Boleyn, a mere slip of a woman, done it, walked to her death? Maybe she pretended she was merely going for a stroll. I don't know.

"But I stopped thinking about what I was presently enduring and the future that I assumed awaited me, and I focused instead on the past, on things that were worth remembering one last time: the unraveling of a woman's hair, a waltz, the last kiss I'd had, would ever have."

She'd paused in her ministrations, and he lowered his gaze, capturing and holding hers. "You, Kathryn, you were there with me and helped me walk down that stone corridor with some dignity."

TEARS WELLED IN her eyes, and he realized he shouldn't have confessed something so personal that involved her. But during the two weeks he was in the Tower and the months following when his life had gone to hell, memories of her had sustained him.

"Hand me the linen. I can finish up here," he said brusquely, probably too briskly, because she seemed to snap into action.

"I'll do it."

It was torture to have her winding the cloth around him. Every time she carried the cloth to his back, she leaned in so close that he could have easily captured her mouth, kissed her throat—and every time he thought of doing both, was so damned tempted, he'd remind himself he was the son of a traitor, was familiar with London's darker corners, had hunted in them, had been responsible for a death. He now ran a club that encouraged sin. Not exactly the sort of gent in whom a woman could take pride. Certainly not the sort for which a lady should give up an inheritance.

"But, thankfully, they didn't take you to the chopping block," she said, finally finished with the tortuous wrapping and sitting back on her heels.

"No. They took me into a room where they sat me in a wooden chair and started asking me questions about my father. It was the first hint I had that the arrest might be a result of something he'd done. I could offer very little insight into his actions, was stunned by the revelation regarding his plans." He glanced toward the window. "When do you think we'll be able to leave?"

"It depends how long the rain continues, but based on how hard it's coming down, probably not until tomorrow."

He bit back a curse, not wanting her to know how desperately he needed to get away from her. Resisting her was becoming more challenging by the minute. When she looked at him with those sultry eyes or when tears gathered or when she touched him—

She'd touched him last night. He remembered it now: it had been as he was drifting off to sleep. He'd luxuriated in her caresses, had taken them into his dreams where he'd returned the favor to her in the wickedest of ways. He wanted to transform the fantasy into reality.

But she was not for him. And he would not risk her losing what she longed to possess. Especially now that he'd seen her here, seen how perfectly it suited her. The innocence of the place where she was free to frolic on the beach, a world so different from the one in which he now lived. An ugliness from his past had touched her, and he intended to ensure it never touched her again. Never had a chance to even come close. He couldn't swear that he'd escaped it completely, that if Marcus sent word to him, he wouldn't answer and return to his brother's side. "I've grown weary. I should sleep for a bit."

"Of course." She rose. "You're healing. You should rest while you're here. I doubt you'll get to do that very much when you've returned to your club."

After gathering up the bowl, the old linens, and the salve, she headed for the door.

"Lady Kathryn?"

Stopping, she turned to glance back at him. Confusion marred her eyes, no doubt because he'd addressed her so formally, but it was imperative to constantly remind himself she was beyond reach. "Thank you for your care."

"While I wish it wasn't necessary, tending to you was my pleasure."

As she left, he slammed his eyes closed as images of another sort of pleasure, hot, sweaty, and extremely carnal, raced through his mind. He flopped down onto the bed, onto his back, and groaned as his side protested the abuse. He cursed Kingsland for having not already married her, for not removing all temptation of her.

CHAPTER 15

*H*E AWOKE TO the light patter of rain. After rolling out of bed, he walked to the window, parted the draperies, and gazed at the gloominess that somehow comforted and brought solace. He understood why Kathryn loved this place, why she'd not considered giving it up for any man who didn't meet the criteria required for her to have it. She was more relaxed, happier, at peace here.

Why the devil hadn't Kingsland asked for her hand already? He'd had months of calling upon her. Was the man blind to the treasure she was? She'd make an excellent duchess, wife, and mother. When he envisioned her with children, he saw them as blond—which was impossible, considering how dark the duke was, how coppery red her own hair—frolicking through the tall grasses, rushing down the trail to the water's edge, and squealing with delight as the sea rolled in to tickle their toes.

He placed his scarred palm on the glass, splayed his calloused fingers. The hand of a brute.

Eventually, if his business continued in the direction it was going, if his investments continued to reap rewards, he could purchase a cottage by the sea. But it was unlikely to be this one, wouldn't hold her memories. If he confessed his feelings for her, asked her to marry him, she wouldn't be the wife of a gentleman but that of a scoundrel and worse: a man willing to do anything to survive.

He cursed the rain that was going to keep them there for another night, keep her within proximity. At the club witnesses—some studying him warily, some glaring openly—served as a reminder they were watched, and so he'd kept his hands off her when he'd dearly wanted to touch her. He'd maintained a distance, not only physically but mentally as well. He'd fought against letting her delve beneath his surface, battled against letting her know that he could survive for weeks on one of her smiles, for months on a single peal of her laughter.

To aid in his quest to shield himself from her, to protect her from him, he'd built a wall, brick by brick, each representing an action in which a gentleman would never engage but that he had—multiple times. The hefting of boxes, the hauling of crates, the pulling on ropes. The pummeling of a fist, the intimidating, the spying. The learning of secrets, the threatening to reveal them. The power that could be used for harm. The night he hadn't hesitated to use it to destroy.

His past should be enough to ensure he kept his hands off her. But when she'd kissed him at the club and in the carriage, the bricks crumbled, and he had been forced to rebuild the wall.

He shouldn't have come here, shouldn't have caught a glimpse of what life with her might be: dances along the shore, the music of her soul on the air, smiles exchanged, laugher shared . . . and peace.

How he longed for peace. Maybe it was the reason Marcus was obsessed with discovering the truth of their father, because without it, for him, peace could not exist. But Griff was learning that the truth didn't bring peace. It brought only misery.

Because the truth was—and had been for longer than he'd realized—he loved Kathryn. Loved her with a strength of conviction and passion that was terrifying. It had prompted him to write the duke in order to ensure she gained what she desired.

The wager had been an afterthought, to provide him with consolation. If he couldn't have her, he'd have his damned club. But the laughter within its walls had not been hers. The smiles had not been hers. The seductive whispers had not been hers. He'd not been able to put her there—until the night she'd walked in. And now he'd not be able to stroll through it without bringing forth images of her in each of the rooms.

He wondered if she would have the same experience, if she would be able to walk through the cottage and not sense the remnants of his presence.

A rap sounded on the door.

"Griff? Dinner is prepared. Will you be joining me?"

He shouldn't. He should have a plate brought to him and eat it in here. Alone.

But he was destined for a good many nights alone, and many lonely nights. No matter how crowded his club became, still he remained alone . . . and lonely.

So he stacked the bricks and shoved mortar between them, making the walls sturdier, as he crossed the room and opened the door. "I'll join you."

FOLLOWING DINNER, HE taught her to play brag, a favorite of the Duke of Kingsland apparently. They wagered with matchsticks, and she won most of his. While he grumbled a lot about her winning, she could tell he enjoyed the competition she provided.

When the clock struck ten and most of the matchsticks were in her possession, he bid her good night and retired to his bedchamber. And she went to hers and readied herself for bed.

But now as she lay beneath the covers, she couldn't sleep for the thoughts of him going through her mind. The way he met her gaze and held it. The manner in which, sometimes, that very same gaze would drift to her lips. The frequency with which he would touch her hand, her elbow, her shoulder—and the naturalness of it. As though he did it without any conscious thought. She'd caught herself touching him a time or two without thinking it through, realizing what she'd done only when the warmth of his skin penetrated the linen of his shirt to taunt her fingers, to remind her of how it had felt to skim her hands over his forbidden flesh.

She would never again be able to visit the cottage without seeing him here. Sitting at her table with wineglass in hand. Lounging on the sofa sipping port. Standing at the window watching the rain.

But it was more than their time here she would be unable to forget. It was everything about him. She knew her thoughts should be focused on Kingsland, that he should occupy her mind at all times, that she should miss him, be anxious for his return—and yet it was Griff who filled every nook and cranny of her mind and, she feared, perhaps even her heart.

In all the months Kingsland had courted her, had she really come to know him? Did she know how his lips twitched when he was teasing? Or how his eyes darkened just before he kissed her? Or how they smoldered when he first caught sight of her in a gown of green? Griff had never said in words how he favored the green, but it was there in the way he looked at her as though he'd just encountered a masterpiece.

She knew so many small things about Griff, and they seemed as important as all the large things she knew about him. His dreams, ambitions, willingness to take any job to survive. He'd watched over Althea until Benedict Trewlove had taken on the task. Then he'd gone to watch over his brother and had nearly sacrificed himself to ensure Marcus remained safe.

Life had thrown challenges at him, and he'd met each and every one of them head-on. No more mornings waking up behind hedgerows. No more nights filled with drink, and play, and . . . women. Were there women? There certainly could be based on the interested way several had watched him at his club, but he'd told her they weren't for him. Would he have returned her kiss at the club or in the carriage if he favored someone?

She listened as the rain pattered the roof and tapped against the windows. She'd always loved this room at the top of the stairs when the weather was rough and wild and should have been frightening. It had always given her strength and made her believe that if she could survive a storm, she could survive anything.

Even a marriage without love.

But what she found herself wondering now was if she could give up love for such a marriage.

HE AWOKE TO a scream. High-pitched. Terrified. The shrill cry of someone being attacked, someone in mortal danger. He scrambled from the bed, snatched up his trousers and drew them on, fastening the buttons and ignoring the pain in his side as he raced out of his chamber before the echo of sound faded. He tore down the hallway and up the stairs.

Only one other person was in this residence with him. The woman who did the cooking and cleaning lived in the village with her husband and returned to him every night. Griff had learned it was that bloke's clothing that had been lent to him. He had no idea where the coachman and footman slept. Perhaps in the village as well, where they liveried the coach and horses. At that moment none of it mattered. All that mattered was her.

Another shriek, his name woven through the wail.

His heart pounding so hard that he was surprised the walls didn't shake with the force of it, he reached the landing. Three doors were visible. Two open, one closed. He went for the one that would have given her privacy when she'd retired. He didn't bother with testing to see if it was locked. He simply kicked it in.

His gaze swept through the room, searching the shadows that evaded the faint moonlight spilling in through the window. But he could make out no dastardly silhouettes or menacing figures cloaked in darkness.

Yet still another shout came, the danger real, but only to her, as she thrashed about in her bed. He'd had enough nightmares over the past several months to know how terrifying it could be when lost in the throes of one. Crossing quickly to the bed, he sat on its edge and grabbed the wrists of her flailing arms, bringing them in close, holding them against her heaving chest. "Kathryn, love, I'm here. I won't let anything hurt you. Wake up."

While speaking the words forcefully and determinedly, he gave her a gentle shake. "Come back to me, sweetheart."

Her eyes fluttered open, wild, unfocused. Then they fell on him and widened. She blinked. Her breaths came in harsh pants. "What are you doing here?"

You were screaming like the hounds of hell were chasing you probably wasn't what she needed to hear at the moment. "You cried out."

"Oh God, I'm sorry." She tried to move an arm, and he realized he still had them clamped tightly, badly needing the touch of her to reassure himself she was safe. He released his hold.

Grateful he had, when her first action was to reach out and cradle his jaw. "I was back by the Thames. You were being attacked only . . . you weren't winning."

He settled his hand over hers, held it in place as he turned his head and pressed a kiss to the heart of her palm, all the while managing not to take his gaze from hers. "I shall always win, Kathryn." Because his father's actions had given him a taste of what it was to lose—and he was determined to never experience a soul-crushing defeat again. While he wasn't going to win Kathryn, it was by choice, a decision not to try, a resolution to ensure she won something far greater than anything he could offer her.

Her enticing lips twitched as she fought a smile. "I would claim you arrogant. Except I've seen you fight."

Then she grew somber because what she'd witnessed had been responsible for the nightmare that had plagued her. If it visited her again, away from here, he wouldn't be near enough to rescue her from it. He needed to give her a better memory to replace the awful one.

After standing, he tossed back the covers, took her hand, and gave a little tug. "Come with me."

She didn't hesitate, didn't question, simply slipped out of the bed, and like an ethereal being, limned by silver moonlight, she came into his arms. He captured her mouth with an urgency that he was grateful didn't seem to frighten her. It was maddening how desperate he was for the taste of her, the feel of her, the warmth of her.

Her fingers scraped up his scalp, tangled in his curls. He wanted them to remain there forever, to hold him in place so he could never stop kissing her.

As for his own hands, they were sliding up and down her back, grateful for the thin linen of her nightdress that allowed him to feel the movement of her muscles as he adjusted the angle to take the kiss deeper.

Perhaps it wasn't his letter to the duke that had seen her selected. If she had put in her missive to the arrogant peer that she kissed with wild abandon, had described the enthusiasm with which she partook, had admitted that she wasn't missish at all when it came to entangling tongues, the duke would have selected her without bothering to read any of the other solicitations he'd received. Griff didn't want to consider that eventually the man would have this, would know what it was to experience her passion.

Drawing back from the kiss, he intertwined their fingers, and it seemed as intimate a thing as entangling bodies lost to rapture. After leading her over to the window, he once again took possession of her glorious mouth. If he'd never been wounded, he wouldn't have this now, her in his arms, moaning low as he plundered. But it wasn't enough, in this darkened room, with only the moonlight. He wanted more, wanted to give her more.

Feasting along her neck, he journeyed up to her ear and took the small lobe between his teeth as he freed the buttons of her nightdress. When he was done, satisfaction swept through him as she gave her slender shoulders a little shrug that eased her out of the linen and sent it gliding down her magnificent curves to the floor, leaving her bared to him, awash in the moon's silver glow.

"My God, but you're beautiful."

She trailed her fingers over his chest, circled the tip of a finger around his nipple, as though mesmerized by the darkened disk, and he was glad he hadn't taken the time to grab a shirt when he'd run from his room. "So are you."

Before she set them on a path of no return, he spun her around, so she faced the stars that seemed even more brilliant as they glowed now that the rain had stopped, draped her plaited hair over one shoulder, pressed himself against her, and settled his mouth at the curve of her neck where it flowed seamlessly into her shoulder. So smooth, so silky.

"Watch the sea, Kathryn."

And in the future, when you look at it, remember me.

SHE SHOULDN'T HAVE brought him here, but this place had always been her sanctuary. After the awfulness they'd endured by the Thames, she'd been in desperate need of a sanctuary and had thought perhaps he'd been as well. Someplace to heal not only the physical wound but any emotional ones as well. She'd seen the toll that the duke's betrayal had taken on Althea, couldn't imagine that it hadn't taken an equal one on Griff. To have plunged from the summit of Society with nothing to soften the landing when he'd hit the nethermost realm of existence.

But now whenever she visited this little corner of the world that she loved, she would be reminded of him. She would hear his laugh in the wind that swept over the cliff, the low deep rumble of his voice sharing secrets in the parlor. She would see his blue-gray eyes as he watched her in the sunlight, his smile in the moonlight.

And in the sea, whenever she looked at the sea, she would recall what it was like to have his hands caressing her breasts, his heated mouth languidly trailing over her back, along her spine, down one side and up the other. While in the distance, the water reflected the moonlight, and she wondered if it absorbed its glow as her flesh did the amazing sensations he created, or if it tossed it back to the sky, more brilliant than it had been when received.

She loved when he glided his bare chest up her back, from her hips to the top of her shoulders. Then his mouth, open and hot, was on her nape, and his fingers were skimming lower, lower, past her ribs, over her belly, circling there, teasing, tracing along her hips, arrowing down slowly, giving her time to object to the intimacy. Instead, she placed her hands over his larger ones, partaking of the journey.

As he neared his destination, she glided her fingers over his wrists and forearms, over the coarse hair that wasn't dark enough to hide the raised veins or the taut muscles that now defined him, clasping the muscles just above his elbow, holding firm as his deft fingers tiptoed over her curls and parted the folds, before circling tenderly over the sensitive bud that had never known a man's touch. The wondrous sensation that tripped through her explained why seasoned women went to his club in search of unfettered companionship.

While Kingsland had called upon her, had even kissed her on occasion, nothing they shared had ever been like this, all-consuming, devouring, passionate. So why should she not indulge in pleasure when neither the duke nor she had committed themselves to the other. Especially when she cared so very much about this man. When she'd thought he might die, she'd wondered how she would go on in a world that didn't include him. Even though he no longer wandered about in high Society, she at least knew he still drew breath.

Even if it did sound as though he was having difficulty doing so now, his panting harsh and heavy.

"You're already so wet and swollen," he rasped near her ear in a strained voice that made her wonder if the knowledge made it as difficult for him to remain standing as the delicious vibrations were making it for her to do so. "I love how quick you are to react."

"Is that not a testament to your prowess?"

"It's a testament to your lack of inhibitions, to your sensuality, to your own power. Your body wouldn't react thus if you didn't want it."

It? It wasn't *it* that she craved, but him. She wanted him. It pleased her that he wasn't boasting or taking credit but was instead crediting them both for creating this fire that was blazing within her. Could the match create a flame if the wood was not receptive to it?

She started to turn—

"Keep looking at the sea that you love."

She would give him that, if it was what he wanted, but she raised her arm and bent it back until she could tangle her fingers in his hair. She hadn't the ability to not touch him when one of his hands was kneading a breast and the other circled her nether regions. Then he slid a finger inside her, and she couldn't stop the whimper or the tautening of her muscles.

"So hot, so tight," he growled low as he worked his finger in and out. Another joined the first as his thumb circled her nubbin, pressing against it, sliding over it. "Christ, this isn't enough for me, Kathryn. I want to taste you."

"Then, kiss me."

Coming around, blocking her view of the sea and the stars and the moon hovering on the distant horizon, he took possession of her mouth, her heart, her very soul. Even as she knew she shouldn't give the last two aspects of herself to him. But she also knew they would never go to the Duke of Kingsland. Her grandmother hadn't made them a condition of receiving her inheritance, hadn't indicated she should marry a man she loved, only a man with a title. Why had she favored status over her heart? Why sacrifice this, a man adoring her, for position?

She'd always admired, respected, and trusted her grandmother. But it was becoming increasingly difficult to have faith in her opinion on this matter, on her future, when the present was so deuced satisfying. When his kiss reached every aspect of her.

"You're so beautiful," he whispered again, reverently. "Cream to be lapped up."

He cupped a breast, plumped it, and scattered a series of kisses over the soft mound. As the heat coursed through her, she dragged her fingers through his thick hair and then down over his shoulders, digging into the hard muscle. Then he closed his mouth around her nipple, sucked hard, tugged, and her whimper was one of pleasure and slight pain. His tongue soothed, and he suckled more gently, pulling glorious sensations up from her toes.

He dedicated himself to ensuring her other breast didn't feel overlooked. She adored the intimacy of being able to touch him as she pleased, wanted to touch all of him, but was careful with his healing wound. Images from the earlier nightmare threatened to return, and she shoved them away. Now was not the time for horror, not when he was doing such wicked things to her body, was causing such riotous sensations to burst forth that she wondered if it was even possible to survive the exquisite commotion that he was stirring to life throughout her, from head to toe to fingertips. How was she to have known that a touch in one spot would travel through every muscle, across every inch of skin?

His large hands cradled her sides as he took a journey along her ribs, leaving a trail of kisses in his wake. Sinking to his knees, he continued his expedition, along her stomach, dipping his tongue in her navel. Kissed one hip and then the other.

Lowering his head, he kissed her right knee and then traced a path along her thigh, spreading her, opening her. He did the same with the other side, and when he was done, she was surprised to discover somewhere along the way she'd abandoned all modesty. She parted her legs farther, and his resulting groan turned her blood to lava. The heat swamped her. Her body tightened in anticipation. She didn't know what he had in mind, what his next move might be, but she knew it would result in gratitude.

He tilted his head back, and his smoldering gaze nearly ignited her. "I used to be jealous of the sun for all the kisses it bestowed upon you. Now, I'm going to kiss you where it never could."

Burying his head between her legs, he kissed her most intimate center just as he kissed her mouth: open with tongue delving and exploring. Crying out, her thighs trembling, she dug her fingers into his shoulders, anchoring herself to him as he plundered. To keep watching him was too much. Falling into the depths of the wonder that he was creating, she looked out to the sea.

In the far distance lightning flashed, hinting at more rain, momentarily illuminating his wide shoulders and broad back, glistening with dew. He was so gorgeous. She wanted more lightning. She wanted sunshine to flow over him and fill her with jealousy because it could touch all of him at once while she could only touch portions at a time.

He suckled and stroked and teased. He swirled his tongue around the tiny bud and then closed his lips around it and tugged. The sensations built. She clutched his shoulders. "Griff?"

"Let it take you under, Kathryn, to the deepest depths, and then the tidal wave can shoot you into the stars." She hadn't known he had such poetry in him or that he could accurately describe the promise that was thrumming through her veins with each stroke of his tongue.

"I can barely stand."

"I have you."

And she knew that he did. Perhaps always had.

When the cataclysm came, it rocked her to her core, a tempest that thrashed her about, wrecked her, and left her lethargic on shore. While tremors cascaded through her, he softened his attentive actions, slowed, licked gently before pressing a kiss to the heart of her. After rising to his feet, he circled his arms around her and tucked her face into the crook of his shoulder. She pressed a kiss against his heated skin.

"I shall never look at the sea in the same way," she said in breathless wonder.

As his laughter circled her, she'd never treasured any sound more and feared she might never have another moment such as this, when she felt so loved and loved so much in return.

Chapter 16

She awoke to faint sunlight streaming in through the windows, disappointed to discover she was alone. But she could see the shallow dip in the pillow where his head had rested while he held her.

After escorting her to the bed, he'd crawled beneath the covers with her. While he'd not removed his trousers, at least she'd had his bare chest to snuggle against, to glide her fingers over. She'd counted his ribs and kissed the hollow in their center. She'd inhaled the earthy fragrance of him. Too sated to speak, she'd merely absorbed his presence and relished the way he held her close with one arm, while his other hand cupped her hip.

Once she'd awoken to discover her back against his chest, his hand cradling her breast, his soft snores near her ear. Contentment had swept over her as incessantly as waves over the shore, constant and never-ending.

But it would end, when they returned to London. Perhaps they'd stay here, one more day, one more night. Only this time, she would give to him as he'd given to her.

With that last remembrance, an ache formed in that secretive place between her thighs, a place he knew so well. While she chastised herself regarding what she had allowed, she couldn't seem to regret it. Not when she cared for him so deeply.

Perhaps she always had. Perhaps the teasing had been a form of defense to protect her heart because she wasn't destined for a rapscallion. She was destined for an heir. If she wanted to hear the wind whistling through the windows, the creaks of the ancient floorboards, the crash of the sea against the shore.

Thinking of him caused a pressure to build, centered in that tiny little bud that he had closed his lips around and suckled. What passed between a man and woman was nothing at all what she had expected it to be.

After Jocelyn had married Chadbourne, she had told Kathryn, "You simply lie there while he moves over you, and when he's done, you clean yourself up because it's a terribly messy affair, and go on about your business." It also had seemed a terribly cold affair.

Last night had seemed anything but cold or messy. Granted, he hadn't mounted her—she knew all about mounting having seen a stallion covering a mare at her family's country estate—but still she couldn't imagine anything with Griff being passionless. Just thinking about him stirred within her things that shouldn't be stirred. And yet, he'd always had the ability to make her feel things she shouldn't—and to always feel them so damned strongly. Whether it was irritation, anger, fear, happiness, joy, contentment . . . passion . . . desire.

He possessed the key that unlocked every emotion within her. Every sensation. Every spark.

She wished he was still here for her to explore, but he'd no doubt left in order to protect her reputation. Mrs. McHenry arrived with the dawn to begin preparing breakfast. The coachman and footman would arrive with her, to manage any tasks that needed doing, such as hauling up water for her bath. Even now, she could hear movements taking place on the floor below hers.

She thought the next time she saw Griff she should feel self-conscious and shy because he knew the intimate details of her, and yet it was inconceivable that she would feel anything but happy to see him. Perhaps she could convince him to dance on the beach with her before breakfast, because she was suddenly of a mood to frolic on the sand and at the edge of the waves.

After easing out of bed, she crossed to the window and snatched up her nightdress from where it had landed the night before. As she retraced her steps to the bed, she caught sight of her reflection in the cheval glass. Tentatively she approached it and held out her arms. Shouldn't a woman well-sated look different in the morning? Only she didn't. Nothing about her revealed the wickedness that had occurred. What an incredibly prudent trick of nature, to keep a woman's wantonness hidden.

Only she and Griff would know. They could exchange secretive smiles with no one the wiser.

After slipping into one of the simple frocks she'd left here on her last visit, she wandered down the stairs. When she reached the hallway, she glanced down it toward the room where Griff had been sleeping and noted that the door was open. Tiptoeing to it, intending to surprise him with her presence, she was disappointed to find it empty.

Nor was he in the parlor or the dining area.

"Morning, milady."

She glanced back at the door that led into the kitchen area. "Good morning, Mrs. McHenry. Have you seen Mr. Stanwick?"

"No, miss. Are you off to enjoy your morning stroll?"

"Yes." Perhaps he was outside.

"I'll have your food ready when you return."

"Thank you."

After stepping outside, she didn't see him at the cliff. A sense of urgency struck her as she raced to its edge and looked down. But he wasn't on the sand, wasn't in the water.

Spinning around, she saw the footman and coachman in the distance, no doubt returning after checking the road. She hurried over to them. "Have either of you seen Mr. Stanwick this morning?"

"Aye," the coachman said. "At the livery before we headed over here. He was seeing about purchasing a horse."

"Why would he need a horse?" Even as she asked the question, she knew. God help her, she knew.

"Don't know, milady. Didn't think it was my place to inquire. But he did ask the fellow who sold him a gelding for directions to London."

She felt as though she'd taken a physical blow. He'd left. After all that had transpired between them, he'd left without so much as a word.

"We was just checking the road out of here, milady. It's heavily mired from the rain. We should probably wait another day before trying to use it."

"But a single horse could traverse it."

"Aye, if you take it careful or travel to the side of it where the grass absorbed the wet."

"Then, he's gone," she murmured, not to anyone in particular. More to herself, confirming what she'd already deduced.

Having brought her exquisite pleasure, he was done with her. It shouldn't hurt, should have been expected. Far easier to leave than to face her. At least her anger at him prevented her from experiencing any sort of sadness at his parting. It was no doubt for the best because she had a duke to marry.

Chapter 17

$\mathcal{H}$E'D HIRED A lad to watch the residence in Whitechapel where his sister had lived before she married, as well as one to watch the residence in Mayfair where she would no doubt reside now that she was the Earl of Tewksbury's wife. So he knew within an hour of her return to London where he would find her.

He waited until the following afternoon to hire a hansom cab in order to call on her.

As the vehicle moved swiftly through the streets, he couldn't help but turn his thoughts to Kathryn, as she was never far from his mind. He was fairly certain Kingsland would bring her pleasure, but it would all be only motions. Touch here, press there, rub, circle, squeeze, take—the actions he'd learned from bedding dozens of women.

Griff knew those actions. He'd wanted Kathryn to know what they felt like when accompanied by love. Not that she'd know the difference immediately. Perhaps she never would. He hoped she didn't.

But he'd also wanted to know what it would be like for him when love was involved because never before had he loved a woman with whom he'd been intimate. Oh, he'd liked them immensely, adored them, cared about them—but what he felt for Kathryn was so much deeper than what he'd experienced with any other woman and couldn't be measured. While he'd not found his own release, it didn't matter. He'd taken as much satisfaction from hers as he might have from his own. No encounter with any other woman had been as satisfying. Now he knew the sounds of her moans and cries. Knew the feel of her thighs quivering before she finally soared. Knew her musky scent when stirred by desire. Knew the sweet taste of her most intimate, secretive place.

Knew she had the tiniest, softest little snore when she slept. For a few hours afterward, he'd merely held her and basked in the wonder of watching her. She'd always despised what he'd considered an endearment. Freckles.

He'd known, of course, how she felt about it, and so he'd teased her with it—until teasing her had no longer been what he wanted to do. And so he'd locked the pet name away in a special corner of his heart where he'd store all the other memories of her.

A little over a week had passed since he'd left her sleeping—so beautiful, so at peace—just before dawn, gone into the village, and paid handsomely for a horse to get himself back to London. After all the rain, he'd been concerned their journey was going to be delayed for another day, perhaps two. Or if he had his way, forever.

Since his return to London, every night he stood at the top of the stairs at his club, waiting and watching for her to stride through the door in all her glorious and righteous anger because he'd left her. Simply slipped out of her bed and gone on his merry way.

Only he hadn't simply slipped out and gone on. He'd stood there and catalogued each of her features, had taken a few of her curls between his finger and thumb to rub and absorb the texture. Had inhaled her orange and cinnamon fragrance. Had considered easing back into bed, beneath the covers, and taking possession of her body, heart, and soul—properly and completely—making her his.

The indulged second son he'd once been would have done it, would have put his own pleasures and wants and needs ahead of hers. But he no longer was that man. He'd had his sense of privilege slowly ground out of him through toil and labor and deprivation. He'd come to appreciate what he'd had only when he'd no longer had it. To take her would have meant seeing her deprived of what she yearned to possess—and where she was concerned, he refused to be that selfish.

But if she'd come to him, if she'd come to his club, if she'd chosen him—

Only she hadn't. Although he'd considered going to her, he could offer her only a few nights, not eternity. But then why would she want a man who'd been broken, slowly pieced himself back together, but remained cracked? Not for the long haul, and it wasn't fair to either of them to settle for the short haul.

So he'd left, trusting the footman and driver to see her safely to her residence. He knew they had, the day after he left, because the boy he'd hired to keep watch had reported to him when she returned.

After that, like a fool, he'd begun his vigil at the top of the stairs, ignoring everyone around him, focusing on the door through which she never walked. Her absence didn't stop his heart from thundering each time someone came into the club until he realized it wasn't Kathryn. He needed to accept that never again would it be her.

The club now seemed duller because she would never again grace it. The din and cacophony of voices flatter because her laughter would no longer lighten it. The fragrance staler because her orange and cinnamon scent would no longer tease it. Tonight, he would cease his fruitless watch and begin wandering through the rooms again, even as he dreaded the memories of her that each would visit upon him and the loneliness they would leave in their wake.

The cab pulled into the drive of the massive manor in Mayfair. After slipping payment through the opening to the driver, Griff disembarked and studied the well-maintained lawn as the vehicle was driven away. It was strange to be back in Mayfair after all this time, to be on the verge of entering a fancy residence, especially when he no longer felt he belonged here. Maybe he never had.

After ascending the steps, he tapped the knocker against the wood and waited. In short order the door opened, and a butler gave a deferential nod. No doubt a result of Griff's fine attire. He knew that to be successful he had to look the part of already being successful, and he'd made certain to use his coins wisely when it came to his clothing. "Mr. Griffith Stanwick to see his sister, Lady Tewksbury."

The butler opened the door wider. "Do come in, sir. I shall see if her ladyship is at home."

Standing in the grand foyer, Griff would be surprised if she wasn't. She was back in the sort of residence she deserved, with its massive walls and vaulted ceilings and crystal chandeliers. With its claymores and broadswords displayed, revealing a heritage that could be traced back generations.

"Griff!"

He turned as Althea rushed into the foyer, her husband following at what seemed to be a sedate pace, but it was only because his long legs ensured he didn't need to move as quickly to keep up with her. Before he could even greet her, she had her arms snuggly around him and hugged him tightly.

"I've been so worried." She leaned back. "You look well, prosperous in fact. The last time I saw you, you appeared quite . . . menacing, to be truthful."

They'd last seen each other shortly before she married, before she'd gone to Scotland, when he'd still been more involved in Marcus's efforts than his own. "I'm on a different path now."

"I want to hear all about it." She moved aside slightly, held out her arm. "We want to hear all about it."

Trewlove came forward and placed his arm around her, drawing her in close, in a move that seemed as natural to him as breathing in air. He extended his hand. "Stanwick."

Griff took the offering, gripping the man's hand, shaking it solidly. "My lord."

The new Earl of Tewksbury grimaced. "No need to be so formal. *Beast* will do."

"I've rung for tea," Althea said. "Come into the parlor, get comfortable, and tell me everything."

"Scotch might be better, my love," Beast said.

Griff wondered how much his brother-by-marriage already knew. He'd haunted the darker corners of London, had ruled in Whitechapel. He wouldn't be surprised if the man knew a good deal more than he'd ever admit. "Scotch would be appreciated."

They went to the library where he and Beast sipped scotch, while Althea nursed a sherry as she told him about their wedding—which he truly regretted not being able to attend—and their time in Scotland, how she'd fallen in love with its people and majestic lands. He was grateful to see how absolutely happy she was. It was obvious her husband adored her, much more than he suspected Chadbourne ever would have. In spite of the detour her life had taken, he couldn't help but believe she was much better off than she would have been had she been able to remain true to the path chosen for her. She was stronger, more confident. Easily a woman who could conquer any of life's challenges.

A woman like Kathryn, who had saved herself on the banks of the Thames, with a little aid from him. Who hadn't been squeamish about his wound, who had taken charge and seen him cared for. Who would now carry on with her life as though he'd never been in it.

When his sister came to the end of sharing her adventures, he explained about his club.

"I want to see it," she insisted.

"You're married. Membership is only for those who are not."

"I don't want a membership. I want only to peek inside, stroll around perhaps."

He shook his head. "It would have to be when it wasn't open, and then it's simply a building with rooms." It was the membership, the manner in which they interacted that created the atmosphere that was leading to its success, and he needed to ensure they all remained comfortable, trusted that they and their . . . *escapades* . . . were safely kept within those walls.

"Your refusal to let me see it leads me to think wickedness goes on there."

He merely sipped his scotch.

She smiled. "You rapscallion, you. It's the sort of place that would have given Mother the vapors, isn't it?"

"She might have disowned me if she'd ever learned of it."

"I miss her." She glanced out the window. "Sometimes I even miss Father, which I know is so wrong." She looked back at him. "And Marcus, what can you tell me of him?"

He'd known she'd ask, didn't want her to worry, but she deserved to know some of it. "I believe he's getting close to finding what he's been searching for, but he's had to leave London for a while."

She nodded, no doubt expecting what he'd shared. "I wish he'd give up this damned quest of his." She pointedly arched a brow. "Yes, I've taken to using profanity on occasion. Comes from not being a lady for a while."

"Society will welcome you back now."

"Rather reluctantly, but it helps to have married into a powerful family. Speaking of that family, we're having them over for dinner tomorrow evening. I do wish you'd join us. You know the nobles, of course, but you've yet to meet Ben's brothers and sisters. I would very much like for you to."

"I'm not certain it would be wise."

"My family doesn't judge," Beast—the moniker seemed more appropriate than the *Ben* that his sister used—said. "They'd welcome you."

"Please," Althea said softly. "It would be nice if our family could return to some semblance of normalcy. The dinner might help achieve that end. And you did miss the wedding."

Guilt was a powerful motivator. While she and he had never been particularly chummy, what they'd gone through together had created a stronger bond between them, brought them closer, especially as she'd been the one to tend to his hands that working the docks had torn up every day. "I'd be honored."

She smiled brightly. "Wonderful! You're going to love them, and they're going to love you."

He very much doubted love would be involved, but he was glad to see his sister exhibiting such optimism. She'd endured a lot—a broken heart, poverty, working in a tavern, and dangerous circumstances—to come out on the other side strong and knowing exactly who she was.

"YOU'VE NOT RETURNED to the Fair and Spare since that second night," Wilhelmina said slyly, before taking a sip of tea in Kathryn's garden.

She had invited her friend to visit for the exact reason that Wilhelmina had just stated, because Kathryn hadn't been to the club and was hoping to catch a bit of gossip about it, about *him*. She wasn't going to go chasing after him. He'd made his position clear enough when he'd left that morning without even bothering to thank her for her care, without so much as a farewell. But that didn't mean she wasn't interested in gleaning some information regarding him and his club. "My curiosity was satisfied."

"I very much doubt that."

She decided a change in strategy was needed, because she wasn't going to ask questions directly. "Tell me about the fellow with whom you were drinking red wine."

Wilhelmina emitted a tiny mewling as her cheeks blossomed into a deep shade of crimson. "He's merely a gent I met there."

"Merely?"

Her cheeks burned redder. "He makes me laugh."

Kathryn didn't want to consider that Kingsland had never made her laugh, that she didn't even know what his laughter sounded like. Deep, she was rather certain, but did it invite one to join in?

He was always so serious, not one for dancing on the beach, or even taking a moment to look out over the sea.

Griff was in charge of his business, still in the early stages of it, trying to make a go of it, and yet he'd found time to show her around his establishment. He hadn't seemed in a hurry to be rid of her, although that had certainly changed after her nightmare, after he'd taken actions to make her forget it. Anytime thoughts from that horrendous experience on the riverbank threatened, she'd bring forth the memories of the manner in which he'd touched her, tasted her, tormented and appeased her—and they drove the ugliness away. Always. Even when not near, he had the power to bring her solace.

It should be the duke who did so. Perhaps once they were married, once they'd had intimate encounters and she knew the feel of his hands—only she didn't want to forget the abrasiveness of Griff's scarred ones. What madness was this, to be so besotted with a man who was incredibly wrong for her?

"He looks for you, you know."

Snapping out of the musings into which she'd drifted, she furrowed her brow and stared at Wilhelmina. "Why in the world would your gentleman look for me?"

Her light laughter like the ringing of crystal bells trickled forth. "Not my gentleman. Yours. Mr. Stanwick."

She glowered at her friend. "He is not my gentleman."

"Is he not?"

"No. As I mentioned before, he's merely the brother of a friend."

"Interesting."

"What is?"

"I would have expected you to adamantly claim Kingsland was your gentleman."

"Well, of course he is. That goes without saying."

Her friend leaned toward her. "Is he?"

"Wilhelmina, don't be obtuse. You know he is."

"Do you know why I'm a spinster?"

"Because no gent has asked for your hand."

"Because the *right* gent has never asked for my hand."

"Kingsland is the right gent." She wished her words didn't lack conviction. "I am not with Kingsland in order to avoid being a spinster. I am with him because it benefits us both, which is how marriages among the *ton* are decided." Love was not required of the nobility when they married. In truth, it was rare for it to be a factor at all.

Wilhelmina lifted her cup and slowly sipped her tea. "I certainly find no fault with Kingsland."

"He is perfection." Pity she was finding perfection a trifle boring.

"No man is perfection, darling. If you believe that of him, then you don't know him well enough."

She did know one man well enough to know he was far from perfection, and yet it was the little flaws that most intrigued her, that made her care about him so much. That elicited every emotion possible within her. That made her *feel*. That scared her with the strength of those feelings, whether she was angry with him or happy or sad or worried. With Griff, everything was more intense, more immediate. Everything demanded exploration. Everything about him called to her to be an adventuress.

"Kathryn, the choices you make are absolutely none of my business. People marry for myriad reasons. Wants, needs, gains. I find fault with none of them because I do not walk in another lady's slippers. I walk only in my own. But the one thing I do know is that sometimes in life, we have a chance for something more—perhaps for only a night or an hour or a minute. But if we don't take it, it can fill us with an eternity of regrets."

"Have you had a night with your gentleman?" She knew it was rude to ask, but her friend didn't seem at all offended.

"Not yet, but I will."

"If, afterward, he is done with you . . . how will you deal with that?"

"I shall mourn for a while, I suppose, but then I shall go in search of another. One night with a man who makes me feel like a queen is better than no night at all."

"If in taking that night you are unfair to another?"

"Do you honestly believe that since he began courting you, Kingsland has not bedded anyone?"

Kathryn felt the heat suffuse her face because Wilhelmina would be so blunt, wouldn't even pretend to not know who was being discussed. "Women are supposed to remain pure for their husbands."

"Who decided that? Some man? You are not yet wed to him, Kathryn. You are not even officially betrothed. If you need that one night with another, take it before you are engaged, and it becomes lost to you forever."

CHAPTER 18

GRIFF LIKED ALTHEA'S new family. He supposed when one began life under challenging circumstances—and none would argue that being born out of wedlock didn't present challenges—strong bonds developed between those who helped to see you through.

Standing near the fireplace, watching the camaraderie expressed by the six Trewlove siblings toward each other, he couldn't help but feel a bit of regret that he'd gone years without experiencing the same regard toward his own brother and sister. It was only of late, when their circumstances had changed for the worse, that he'd come to realize he would willingly die for either of them. Prior to that he'd kept his emotions, dreams, fears, and disappointments to himself. He'd never shared how his father had made him feel useless, overlooked.

But watching the Trewloves, seeing the absolute joy with which they greeted each other, listening to the news they revealed and observing their obvious interest, he knew beyond a doubt that these people confided everything in each other, never fearing judgment. He was glad to see them embracing Althea, ensuring she understood she was now one of them.

"They can be a bit overwhelming at first."

Griff glanced over at the Duke of Thornley who had married Gillian Trewlove, a tavern owner. It had created scandal at the time—all the marriages had—but Thornley was powerful enough to have weathered the storm and seen his wife accepted by those who would have preferred to shun her. "They're all so comfortable with each other."

"Not exactly the way we were brought up to be, is it?"

"Afraid not. Pity that." He'd been introduced to each of the family members, hadn't sensed them taking offense by his presence. They were all married now, and Althea had included their spouses' siblings as well, which resulted in half a dozen lords being in the room. All together, close to twenty people mingled about. "I'm glad they're making Althea feel as though she is part of their family."

"It's one of their strengths. Accepting people for who they are themselves and not for who their parents might be or for their sire's actions in particular."

"Not seeing after your bastard is hardly a transgression on equal footing with attempting to assassinate a queen."

"It is if you're that bastard."

Griff grimaced, nodded. "Right you are. After all these months, I'm still struggling to reconcile what he did and continue to view it as a major transgression."

"It was that. You'll get no argument from me there. But his transgression shouldn't be visited upon you. Unfortunately, that's not the way the nobility always sees things. I would have viewed it the same way before Gillie came into my life. It's difficult not to reevaluate your viewpoint once you come to know these people. In spite of the unfairness life tossed their way, they've all met with success. Say, I hear you have a club now. A sort of matchmaking venue."

He couldn't stop himself from grinning. "I got tired of being overlooked at the damn balls. Assumed there were others who felt the same."

"I wish you much success with it."

"I apprecia—"

"I'm so sorry we're tardy." The raspy voice, the one that haunted his dreams, his memories, had his gut drawing in tight and his side remembering the tenderness of her touch—as though skin had the ability to recall anything. But it was as though he could feel her fingers there again, pressing gently, skimming over the raised welt. What the devil was she doing here? She wasn't family.

"Nonsense!" Althea said, crossing over to her friend and embracing her. God, Kathryn was more beautiful than any woman had a right to be. She wore yet another gown of green, and he cursed her for that, for the way it made her eyes sparkle emerald. "We were just visiting, catching up. Your Grace, I'm so glad you could join us."

It was only then that he noticed Kingsland standing beside her. He didn't want to see them together, but even as he acknowledged the thought, he realized it was for the best. He'd begun to have fantasies in which he imagined the life he'd led wouldn't turn her away from him if he asked for her hand. That the realities of his club wouldn't cause matrons to have the vapors, and fathers, recalling the escapades of their youth, not to express disapproval.

Ever the perfect hostess, Althea began making introductions, ensuring everyone knew each other. Thornley left his side to greet the newcomers, and Griff knew that he should do the same—or better yet leave entirely. Simply slip out without being seen or acknowledged, but then Althea was headed his way, the recent arrivals in tow.

"You remember my brother, Griff."

"Yes, of course," Kathryn said, and he couldn't judge her mood, her thoughts. "It's lovely to see you looking so well after all the trials and tribulations your family has endured."

And he translated her words into what she truly meant to convey by her tone: after leaving me with nary a word.

"It's a pleasure, Lady Kathryn." He turned to the duke. "Good to see you, Your Grace."

"And you, Stanwick. I've not forgotten that I owe you for directing me toward this charming lady."

"You don't owe me."

Althea's brows pinched, and he realized she probably hadn't a clue what the daft duke was referring to. "May I offer you some refreshment? Some before-dinner port, perhaps?" she asked.

"Yes, please," Kathryn said.

"Why don't you go on?" Kingsland suggested. "I'll join you in a minute. I'd like a private word with Mr. Stanwick."

As the ladies walked away, Griff suspected his sister was going to learn about the letter he'd written, and if she didn't already know about it, the damned wager he'd made. Not that any of it mattered. It was so long ago. Or it shouldn't have mattered. But he was finding that he regretted rather strongly that he'd done both. Especially when it was so difficult to see Kathryn with this lordly paragon. He was grateful Beast had offered him a glass of scotch earlier and he hadn't yet finished it off. He took a casual sip as he waited for Kingsland to have his say, whatever it was, although he had a good idea what it would entail.

"You threatened my brother." Four words that came out flat, casual, as though he'd stated he took four lumps of sugar with his tea, but they were edged with warning.

Griff held the duke's gaze and lifted a corner of his mouth in a mockery of a smile. "Did I?"

Kingsland studied him for all of a heartbeat. "Not that I blame you. He owed you what should have already been paid. But I am curious. Did you intend to punch him or expose a secret?"

"A secret."

The duke's jaw tightened. Obviously, he'd have preferred *punch* as the answer. "I don't suppose you'd be good enough to share what it was."

"He paid. It stays with me."

Kingsland nodded. "Was it easily uncovered, so others might use it against him, possibly to blackmail him?"

A year earlier, Griff hadn't known what it was to want to protect one's brother, to be willing to do anything for him. He knew now, and he recognized in the duke the same desire. Kingsland wanted to shield his younger brother from harm. Ah, hell. He might as well confess. "I don't know what the secret is."

Apparently quite stunned, Kingsland blinked at him. "I beg your pardon?"

"Everyone has secrets, Your Grace. All I did was imply that I knew his and would reveal it."

"Bloody hell. Brilliant. And if he hadn't paid?"

He shrugged. "Then I would have gone to the bother to figure out what it was."

"Well played, Stanwick. I might have to employ the same tactic the next time I'm on the losing end of a negotiation."

"When have you ever been on the losing end of anything?"

"Quite right. You collected all you were owed, I assume."

"With interest."

"Jolly good for you. Made a few enemies, I suspect."

"They already considered themselves my enemies." But he'd settled the ruffled feathers of those who qualified by granting them a six-month membership in his club. It had been a way to spread the word about his enterprise, and most, if not all, would no doubt continue their membership once their time was up. An initial small loss for a greater gain.

"For what it's worth, I don't believe in visiting the sins of the father upon the sons."

"I appreciate it." Even if the duke was only one of the few who held that opinion.

"Now, if you'll excuse me, I could use some scotch and a word with Thornley regarding a bill we're working on."

He started to walk away.

"She has to marry before her twenty-fifth birthday," Griff said quietly enough that no one else would hear.

The duke paused before glancing back at him. "I beg your pardon?"

"Lady Kathryn. She has to marry before her twenty-fifth birthday in order to gain an inheritance her grandmother left to her. She reaches that quarter of a century mark on August fifteenth."

"I see."

"That's not a reason to marry her, of course, or for her to marry you, but if you're going to marry, you might as well do it in time for her to receive an additional benefit." He shook his head. "Why *haven't* you asked?"

"I have my reasons."

"It can't be that you find fault with her."

"'Tis true. I find no fault with her. I simply want to ensure she finds none with me. And that takes time. Especially when I've had to travel so much of late. But I shall take this new information into consideration." He gave a brusque nod. "I appreciate it."

Then he strode off to talk with Thornley about some blasted bill that wasn't nearly as important as Kathryn. It probably wasn't his place to tell the duke about the damned inheritance, but if he wasn't going to marry her in a timely fashion, there was no point in his marrying her at all.

Inwardly, he strung together a slew of curses. Even if the duke missed her deadline, Griff couldn't marry her. The duke was offering her power, prestige, influence. Griff could offer her little more than a life away from all that was familiar.

Being admitted into this parlor was not being admitted back into Society. He wasn't fool enough to think it was.

Besides, she deserved far better than a man with a soul as tainted as his.

BECAUSE THE DINNER involved family, Althea hadn't bothered with any sort of formal seating arrangement. Therefore, Kathryn sat across from Griff and beside Kingsland. When her dear friend had invited her to dinner, Althea's first formal event since returning from Scotland, Kathryn had been more than happy to accept, especially since Althea had mentioned that Griff would be in attendance. She'd wanted to know exactly how he fared.

She was relieved to see him looking so well, with no sallowness to his skin. When she'd first caught sight of him standing by the fireplace, she'd noticed his left arm rested at an angle, an attempt to shield that side of his body from any unexpected knocks or blows. His wound was probably still healing and tender, or perhaps it was merely a habit he'd developed when it had been, and he'd strode through his dominion. She doubted anyone else would notice the protective stance, that anyone else would drink him in like he provided sustenance to a parched soul.

It rather irritated her that she did. She'd not had an opportunity to speak with him alone, so she had yet to reveal her upset with him for sneaking away without so much as a farewell. Although perhaps he'd wanted to avoid facing any awkwardness between them.

What had transpired shouldn't have. Yet it had seemed as natural as reaching for the saltshaker—which at that particular moment they both did, their fingers touching, pausing, before he drew his back.

"I was in Scotland recently," Kingsland said to their host at the head of the table, to his right. "I'm thinking of investing in a distillery."

"The Scots do know how to make a good whisky," the Duchess of Thornley said.

"Might you carry it in your tavern?"

"I would have to sample it first."

"I'd be willing to give it a taste as well," Aiden Trewlove said. "Might carry it in my clubs." His clubs being the Elysium she visited and a gaming hell for men.

"What of you, Mr. Stanwick?" Kingsland said, as he sliced his beef. "Might you serve it in your club as well?"

She went still, except for her thundering heart, and wondered how he knew of the club. He certainly wouldn't qualify for a membership. Griff met her gaze before sliding it over to the duke. "Depends how smoothly it went down."

"Well, if I might possibly already have three avenues for distributing it, I shall give it more serious consideration."

"I found Scotland to be beautiful," Althea said, lightly as though she could sense some tension building between the two men.

Perhaps Kathryn should have come alone, but Althea had suggested the duke accompany her, and it seemed inappropriate not to extend the invitation to him. Besides, she hadn't wanted to explain that her main reason for coming was to see Griff, and having Kingsland beside her reminded her that it shouldn't be. She wasn't even certain she should consider Griff a friend. Except a friend wouldn't have done with her what he had. They'd been the actions of a lover. Oddly, she didn't feel guilty about the liberties she'd allowed him to take. If anything, she wanted him to take them again. Only then, she probably would feel guilty, even if Wilhelmina had advised her that she shouldn't.

The conversation drifted to specific aspects of Scotland, various areas they'd each visited. She'd never been and couldn't contribute anything. Other discussions were taking place, as was the practice when one dined. She listened with half an ear as Lavinia Trewlove, wife to Finn, spoke with Griff about the horses her husband bred and about the home they provided for orphans. All the while Kathryn gave the impression she was giving her full attention to the youngest Trewlove, who had married the Earl of Rosemont. Fancy owned a bookshop, had met her future husband there, and so it seemed natural to discuss the latest novels she'd read.

Yet in reality, she only longed for a moment alone with Griff.

It finally came, following dinner, after they were all assembled in the billiards room. Apparently the Trewloves didn't hold with the tradition of gents going off for a bit of port while ladies sipped tea. They'd all gathered in the large room that even the billiards table couldn't dominate. It was spacious with various sitting areas and a fireplace at either end. Paned doors left open to allow in a bit of breeze led out onto the terrace.

The Duke of Thornley had challenged the Duke of Kingsland to a game of billiards. They'd removed their jackets and rolled up their shirtsleeves. She didn't think either of them could have taken the game more seriously if the fate of a nation was involved, so all conversation had to take place a good distance away from the dueling dukes so as not to interfere with their concentration.

When she saw Griff slip outside, apparently without catching anyone's attention, she made her excuses to Althea and Selena, Aiden Trewlove's wife, claiming to need just a short respite for some fresh air. Neither offered to join her, perhaps because they sensed she wanted some time alone. Or perhaps she'd been wrong, and they had noticed Griff slipping out and guessed her true purpose. Although, neither knew what had recently transpired, and Althea would see her visiting with her brother as a completely innocent act, just as it had been during all the early years that she'd known her.

She spotted him at the end of the terrace, away from any direct light, bent slightly, his elbows resting on the stone wall as he gazed out into the gardens that were only shadows in the darkness. Her heart shouldn't have sped up with each step that brought her nearer to him.

"You shouldn't be out here," he said quietly, without even looking at her, without confirming it was her. But then, perhaps he was as attuned to her presence as she was to his.

"You just left." She didn't bother to clarify, was rather certain that her abrupt tone indicated she wasn't referring to his just now leaving the billiards room.

"I needed to get back to my business. The roads couldn't be traveled by coach."

"Knew that before dawn, did you?"

He released a long, frustrated sigh, straightened, and faced her. "You make a handsome couple."

If he thought she was going to move on to another topic of conversation, he was sadly mistaken. "You could at least have bidden me farewell."

"If I'd stayed, Lady Kathryn, you'd have not left there untouched."

His emphasis on the *untouched* let her know the exact type of touching that would have taken place. Far more involved, far more intimate than what already had. Deep, penetrating. She'd have not left there a virgin. He would have ruined her. Yet for the life of her, she couldn't imagine she would have felt ruined.

Nor was she quite certain that Kingsland would have cared. He did not seem the possessive sort. Certainly, he gave her attention when they were together and sent her trinkets when they weren't, but she'd never had the sense that anything she did would spark jealousy in him. They would have a very calm, cool marriage.

Whereas Griff seemed capable of making every emotion in her burn with a fiery passion. Especially her anger.

"I found your departure rude and inappreciative. If not for my gentle care, you might have died."

"The wound wasn't that bad."

With a quickness that surprised him, she leapt forward and made a swiping motion at his side. He jerked back and brought his arm up to protect it before he realized that her movement had been a feint. Even in the encroaching darkness, she could sense his displeased scowl. "For a wound that *wasn't that bad*, it seems to still be tender and perhaps healing," she said.

"Coming at me wasn't very sporting of you."

She wasn't in the mood to be sporting. "I was hurt, Griff. Hurt to wake up and find you gone." Not to mention disappointed and saddened.

"Kathryn—"

"Not from the bed. That I understood. But from the cottage. I woke up and imagined us taking a walk along the shore."

"Nothing good would have come from my staying."

"Nothing good came from your leaving."

Turning back toward the garden, he once more crossed his forearms on the stone. "A great deal of good came from my leaving. You just don't realize how much."

"Then, tell me."

"You're being difficult, Lady Kathryn. I already told you."

"So you left without bothering to wake me in order to protect my reputation when no one was about to declare my reputation sullied."

"Someone would have whispered it. A footman striving to impress a chambermaid. A coachman wanting more pay."

"I was alone in the cottage with a man. By itself that was enough for scandal. Anything else would have been speculation."

"I have known speculation to ruin lives."

She slammed her eyes closed. People had speculated that he and his brother were complicit in their father's conspiracy. While tonight it seemed that he'd been welcomed back into the fold, it was only into this tiny pleat. And even then, she noted it didn't seem to be an entirely comfortable fit for all involved.

After moving up to the wall, she set her own forearms atop it, felt the grit beneath her silken skin and suspected his was too tough to be bothered by it. Although at one time, it probably hadn't been. "Why do you suppose it is that women are expected to remain pure while men are not?"

His response was only silence.

"Lady Wilhelmina speculates that it's because men make the rules. Although, I think it's women who made this particular one, out of fear that without it they would succumb to the lure of pleasure."

He didn't say anything. Perhaps he didn't want to get into a debate regarding how it was that Society had evolved in such a way that different rules applied to men than to women. But then, it wasn't her reason for coming out here to confront him. "Once again, Griff, I felt ill-used. Even though it was the most glorious ill-using I shall ever experience."

He released a long-suffering sigh. "Kathryn—"

"Your leaving made what had passed between us seem tawdry, as though you were ashamed of having been with me."

"God, no." Turning, he cradled her face as though it were a fledging bird that had fallen from its nest and he wanted to see it safely placed back where it belonged. "But I knew I'd taken actions I shouldn't have . . . I"—he moved his hands away from her and held them up before her—"I should never have touched you. You know what these have done. They should never be anywhere near you."

"What poppycock." Taking one, she pressed a kiss to his scarred palm. "They saved your brother. They saved me."

They studied each other as though in no rush to carry on with their lives, until he finally said, "I should have woken you. I should have told you I was leaving, but I thought it would make it harder to go, to return to London without you."

"So you took the easy way."

"Leaving you has never been easy, Kathryn." He released a harsh laugh. "Nothing about you has ever been easy."

She should not have been so pleased by that confession.

"Kathryn?"

The deep voice in the darkness startled her, but when she glanced over her shoulder, she discovered the Duke of Kingsland wasn't as near as she'd feared, certainly not near enough to have heard their conversation. She didn't think. Desperately hoped not.

She'd felt Griff stiffen, preparing himself to come to her defense if needed. Releasing his hand, she pivoted to face Kingsland. "Your Grace."

"I thought it time we took our leave."

"Did you beat Thornley?"

"Of course. I am not known to lose at anything."

"Doesn't that grow boring?" Griff asked. "Always winning? I've found the occasional loss makes the next win all the sweeter."

"An interesting hypothesis. However, not one I care to test." He extended his arm. "Kathryn?"

She turned to Griff. "I'm glad to know you're doing well. I wish you the best with your club." Then she walked up to Kingsland and wound her arm around his. "Shall we?"

He escorted her inside, and they gave their farewells to everyone. When she reached Althea, she hugged her tightly. "Thank you so much for including us in your family gathering."

"You're the sister I never had."

From there, she followed Kingsland out to the drive where his coach waited. It wasn't until they settled inside, sitting opposite each other, the vehicle rumbling over the street, that he spoke. "Why didn't you tell me that you need to marry before you're five and twenty in order to gain an inheritance?"

It was not what she'd expected him to ask. She'd thought he might inquire about her time on the terrace with Griff. She wondered when and where he'd learned the information. Obviously tonight, probably from Griff. "I didn't want you to feel the pressure of the deadline, to think you had to marry me before you had decided that you wanted me for your wife."

"If we didn't marry before you turned twenty-five?"

"A part of me thought it might be a bit freeing." She looked out the window. "It's begun to seem a trivial matter on which to marry."

"I've known lords to marry for much more trivial matters than an inheritance."

"You don't even know what it entails."

"It doesn't matter. By its very nature, an inheritance implies that it is something of worth, whether monetary or sentimental. It is something you should have. I'll speak with your father in the next few days."

For a second there, it felt like her heart had stopped beating. After all these years of yearning for the cottage to be her own, she wasn't certain she'd ever fully accepted that it would be. He'd been a last resort. Perhaps she hadn't told him about the conditions because she hadn't wanted them to influence *her* decision to marry him, had tried to pretend they didn't exist. She'd wanted to marry him because she desired him. But she didn't know if she'd ever grow accustomed to his arrogance, his entitlement, and his belief that losing wasn't for him. "It's been nearly a year since you called out my name, but the reality is that with all the businesses you've had to see to, we've had very little time to truly get to know each other."

"I know enough to deduce you'd be an excellent duchess. Besides, I mentioned when I announced your name that we would marry before the next Season ended. I'm one for keeping my word. And in doing so, we'll both benefit."

"Yes, I suppose we shall." She should have been excited beyond measure by the prospect. Instead, she felt another sort of clock was ticking, one that involved Mr. Griffith Stanwick.

CHAPTER 19

$\mathcal{G}$RIFF DIDN'T HAVE to look at the clock on the mantel to know that it was a little after two, because his club had gone still and quiet. Even in his office, sitting at his desk, going over his accounts, he could hear the hum of activity, feel the shimmering thrill of interest returned, and sense the moment when two lonely souls realized that for a few hours at least, the loneliness would cease to matter. For a lucky few, it might dissipate forever.

While he'd never considered his club to be a matchmaking service that would lead members to the ringing of wedding bells, he suspected one couple might be headed in that direction—if the daughter of an earl could convince her family to accept the son of a tradesman, who was in trade himself and thriving at it.

That was always the key: getting the family to accept the one chosen. Now with his past and being owner of this scandalous club, he'd taken marriage completely off the table. Not that it mattered. As he'd watched Kingsland escort Kathryn from the terrace earlier in the evening, the tightening in his chest until he could scarcely draw in a breath had confirmed that his heart had been claimed, and he doubted it would ever be untethered and free enough to be given to another.

Footsteps echoed along the hallway: Gertie delivering the night's take. As they went silent, he glanced up. Only it wasn't

Gertie at all. At the vision in green hovering in the doorway, he shot to his feet. "What are you doing here? We're closed up for the night."

Lady Kathryn Lambert smiled a saucy smile, one filled with temptation and promise, the sort the women who visited here were hesitant to give the first night but were more willing to offer by the third or fourth, once they were comfortable with all the flirtation that had been absent from their lives until that point. But from her, it came naturally, a turning up at the corners of her mouth, a flash of white. "I know. Billy granted me entrance." She held up a long length of brass. "And Gertie gave me a key. I wondered if you could direct me to the red room."

Her words came like a punch to the gut. Four chambers— green, blue, red, pink—on this floor had been designed and designated to provide privacy for a couple. A small sofa. A table with decanters, cheeses, and fruit. A bed. For couples to explore compatibility or have a single night of needs met. The rooms had been used less often than he'd anticipated. But then he'd learned that companionship, needs, and desires took all forms. "What are you doing here, Lady Kathryn?"

She reached into her reticule and removed a stack of cards bound by ribbon. "I want to play cards with you."

"The cardroom is on the floor below."

"A closed door is required for the type of game I wish to play."

Through his mind flashed images of wagers made that resulted in clothing being removed. "Lady Kathryn"—did his voice have to sound so rough and raw?—"you're playing a dangerous game here."

"I'm well aware." She gave him a look that was pure seductress. "I'm willing to find the room on my own."

Her gaze never left his as she turned, and when she disappeared from his sight her message was clear: *I dare you to follow me.*

Hell and damnation if he didn't do exactly that, with such haste that he failed to clear his desk completely, which resulted in slamming his thigh against the hard corner and grounding out a harsh curse. He'd have a bruise there in the morning, but he suspected he was going to have deeper bruises, ones that couldn't be seen, when he was done with this night, done with her.

Emerging into the hallway, he came to an abrupt stop and watched as she slipped the brass into a keyhole. Taking a few seconds, he strained to hear any noises below, any hint of activity, and detected none. Staff had already finished their tasks and gone. Gertie had left without bringing him the night's tallies, but they would remain safe. Billy would have locked everything up tight when he departed. So it was only the two of them, he and Kathryn. If that wasn't a recipe for disaster, he didn't know what was.

"Not that one," he said. She glanced over at him, and he wished he had it within him not to give her what she wanted. "This way."

He led her in the opposite direction, to a corner room beside his office. No key was needed as it wasn't locked, didn't require privacy. Or at least it hadn't before tonight. He swung open the door and waited for her to precede him inside, her skirts brushing up against his legs, and he could have sworn she'd come that close to him intentionally, to make him drunk on her orange and cinnamon fragrance. He'd taken it in with the same care he did the smoke of a cheroot, for the sole purpose of savoring it.

After adjusting the glow of gaslight in the sconce so he could see her more clearly but not enough to chase off all the shadows, he closed the door behind him, the hushed snick reverberating between the walls like a rifle report. Or at least it had sounded that way to him. She seemed not to notice as she wandered through the room, taking in everything. The bed, the wardrobe, the bedside table, the washstand, the small sideboard with its decanters, the single dark brown padded wingback chair in front of the fireplace.

She picked up the book from the bedside table, and he hoped she didn't recognize that the faded and frayed ribbon marking his place had once been used to tie off her plait. He'd carried it in his waistcoat pocket until it had become threadbare from his constant rubbing of it and he'd realized if he kept it there, it would eventually disintegrate into nothing. So he'd begun using it to mark his place, to greet him at the end of a long night when he finally settled in for a few minutes of escape.

"It looks more lived in than I would have expected of a chamber designed for assignations." After returning the book to its spot, she glanced back at him. "You reside here."

He hadn't wanted her in a room where others had sinned. "What are you doing here, Lady Kathryn?"

"I told you. I wish to play cards."

"Is this some sort of punishment you've designed for me because I left the cottage without telling you I was going?"

"How can it be punishment when I'm being extremely reasonable and calm? I'm not shouting at you or making snide remarks. I find I'm being quite pleasant." She glanced around again. "But you lack a table. I suppose we can sit on the bed."

Without waiting for his permission or even his agreement, she climbed onto the duvet and sat in such a way that it was obvious she'd folded her legs beneath her, her skirts circling her. She gave him an expectant look that harbored another dare.

He strode over to the decanters. He was going to need whisky for this. "Brandy?"

"Yes, please."

After pouring a splash of brandy into a snifter for her and a hefty dose of whisky into a tumbler for himself, he carried both glasses over and set them on the table, only then noticing her slippers resting on the floor, as though she'd merely stepped out of them. He didn't want to contemplate how much he'd enjoy seeing her slippers beside his bed every night.

Tugging off his boots, he tossed them across the room as though if they were anywhere near her slippers, they would be giving him permission to do what he ought not. As though she wasn't giving him permission with her sultry eyes and her plump lower lip that glistened after she ran her tongue over it.

Grabbing his glass, he launched himself at the foot of the bed, fitting his spine to the post, and stretching his legs out at an angle that stopped any portion of him from touching any portion of her. "What are we going to play then? Whist?"

"Don't be ridiculous. Four-card brag."

"You have the matchsticks for wagering?"

That smile again, the one that said she knew things, the one she'd never given him before she'd come to his club, before he'd exposed her to the sort of flirtation that did not take place in proper ballrooms. The kind of flirtation that promised a journey into sin.

Watching as her bodice stretched across her breasts, as the visible mounds plumped up as she stretched her arms behind her head and retrieved a pearl comb, he cursed her for ever coming here, cursed himself for ever giving her this place to come to. She was more dangerous to his heart than the dregs that lurked in the darkest corners of London. They'd use a knife to create the sharp pain that would kill him while she used every feminine wile at her disposal to utterly destroy him. When she strolled out of here, he would continue to breathe, but his heart would be going with her.

She set the comb between them. "My wager. If you win it, I'll let down my hair."

As though he wouldn't do everything within his power to gain that reward.

She arched a brow. "You?"

"My neckcloth. But it stays on until you win it."

"That hardly seems fair."

"It's how the game is played. You don't take anything off until it's been won."

"Ah, it seems I misunderstood the details of the game." She began shuffling the cards. "Since it's only the two of us, we'll play a simplified version. Cards are dealt. We'll toss aside one. Show our hand. The best wins."

After giving a curt nod, he sipped his whisky and watched as she deftly dealt the cards, no doubt from all her experience at whist. At the cottage, he'd been the one dealing, the one teaching her. She set the deck aside and picked up her cards. With no place to rest his glass, with one hand, he gathered his, managed to fan them out, and rid himself of the lowest card.

"You first," she said.

He tossed his cards down, face up. A lousy showing, with no matches of any kind, but his jack of hearts beat her two, seven, and nine. And everything inside him went still as he waited for the unraveling.

She moved the comb to the bedside table. He didn't object. The pearl adornment wasn't his to possess forever, only for the span of this ridiculous game. Then she was plucking out pins and placing them beside the pearl comb, and he decided he liked the game very much indeed as the coppery curls began to spill around her.

If only he was as unencumbered. If only he could reach across and bury his hands in them. But she was not his to touch. Apparently, however, he was hers to torture and torment. If her victorious smile was any indication, she knew exactly how she was twisting him with need. A quick glance at his lap would be enough to confirm that.

When the last of the strands cascaded around her shoulders, she shook her head, sending the tresses flying around to land in a wild disarray when she went still. Why in God's name did she ever pin up her magnificent hair? If a woman's hair was considered her crowning glory, then hers was worthy of being associated with the Crown Jewels.

"My gloves."

"What of them?"

She smiled as though he amused her, although he suspected it was his croak that delighted her. "I'm wagering them next."

And lost them, her king no match for his pair of threes.

The torment began again, with her taking her time to remove the gloves, as though she had all night to do so. Rolling them down from her elbow to her wrist, before tugging on the fingertips.

"I assume your parents are still in Paris and don't know you're here."

"They returned a few days ago but had long since retired before I snuck out."

"And your trusted coachman?"

"Is as loyal as they come. He won't tell. No one saw me enter. I waited until I was sure all your members had left. And I know you'll ensure that your staff holds our little secret."

"They hold all secrets. It's what they're paid to do, and they know they'll answer to me if they don't."

The first glove came off to reveal her silky-smooth skin. Not a blemish in sight, although he recalled the freckles that had adorned her arms and hands in her youth. He took a quick glance at his right palm, at the scars there, saw the ones that were visible, the ones that were not, the ones that would take a lifetime to wash off. For the first time in a long while, he had a strong urge to hide them. He tossed back what was left of his whisky and set the glass off to the far side of the bed.

The second glove was gone, and she was arranging it, along with the first, across one of his pillows. Then her gaze was back on him. She took a sip of her brandy, and he watched the delicate muscles at her throat work as she swallowed. He didn't want to remember how close that elegant slope of her neck had come to being sliced.

Following the attack, he should have seen her home. Not gone to the cottage with her, not kissed her there, not seen the moonlight glowing over her skin. Skin, that even now, though hidden from him, tempted him.

He saw a flicker of doubt in her eyes, before she took another taste of the brandy, as though she needed it for fortification. She had a string of pearls at her throat. Surely they would be next. Or her stockings. Not her gown, not something that would require his help in removing.

She set the snifter aside and licked those sweet, pink lips that he desperately wanted to taste. But he wanted another taste of other lips as well. She shouldn't be here. He should drag her from the bed, toss her over his shoulder, and haul her down to the coach that was no doubt waiting in the mews. Instead, he watched, mesmerized, as she slipped two fingers down the front of her bodice.

"I wager this next." She brought forth a gold medallion and chain—no, a pocket watch and fob—and placed the items between them.

He stared at the gold cover, plain save for the engraved ivy circling the outer edge, enclosing the G and S that resided in the center. Something was wrong with his throat. It was having some strange reaction to the whisky, swelling or knotting up so it was becoming difficult to swallow. Even more difficult to speak. Finally, he managed to lift his gaze to hers, to discover her studying him expectantly, perhaps a little nervously. "You're going to deliberately lose the next hand."

She gave the barest hint of a nod. And he knew she'd intentionally lost the previous hands as well, had probably tossed away a card that would have seen her win. After each hand, the played cards were returned to the bottom of the deck. If he sorted through them, he could probably figure it out, but there was no need. He knew what she'd done.

"I don't get to keep the comb or the gloves, but this—"

"Will become yours."

"Why go through the elaborate ruse? Why not just give it to me?"

"Because a lady shouldn't give a gentleman a gift such as this"—an expensive, personal item—"nor should a gentleman accept it."

"You really think a man who owns a place such as this, where people are encouraged to do what they ought not, is any sort of gentleman at all and is going to say no to your gift?"

"Would you have?"

He gave a dark chuckle. "Probably."

"A man of business should have a timepiece, don't you think? I noticed you still didn't."

Reaching out, she turned it over, and he read the inscription. "'To seizing dreams.'"

"You helped me gain mine when you wrote Kingsland," she said quietly. "Now you have yours."

Only he didn't. Not if he was honest. He had acquired one dream, certainly, but another would always elude him. Justifiably so.

After picking it up, she scooted forward until her knee nudged against his thigh, and God help him, he felt the touch clear down to his toes. Easing the front of his coat aside, she tucked the time-piece into the pocket of his waistcoat and attached the end of the fob to a buttonhole. All he could do was be amazed by her expression, as though it brought her unbridled joy to perform such a service for him.

"I can't accept it."

She patted his chest. "Too late, it's already yours." Her gaze landed softly on his. "And it won't fray like my hair ribbon."

So she had recognized the marker in his book. Because she was incredibly near, he plowed his hands into her hair, relishing the feel of silk over his skin. "You shouldn't have come. Not to this place. Not to me."

"I won't again. Only tonight. To have one more dream. To give to you as you gave to me."

"If it's a dream you want, sweetheart, we're going to give to each other." He took possession of her mouth, a mouth that tart words had often escaped, a mouth that could drop him to his knees. She belonged to no one at the moment, but soon she would. She would belong to a duke, and as much as he wanted that for her, it tore him up inside as well.

So he would take what she was offering and strive to ensure she had no regrets. Surely, a duke wouldn't expect a woman of her age to be completely untouched. Perhaps he'd even appreciate that she came with a bit of experience. If Griff's club succeeded, maybe fewer women would fear the marriage bed.

While the duke may never love her, Griff wanted to ensure she had one night with a man who did. But that he couldn't confess to her. No regrets, no remorse, no looking back. No wondering what if.

They would have tonight. Then he would have his club, and she would have her cottage—and they'd have the shared memories.

Laces were undone, hooks untethered, silk and satin, linen and lace tossed aside until she was bared to him. "It never ceases to amaze me how beautiful, how magnificent, you are," he told her, his voice raw with desire. "You seemed ethereal in the moonlight, but in the glow of this room, I can see all the shades. You're as fair as I envisioned." Pale, pink, and perfect. With a thatch of curls that matched her hair.

"I've only seen a portion of you, and I want to see all of you."

With care, he removed the pocket watch she'd given him and positioned it on the table beside her comb. With much less care, he shrugged out of his jacket and tossed it to the floor. His waistcoat, shirt, and trousers followed.

Tentatively, she reached out and touched the healing welt that had formed in his side and would eventually leave a scar in its wake. "This nearly took you from me."

He cradled her face. "No sadness tonight. No bad memories. The past doesn't matter. All that matters is now."

"That's what this place is, isn't it? Someplace to escape to, for a bit. Not to be who you are, but for a while to be who you want to be or who you wished you were."

"I think it is different things to different people. Is that why you go to the cottage? To escape?"

"Sometimes. Sometimes I go to remember." Flattening herself against him, she wound her arms around his neck. "In the future, when I go, I will think of you."

SHE SHOULDN'T BE here, shouldn't be doing this, but the way he'd looked at her as though he'd never seen anything he wanted more made it so that for now *shouldn't*s no longer mattered.

He didn't take her mouth gently, but claimed it with a fury equal to that of a tempest that had the strength to destroy ships. Powerful, strong, determined to have its way. She desperately wanted him to have his way with her.

Even if this was wrong. But how could it be when it felt so right, when she was so comfortable with her body flattened against his while he devoured? She could taste the whisky on his tongue, was certain he could taste the brandy on hers.

She scraped her fingers up through his hair, remembering how the wind off the sea had blown it into disarray. Every aspect of Kent reminded her of him. She wouldn't be able to return here after tonight, because every facet of him would make her want him. Again. Forever.

But she was following Wilhelmina's advice, taking once for herself what a proper lady should not have. The rough and scarred hands of a man she couldn't marry skimming over her, weakening her knees until she wondered how she was able to stand.

She released the tiniest of squeals when he lifted her and tumbled them both onto the bed, his body coming to rest halfway over her.

"I used to imagine your hair across my pillow." Combing his fingers through it, he spread the strands out over the pillow where her gloves rested. "So incredibly beautiful. I wanted to do this that night you unraveled your plait for me." After gathering up her tresses until they filled his hand and spilled over, he buried his face in them. "So soft. So thick."

"I've always loved your eyes, the same shade as Althea's, but I've never wanted to stare into hers. I think because yours always have a bit of wickedness twinkling in them, as though you're thinking thoughts that should never be said aloud."

"Hmm." He trailed his mouth up and down her throat, over and over, moving along it only an inch at a time. "You smell of oranges. I love eating oranges. That's probably what I'm thinking when my eyes are twinkling. I'm thinking of feasting on you."

"I can be tart sometimes."

He lifted his head, grinned at her. "I like tart."

She scraped her fingers along his jaw, loving the rasp of his stubble. "Take all of me tonight," she whispered.

His growl, unrestrained, unfettered, echoed around them as he brought his mouth back to hers and took possession of it as though he owned it already—and perhaps he did. Because when he was near, she thought about kissing him. When he was away, she thought about kissing him. No other man had ever stirred her as he did.

Then they were exploring each other with abandon. Hands and tongues, fingers and mouths. She loved the various textures of him, loved that all was available to her.

Second thoughts and guilt might come later, and she would deal with them then. But she would never regret her brazen move or his groans of pleasure, of want. She would never forget the way he'd looked at the timepiece as though she'd given him the most precious thing in all the world. She would never forget the manner in which he'd looked at her: as though *she* was the most precious person in all the world.

As he gave attention to her breast, kissing and licking the pink bud that pearled for him, she moaned, deep in her throat, creating a vibration that traveled through her chest and lower, to the secretive spot that she had guarded with chastity. Suddenly it seemed to be screaming for release, release that he would provide.

Tenderly, he parted her folds. "You're so wet. Ready for me."

He lifted himself up, and she felt him nudging at her entrance. Slipping her arms beneath his, around his sides, she dragged her fingers along his powerful back, a back that had hefted crates and sacks on the docks. While others might have seen the labor as beneath him, the son of a duke, she saw it as his determination to survive. He would do what had to be done. It was one of the reasons she knew he would have success here. He was not the laggard that people—she, to her shame—had assumed. He would make his way; he would succeed.

He eased his way into her, slowly, inch by inch, the breadth of him filling her, stretching her. She pressed her feet flat, her knees bent, creating a cradle for him, and pushed herself up to meet him. Nothing had ever felt more right as his groan shimmied through him, through her.

As he rocked against her, the sensations began to build. Whimpers she couldn't contain circled around her. Their movements became more frantic, and when the cataclysm came, it tore through her with the force of a great wave hurled to shore by a storm. A wave big enough to take both of them, because his growl followed quickly on the end of her cry, both sounds echoing around them.

But it was only as she came back into herself that she realized he'd left her, that his seed coated her belly. It was the right thing to do, to ensure she didn't get with babe, didn't risk giving the duke she would marry another man's offspring—and yet, she felt a momentary sadness that she would never have Griff's child growing within her.

He kissed her lips, each of her breasts, the valley between. "Wait here. I'll clean you up."

Her grandmother had often told her not to think about what she didn't have, but to concentrate on what she did. She'd had a glorious experience, and for tonight, for the remainder of her life, it had to be enough.

"HE'S GOING TO ask me to marry him. Sometime in the next few days he's going to speak with Father." She was snuggled against Griff's side, his arm around her, his fingers drawing circles on her shoulder while she did the same on his chest. She knew she didn't need to tell him who. She didn't want to bring his name into the room.

"Took him long enough."

"You're not bothered by it?"

"Why would I be bothered by it? I arranged it."

"To win a wager."

He held silent, not that she blamed him. What was there to say? He might not have initially collected the winnings, but eventually he had. From his duplicity, he had built this place. She no longer resented it, but still she wished he'd admitted that what he would have gained had not been his primary motivation, that he'd sent the letter because of his feelings for her, his desire to see her gain what she wanted. She didn't know why she was disappointed, why she wanted more. He'd never proclaimed his love for her.

She was here now not because of his feelings toward her but hers toward him.

How often had women made that very mistake? She thought the Trewloves were probably examples of it happening six times at least. Fortunately, however, she wouldn't bring an unwanted child into the world. No, not unwanted. She'd have wanted it. Her parents, not so much. They might have even sent her packing. But she would be spared all that because he had experience, he'd thought ahead, he'd taken precautions.

She wanted another woman never to be in this room. But she thought that unlikely to happen. He would carry on with his life, and she would move on with hers. She wanted him to be happy, to have someone. While she would have the duke. "You assume I'll say yes."

He shifted until he was resting on his elbow, looking down on her. "Of course, you'll say yes. It's the opportunity to have what you've always desired." He curled his fingers around the side of her neck, stroked his thumb along the length of her jaw. "I've been there, Kathryn. I understand why you love it, why you want it. It belongs with you. The cottage, the sea, the shoreline. The dawn. I'll always see you there."

In his memories.

She would see him there as well. And here. In this once-abandoned building that he had transformed into something that held the power to change lives, hearts, and futures. He'd been betrayed by his father, by Society. But he'd come out the other side, a stronger, better man. A man capable of achieving his ambitions.

"I can't come back here. Ever."

"No, you can't. I'll be cancelling your membership."

"What if I told him no?"

"You won't."

After rolling out of the bed, he snatched up his trousers. She sat up abruptly, pulling the sheet over her chest. "What are you doing?"

He tossed her chemise and drawers toward her. "Start getting dressed."

"I don't understand." He seemed angry, furious in fact.

"It's time you left. I'll escort you to your carriage."

"Why are you doing this?"

He swung around and faced her. Oh yes, he was definitely fuming.

"Why would you even consider telling him no? After all the trouble I went to in order to see this match happen? Why not take advantage of it?"

"All the trouble you went to?" She scrambled out of the bed, balled up her hands, and glared at him. His fury was now hers. "What have you done? Did you make another wager that he would indeed marry me?"

"Don't be absurd."

With no conviction in his tone, she rather feared that he'd done exactly that. "Then, why are you so concerned with my marrying him?"

"This is exactly why I left the cottage. Because I knew I'd give in to temptation and have you. And you would mistake passion for love and latch on to this ridiculous notion that there could be more between us. Do you know what you would lose if you married me? Other than the obvious: your inheritance? You would lose Society. No more dinners. No more balls. No more being called upon."

"Althea's family welcomed you."

"Because we are now related. But the rest of those who presently surround you? They want nothing to do with me. I know their secrets, and they know I know them. And those who come here? Their visits are clandestine. They're not proud to be seen here. They're not proud of what they're doing. They know what this place encourages. What I encourage. They're not going to welcome a man such as me into their homes. And they won't welcome you if you're at my side."

"You don't know that."

"I do know that." He shook his head. "But it's all moot, sweetheart. Because the shackles of marriage are not for me. They never have been. You asked for one night. That's all I'm willing to give you. You fell into the trappings of this place. It's all only fantasy. It's time you go back to your duke."

SHE STOOD BEFORE him in all her splendor, trembling with her righteous indignation. He could see the various spots where his stubble had abraded her delicate skin. He could see the fading blush that their shared passions had brought to the fore.

Could see the hurt and disbelief in her eyes, and the sight flayed his heart.

But he couldn't have her giving up her dreams for him.

She didn't know what it was to be cast out. How it battered and bruised. For her, it would be so much worse, because she'd been embraced by the Society that would turn against her. It would hurt, would devastate her. Eventually she would resent what being with him cost her.

He wouldn't be responsible for any of that befalling her. He wouldn't see her embarrassed, mortified, or shamed.

"I thought you'd changed." She jerked on her undergarments. "But you're still a scapegrace, a scoundrel."

"I will always be. It suits me." Even if at the moment it was tearing him up inside. Shredding his soul, inviting him into hell.

She stepped into her gown, brought it up. He stepped forward to help with the lacings. Her glare stopped him cold. "I don't require your assistance. I don't require anything of you any longer."

While she struggled to do herself up, he pulled on his trousers, dragged on his shirt, tugged on his boots. He didn't know how she'd done it, but she was dressed and heading for the door before he'd finished. He hastened to follow.

"I don't need you to escort me," she said tartly.

"Is your carriage in the mews? There's a rear door that will get you there directly."

She didn't speak until they reached the lowest level. "Well, show me."

He led her down the hallway, through the kitchens. Throwing the bolt on the door, he swung it open. She edged past him, taking deliberate care to ensure her skirts didn't brush against him this time.

It was like a blow to the gut. Even though it was deserved.

With her shoulders back, her head held high, she marched forward. The footman opened the carriage door and handed her up.

She settled in, becoming lost in the shadows, without looking out the window. Then she was gone.

And everything grew quiet.

He dropped to his knees, threw his head back, and howled as the pain of letting her go threatened to destroy him.

CHAPTER 20

SHE'D GONE THROUGH her day in a haze, her well-sated body continuing to thrum, her mind constantly drifting to thoughts of Griff and the manner in which he'd made her feel loved, cherished, and desired. Until he'd snatched it all away with the brutal truth.

When Althea had called on her and they'd enjoyed tea in the garden, she'd almost confessed, "I made the mistake of falling madly in love with your brother."

When Wilhelmina had invited her for a stroll through the park, she'd almost confided, "You were right. A woman should be wicked at least once in her life." But she should take great care in choosing the one with whom she'd be wicked.

When she had wandered into the library and caught her mother sitting on her father's lap, their mouths clamped together, a book resting on the floor nearby, she envisioned her mother interrupting his reading to offer him something more enticing. Her chest had tightened painfully as she'd backed quietly out of the room, wondering if she would be sacrificing spontaneous moments of affection in the future.

Would the duke's eyes darken with yearning? Would his hands reach with purpose? Would he want to taste all of her? Would his voice go rough and raw when he murmured how much he took delight in every aspect of her, when he encouraged her touches, asked where she wanted to be caressed?

When ladies called in the afternoon, she wished them away, barely listening as they gossiped about this lady or that one and some gent. All she wanted was to curl up on her bed and think of Griff, relive the moments of their night together, mourn for what would never again be, for what might never have been to begin with.

She had a different future, away from him, one that had been designed for her by a woman she'd always believed loved her beyond measure. Who'd wanted only the best for her and would reward her when she acquired it. But what if the reward was not worth the cost?

She needed away from here, needed the only place where she'd ever truly been herself, where she could think without interruption. Where no one would call upon her. Where no one would stop by to offer a bit of gossip. After finally managing to catch her parents when they weren't pressed up against each other, she informed them that she was away to Kent for a few days and set her maid to the task of packing a small trunk for her.

She had only just changed into her traveling frock when a knock on her door sounded a heartbeat before her mother barged in, apparently too impatient to wait for Kathryn to bid her entry. Excitement was fairly shimmering off her.

"Oh, my dear girl, the duke has asked for a private audience with your father. He's speaking with him in the library at this very minute." Her mother released a tiny squeal and squeezed her hands. "You'll be betrothed before the night is done. I'm sure of it. Quickly now, you must change. You must be prepared for an audience with him."

He'd told her he intended to speak with her father. She simply hadn't expected it to be so soon. "It's possible that he's discussing an investment opportunity."

"Posh!" Her mother fluttered a hand through the air. "He's discussing a marriage opportunity. You'll be a duchess. Your grandmother would be so thrilled."

"Would she?"

"Absolutely. She wanted to see you well cared for. I daresay there isn't a peer in all of England who could see you more well cared for than the Duke of Kingsland."

Lowering herself onto the vanity bench, Kathryn knew her mother spoke true. She would have a lovely residence, beautiful clothes, and attentive servants. But she didn't yearn for Kingsland, didn't grow warm thinking about kissing him, didn't long for his touch, or find herself worrying over him several times a day. Was that fair to him? Was it fair to herself? "But was it the sort of care she had in mind? I see so little of him."

"He is a busy man. Rumor is that he's increased his income twice over this year alone . . . and the year is not yet done."

"But he was wealthy without that."

"Now he is wealthier. What is wrong with you? I daresay it seems you are searching for excuses to turn him away."

"I'm not searching for excuses, but now that the moment is upon me, I worry that I know so few details about him. I don't know what he likes to read. I know little at all about his business"— except for the couple of ventures he'd spoken about of late—"or how he enjoys spending his leisure hours."

"What are you carrying on about? You will have the sort of marriage you have been working toward your entire life."

"Is it really what I've been working toward?"

"You have been acting deuced odd of late. Is it because your father has given you permission to visit with Althea again, now that she has married a respectable man? Is she filling your mind with peculiar ideas?"

"No." She got up and walked to the window. She could see the duke's black coach in the drive, but where was the sea? She needed the sea. But if she didn't marry him, she would lose it. No, she wouldn't. She could go to Brighton. Although, it wouldn't be the same. She had no memories of Griff there. Why should she want memories of him when he didn't want her?

"My darling, whatever is wrong?" Her mother had come up beside her and was patting the curls that were streaming down Kathryn's back. "You're acting as though Kingsland is discussing your funeral, not your wedding."

Turning, she faced the woman who had brought her into the world. "You waited thirty years for love, Mother. Do you not ever wish you'd had it sooner?"

Her mother stopped fiddling with her hair and gazed out the window. Kathryn wondered what she was looking for or what she saw. "Some women go their entire lives without love, Kathryn. 'Tis better to have it late than not at all."

"That's not an answer to my question."

"Of course, I wish I'd had it sooner." Her mother squared her shoulders and faced her, tilting up her chin until she no longer had the mien of a mother but only that of a countess. "But in all the years I didn't have it, I never went hungry, I never was cold, I never went without. Love is a lovely thing to have, but it cannot provide. You must be practical. When your father dies, your uncle—and then his son—will give you nothing. They will not see to your care. They will not give you influence, power, or prestige. Being a duchess will. Being the Duke of Kingsland's duchess will give it to you tenfold. If you do not take this offer, you will not only disappoint your grandmother but me and your father as well. And I suspect in time, you'll be disappointed in yourself." Her mother squeezed her hands. "I heard he received over a hundred letters. And he chose you, dear girl. Perhaps there is a hint of love in that."

"You know, Mother, I think there very well may have been." Just not in the manner the dear woman thought.

Her mother tugged on the sleeves of Kathryn's frock. "Now, let's get you into something a bit more enticing. Sarah, the green."

"Yes, my lady," her maid said.

"I don't think I need to go to the bother of changing again."

"Of course you do." Her mother took her face in her hands. "His proposal will be a memory you will long cherish. And it is something he will often reflect on. You want your beauty to shine."

For some reason, she couldn't imagine Kingsland reflecting on the moment at all.

The knock came softly, but with a bit of urgency.

"Come!" her mother called out.

One of the maids opened the door, stepped into the room, and bobbed a quick curtsy. "The Duke of Kingsland is waiting in the front parlor. He'd like a word with Lady Kathryn."

Her mother released a deep sigh of relief. "Inform His Grace that we shall be down momentarily." She turned to Kathryn. "Now, let's get you properly attired."

Off came her traveling dress. On went the green gown. She felt as though she was an actress being readied for a play as her mother began providing her with lines. "You'll want to thank him profusely for choosing you. Tell him you are honored. Ensure—"

"Mother, I don't need you to tell me what to say. I have been brought up to know how to respond."

After Kathryn was put back to rights, her mother squeezed her arms. "I am just so happy for you. Let's go see what he wants, shall we?"

"Quiet."

Her mother glowered at her. "I beg your pardon?"

"That's what he wants. Quiet." She wound her arm around her mother's. "But, yes, certainly, let's go see what he has to say."

As they descended the stairs, the countess described how she envisioned Kathryn's wedding gown. All the tulle, satin, and lace. The length of the veil. The length of the train. It all seemed so tedious. Where was Kathryn's excitement? Where was her joy, her anticipation?

Her mother accompanied her into the parlor. The Duke of Kingsland was standing by the fireplace, his forearm pressed to the mantel, his head bent slightly as he gazed into the empty hearth. At the sound of their footsteps, he turned.

He was so devastatingly handsome, dark hair and strong features. Yet she could have been looking at a cup of cool tea for all the thrill that went through her at the sight of him. She didn't want to comb her fingers through his hair or trail them over his shoulders. She couldn't imagine herself ever running into his arms.

"Your Grace," her mother sang out as she glided toward him and curtsied. "We're so thrilled you've come to call."

"Lady Ridgeway, as always it's a pleasure to see you."

"But I understand it is not me you are here to see. Rather, you wish to have a word with Kathryn. I shall leave you to it."

As she floated toward the door, she passed Kathryn and gave her a pointed look which communicated effectively *Mind how you go here.*

When her mother was no longer about, Kathryn offered the duke a small smile. "Your Grace, shall I send for tea?"

"No, thank you. Would you care to sit?"

She approached him, stopping only a couple of feet shy of him. "Actually, I think I prefer to stand."

"As you wish." He cleared his throat. "I've just had a meeting with your father. I'm certain you're aware of what that portends."

"Since I wasn't privy to the conversation, I cannot say with any degree of confidence." It was what she would have said to Griff had he made such an absurd statement. He might not have liked it, but she would have seen appreciation in his eyes. In the duke's she saw merely impatience.

"You're not going to be this contrary as a wife, are you?"

"Having never been a wife, to be honest I can't say how I will be as one."

"Is that the reason you didn't write me a letter, describing yourself?"

"There are a lot of reasons I didn't write the letter."

"Mmm. I see. Well. Be that as it may, I have spoken with your father, and we have come to terms. So all that is left"—he took a step forward, bowed his head slightly—"Lady Kathryn, will you honor me by becoming my wife?"

She studied him for a full minute. He waited, unmoving. "You didn't go down on one knee."

"Don't take offense, but I kneel for no one."

She thought of Griff who had gone to both knees, without hesitation, when it might have meant death. Griff who had come to her when she was lost in the throes of a nightmare and guided her out of it. Giving her a memory to replace it, another that involved going to his knees. But he'd told her it was all fantasy. That she should return to her duke. Griffith Stanwick would only give her one night. But what if *she* wanted more?

"You're not going to be this contrary as a husband, are you?"

He barked out a short laugh, and she realized she'd never heard him laugh before. He had a good laugh, but it didn't reach down into her soul, didn't seek to take up residence there. She suspected an hour after he left, she wouldn't even be able to recall how it sounded.

"Having never been a husband, to be honest I can't say how I will be as one." He shook his head. "No, that's not true."

"You have been a husband before?"

He grinned, and this time she thought maybe he did appreciate her tease. "No, but I know how I will be as a husband. Insufferable, no doubt. I have expectations and don't like for them not to be met. You know at least one of them. You had Griffith Stanwick make inquiries on your behalf to determine what I wanted in a wife."

She rolled her eyes. "Yes, that day in the park I thought you'd figured it out."

"You may take some comfort in knowing that while I have expectations for a wife, I have much more stringent expectations for myself. I will be as good a husband as I can be. I will never strike you. I will never intentionally hurt your feelings. I will never be unfaithful. I will never give you cause to doubt my devotion."

"Devotion is not love."

"No. Love is not an emotion I believe myself capable of. But perhaps you shall prove me wrong."

"You don't strike me as a man who likes to be proven wrong."

"Look how well you already know me, Lady Kathryn."

"Unfortunately, I feel we know each other hardly at all. How well will we know each other five years from now? Or ten? And if I do not prove you wrong, if you do not come to love me—"

"You will have your inheritance. Your father explained to me what it entails. I should think you would be content with it."

"One would think. My grandmother thought so, but I am beginning to suspect that she didn't know me very well." She gave a small, harsh laugh. "Until this moment, I'm not sure if I knew myself all that well, either. I was twelve when my grandmother died. All I wanted was to have her back, to have her love surrounding me again. But the cottage won't give her back to me because her love isn't housed within it." She placed her hand over her heart. "It's here within me, woven through all the memories."

"I'm not certain I know where this is leading."

"No, you probably don't." She wasn't certain she'd known when she began. But she knew if she accepted his offer of marriage, she would be sacrificing a lifetime of memories filled with love.

"Someday, Your Grace, I hope you will find a woman for whom you willingly drop to your knees without hesitation. But as she is not me, my answer to your lovely proposal is no, I will not—I cannot—marry you."

"THERE'S A DUKE tryin' to get in."

Griff was in the receiving room, watching as the artist he'd hired was quickly etching the features of the most recent lady to join the club onto the card that would identify her as a member. The man had begun working for him a few days after Kathryn had made the suggestion. He was quick, efficient, and damned accurate.

Kathryn's idea had been brilliant, got people through the doors more quickly. They simply showed their card to Billy, and he let them in. He was usually quite skilled at sending away those who didn't belong. Moving away from the artist, Griff gave his attention to the big bruiser.

"Told 'im dukes wasn't allowed no entry, but 'e said 'e was allowed. Pompous bugger. I almost punched 'im to get 'im moving on, but thought I best check first, in case 'e had the right of it."

He knew of only one duke that obnoxious. "Dukes aren't allowed, but I'll see to this one personally."

When he stepped into the hallway, he wasn't surprised to find that Kingsland hadn't waited outside as he would have been ordered to but had come in far enough that he could get a better view of everything, was looking up at the floors visible from his position. "Your Grace."

Kingsland lowered his gaze. "I've heard the rumors about this club. They say it's not good enough for firstborn sons who are to inherit."

"*They're* not good enough for *it*."

Kingsland chuckled low. "Spoken like a true second son. It seems to be flourishing, but you would benefit from having a man of influence speaking highly of this place."

"I have men—and women—of influence speaking highly of it."

He grinned. "Ah, yes, the Trewloves, I imagine. Chadbourne turned out to be a rotter, there, didn't he? Turning his back on your sister as he did, although she recovered nicely."

"My brother and I took our fists to him. I'll do the same to you if you cause Lady Kathryn any unhappiness."

"Her happiness is not my responsibility."

"It damned sure will be when you're her husband."

"I'm not to be her husband."

Fury like molten lava burst through him. "After all this time, you tossed her over?"

"She tossed me, old chap. Turned me down flat. Seemed to take exception to my not going down on a knee when I proposed, if you can believe it. Should have expected her rejection of my proposal, I suppose. It was a gamble on my part to choose a woman who had not sent me a letter."

Everything within Griff stilled. "What do you mean she didn't send you a letter?"

"Here, I always thought you had a semblance of intelligence about you. Am I using words that are too large, so it makes comprehension difficult?"

Damn, but he wanted to plow his fist into that perfect aristocratic nose. "You are either too daft to have recognized her name, to have known it was from her, or you overlooked it. I saw her working on it."

"She may have written the bloody thing, but she never sent it. After meeting her at the park, I paid particular attention to the letters, reading each one, carefully searching for hers, interested in finding out what she had to say."

"You didn't meet her at the park. You met her at a ball two years earlier. You bloody well danced with her."

"Did I? Hmm. Fancy that." He studied Griff. "I got *your* letter, though. Thought perhaps she had decided to have you write me. Decided it was brilliant strategy. But then, while she and I were dancing, I discovered she knew nothing at all about it. I found that even more intriguing. Why did you write it?"

He wanted to tell the man to go to the devil. Instead he confessed. "Because of the wager I'd made that you would select her. I wanted to influence your decision." And he'd done it for her, to see she gained what she wanted. But he wasn't going to tell this buffoon that.

"As good a reason as any, I suppose." He glanced around. "Well, good luck with your enterprise here. Wish I'd thought of it. It has the potential to make a good deal of money."

The Duke of Kingsland turned on his heel and headed for the door.

Griff took two steps forward. "Why did you take so blasted long to ask her? The truth this time."

The duke glanced back over his shoulder. "A foolish whim on my part. I was waiting for her to look at me with as much yearning as she'd directed your way that day in the park."

CHAPTER 21

WITH HIS USUAL confidence, the Duke of Kingsland strode into his favorite gentlemen's club and headed straight for the library where he knew the others waited. He was not a man accustomed to losing, and it didn't sit particularly well with him. Ruthless strategy was the watchword. It was the watchword of all the Chessmen—he and his friends so dubbed when they attended Oxford. They knew well how to play the game. Any game. With a cunning and merciless strategy that ensured they won, and that was the reason they'd been both feared and revered. They knew the intricacies of rules, and knowing the particulars meant knowing how to successfully break any rule in order to ensure the Chessmen were always victorious.

He easily spotted the trio sitting in leather wingback chairs in the far corner of the chamber where their words would not be overheard by others. A tumbler of scotch stood at the ready resting on a table near an empty chair. They'd been anticipating his arrival.

Without ceremony, he dropped onto the thick leather cushion, grabbed the glass, and lifted it. "Pay up, gents."

"Bloody hell," Bishop said. "She turned down your proposal."

After tossing back a good bit of his scotch, he gave a half-hearted grin. "She did, indeed. She chose the pawn over the king."

"How did you know she would?" Rook asked. "I've never known you to bet against yourself, and yet in this instance you didn't hesitate to do so."

"How do I know anything? I observe. That long-ago day in the park, I could have cut the sexual tension between them with a knife, so thick was it. They just hadn't recognized it yet for what it was."

"This outcome is going to make you appear rather foolish after investing all this time in her."

"What choice did I have? His traitorous father mucked things up, which resulted in the young lord being sent out of our orbit for a while. But as soon as I heard he was back in it, I knew it wouldn't take long for matters to be put to rights."

"If he hadn't come back?"

"Marrying her would have been no hardship. I found her re-markably interesting." Not particularly quiet, but interesting.

"I suppose the question now, however, is whether the pawn will choose Lady Kathryn as his queen," Bishop mused.

"A thousand quid says they are married before August," King said, striving not to give the impression he was already counting his winnings.

"That's rather specific, which leads me to believe I would be a fool to take you up on that wager."

"You would, indeed. Perhaps I'll place it in the betting books."

Knight studied him. "For a man all of London will deem to have lost, you don't seem particularly troubled."

"I didn't lose. I'm going to receive a thousand quid from each of you blokes. Besides, I never expected to truly win her. Even if she'd consented to marry me, I think her passions would have al-ways resided elsewhere." He could have lived with that, because his resided elsewhere as well. Love was not something he sought. But power, influence, and wealth were other matters entirely.

"I heard through one of our contacts that Marcus Stanwick is striving to bring honor back to the family," Knight said.

"Two thousand quid says he'll succeed," King challenged.

"You'll not get any takers from us for that wager."

"I don't envy him his task." But he had little doubt the once-future duke was up to the undertaking.

"You still need a wife," Bishop said unnecessarily, as though it was something King could forget.

"We all need wives."

"Will you go about finding yours in the same manner?"

"I see no reason not to. It saves me a lot of bother." Only the next time, he'd select for his queen a woman who would be in no danger of spending her marriage pining for another.

CHAPTER 22

WEARING ONLY HER chemise and drawers, Kathryn sat on a blanket on the sand and watched the waves lap at the shore, enjoying the motion and the constant slapping. Earlier she'd discarded her frock and taken a quick dip into the frigid water. Now the late morning sun had almost dried her and was presently kissing her skin.

When she departed this place the day after her birthday, when the promise of it was no longer hers but had transferred to her cousin, she would no doubt again be marred by freckles, and she no longer cared. They would mark spots where not only the sun had kissed her, but Griff had as well. And she wanted those reminders of him.

Her parents had been none too pleased with her for not accepting the duke's proposal, but she wouldn't have been happy with him, nor would he have been happy with her. While it was very unkind of her, she did hope that somewhere was a woman who would bring him to his knees. She would take great delight in that outcome.

After he'd left, and after facing her parents' disappointment, she'd had her packed trunk loaded onto the carriage and come to the cottage. She'd sent the coach and driver back to London as she had no plans to leave here before she reached the ripe old age of five and twenty. She'd been here a fortnight already, absorbing the calm and peace, allowing enough to fill her that it would see her through long after her hair turned silver and her eyesight faded.

She'd wanted to be alone with nothing to distract her from her purpose of hoarding memories. She'd not even bothered to hire Mrs. McHenry to see after things. Kathryn strolled into the village each day to purchase the food for her simple meals—fruit, cheese, bread, butter, and wine, lots of wine. She went to bed when she was sleepy, woke when she was rested. She read and embroidered and walked. And danced along the shoreline.

She was happy. Fairly happy. She required one more thing for absolute happiness: Griff. But she didn't know how to obtain him. He'd made his position clear. He didn't consider himself worthy of her. As long as there was the possibility of having the cottage, even if a hasty marriage to a stranger was the only solution to acquiring it, he would always feel that he'd somehow taken it from her.

But after her birthday, once she had no hope at all of ever having it, then how could he possibly be responsible for keeping it from her? She would gain a membership in his club and taunt him with her presence. She would wear provocative gowns and flirt outrageously. She would give him sultry looks and knowing smiles. If it took the remainder of her life to entice him back into her arms, so be it.

Without possession of the cottage hovering over her, she was free of all constraints. And she rather liked knowing she no longer had to worry about getting married. Marriage now was a choice that it had never been before. Who she married was more of a choice. She could wed the blacksmith's son and not lose more than she would gain.

Unintentionally her grandmother had placed a burden on her shoulders that she suddenly found herself grateful to be rid of. The cottage was not her life. It never had been. Only now had she begun to realize it.

While her father was put out with her, she had little doubt that he would eventually set up a trust for her so she would have the funds needed to live comfortably after his brother inherited the vast majority of his holdings. And if he didn't—

Well, if Griff could work the docks, she most certainly could find some sort of employment somewhere. Whoever hired her would be lucky to have her.

She caught a movement out of the corner of her eye and glanced to the side. Passion ignited, desire thrummed through her veins. Tall and lean, all muscle and sinew, Griff strode toward her. His feet were bare, his trouser legs turned up to expose his calves. Rolled up to nearly his elbows, his shirtsleeves billowed in the breeze. She wondered where his neckcloth, waistcoat, and coat were. Then decided it didn't matter. Those sorts of accessories had no place here.

Nevertheless, without the trappings of them, he still managed to exude all the bearing of a lord. Even though the Crown had stripped him of his place in Society, he had climbed through the muck to reclaim it with his comportment, if nothing else. She could barely breathe for the perfection of him.

When he reached her, he lowered himself to the blanket in such a way that he faced her, his legs stretched out in the opposite direction from hers. His thigh touched hers, and while cloth separated them, flimsy cloth on her part, the familiarity of it seemed almost as intimate as her lying beneath him.

"Last year, you didn't send Kingsland a letter, didn't *interview* for him."

Not what she'd expected. An apology, perhaps. An *I've realized I can't live without you* would have been preferable. "Hello to you as well. This is a surprise. How did you know where to find me?"

"I went to your residence and spoke with your parents. After a lengthy discussion, they reluctantly divulged your whereabouts." He studied her for three heartbeats, four. "Why?"

Apparently, he had no intention of letting his original inquiry go without some answers, even if he'd only made a statement and not presented a direct question. He expected her to address it. She shook her head. How to explain? She bit her lower lip, tried to think of the right words. "Because I can't be quiet. Because I couldn't imagine that a man who wanted a quiet wife would be happy with one who likes to dance on the beach. And I don't just dance on the beach, Griff. I dance when I wake up in the morning, after I crawl out of bed. Sometimes late at night, I dance through empty rooms. But mostly because as I said . . . I can't be quiet. I want to talk to my husband. I want to tell him my troubles. I want to hear his. I want to share my opinions on matters large and small. I want to offer suggestions and have him think that even the ones that aren't good still have value."

"But after he called out your name, you didn't turn him away from courting you."

She shrugged. "You'd gone to such trouble and inconvenience that it seemed the least I could do was give Kingsland the opportunity to impress me." Besides, Griff had disappeared, and she had wanted what marriage to the duke would gain her. A year ago, at least. The cottage had dominated her thoughts. For far too long it had dominated her life. Now she wanted something else entirely, and it was important he understand that. "He did finally ask for my hand. I told him no."

"I know. He came to see me." Well, that was a surprising development, and no doubt how he'd learned of her not sending a letter. "In turning him away, you will lose the cottage if you don't find a titled gent to marry rather quickly."

"I'm not even going to the bother to look. I've decided I don't want a titled gent. Which is the reason I'm here. To gather all the memories of this place while I may."

"And then?"

"You said that leaving me had never been easy. When did it become difficult?"

He glanced off to the side, toward the curved end of the small alcove that allowed for privacy. It was one of the reasons she'd always felt safe here. She could dance with no one watching, could be carefree and lighthearted, and not worry if she behaved like a hoyden rather than a lady. His gaze came back to her. "The night I kissed you in Kingsland's garden. Long before that, probably."

She felt as though she'd unlocked a wooden chest and unearthed a secret treasure. Leaving her had never been easy. Nothing about her had ever been easy. Just as nothing about him had ever been easy. But she'd only recently realized why. "How long have you loved me?"

He closed his eyes, and she watched the muscles at his throat work as he swallowed. His sigh was carried off by the breeze. Finally, he opened his eyes and captured her gaze. "Forever."

The tears stung her eyes, and her chest felt as though it was caving in on itself. Her heart sped up and slowed and seemed to have lost its ability to beat with any sort of rhythm. "Why did you never tell me? Why did you never let on how you felt?"

"Because I'm a second son, and years before I knew about the conditions related to your inheritance, I overheard you tell Althea that you would only marry a man with a title. I would never have one. And now, Kathryn . . ." Once more his gaze slid past her. "God, the things I've done. As you know the blood on my hands wasn't always mine."

She was no longer shocked by the truth of what he'd done, but it seemed he still struggled to come to terms with it. "But it was there in defense of others. Whether you were working the docks to provide for Althea or battling dangerous men in order to protect Marcus . . . or to protect me. Kingsland wouldn't go down on one solitary knee for me. You went down on both. With no hesitation, even knowing if you misjudged my ability to decipher your message, you would likely be killed. You sacrifice for others, asking nothing in return."

"I deserve nothing in return. Want nothing in return. I don't do it for personal gain."

She'd come to realize even the letter he'd written to Kingsland hadn't been because of his damned wager. He'd been seeking to give her what she longed for. But just as he had changed over the passing months, so had she. What she yearned to possess, what she considered important. What mattered.

She placed her palm against his jaw. "I love you, Griffith Stanwick. I turned the duke away because I would rather have a lifetime with you than a cottage by the sea."

With a groan that sounded as though he was in pain, he placed his hand over hers, turned his head, and pressed a kiss to the center of her palm. "Ah, Kathryn, you deserve so much better than a man who has done the things I have done."

"You're wrong there. I want to spend my life proving it to you, showing you that you aren't an afterthought, a spare, or being held in reserve. That nothing you've ever done makes you unworthy of anything. To me, you'll always come first, my first love, my only love. And I promise I won't be quiet while proving it, nor require that you be quiet, either. Will you honor me by becoming my husband?"

SHE BROUGHT HIM to his knees. Even though he was sitting, he still felt as though he'd dropped to them. Somehow, it seemed appropriate that this woman who thought rules should apply equally to both genders would be the one issuing the proposal.

He scooted up, scooted nearer, and cradled her beautiful face between his scarred hands, hands that no longer seemed to define him. Within her eyes, the ugliness of his past didn't matter—and that was all that concerned him. How she viewed him. "Do you fully understand what you'll be giving up?"

"I fully understand what I'll be gaining—all that I've ever dreamed of acquiring."

He pressed his forehead to hers. "Ah, Kathryn, you humble me. The honor will be all mine, sweetheart. Yes, I'll be your husband

and love every minute of it. Just as I love you, with everything within me."

He claimed her mouth as he'd longed to do from the beginning, as though it belonged to him and him alone. She was sustenance, air, life. She was all that was good in the world. She was all that mattered in his. Brave, beautiful, and bold.

She had never written to the duke, had never wanted Kingsland, and Griff had done her a disservice by striving to determine her destiny. He would spend the remainder of his life making that up to her. She would be his partner in all things. His helpmate. The one he turned to when decisions were needed, the one whose opinion he sought above all others. The woman who had turned down a duke for a second son. Turned away a gentleman in favor of a scoundrel.

She was on the verge of discovering how much of a scoundrel he could truly be.

Without taking his mouth from hers, gently he eased her down to the blanket and swung his body around so he lay beside her. He eased his mouth from hers, returned for another taste. God, he'd never have enough of tasting her.

Only now no guilt was associated with the indulgence. He was no longer in danger of taking anything from her. She'd chosen him.

With a growl, he took her mouth again, thoroughly and completely, relishing the feel of her hands digging into his shoulders, into his back. Rolling to her side, she swung her leg over his hip, hooking her calf against his buttocks, and sliding herself closer until her soft haven was pressed against his straining cock.

Her hand skimmed along his chest, freeing buttons as it went. When she ran out of buttons on his shirt, she started on the ones at his trousers.

Tearing his mouth from hers, he went to work on the ribbons of her chemise. With a laugh, she separated from him and began tugging off what little clothing she wore, tossing it aside, seemingly unbothered by the wind catching it and carrying it a short distance away.

He pulled his shirt over his head. Shucked off his trousers.

With dual laughs, smiles, and eyes sparkling, they came to-gether. He'd never known such freedom, such joy.

Her skin was so pale glistening in the sunlight, and he imagined freckles were forming even as he dotted her breasts with kisses. "I have long wanted to see you in the brightest of lights."

"It'll be brighter at noon."

"I can't wait that long to have you." He circled his tongue around her nipple, drew the little pearl into his mouth.

Moaning low, she writhed beneath him. "I've come to enjoy the manner in which you tease me."

"You tease equally."

As though to prove his point, she shoved him onto his back and proceeded to taunt and torment with touches, licks, and bites, while he used his hands to pinch and console. There was no part of her he didn't touch, no part of her he left bereft. He worshipped every inch of her.

Then he cupped her face between his hands, guided her gaze to his. "I don't want a quiet wife, Kathryn. I want you to scream my name."

"Only if you'll scream mine."

SHE COULD HARDLY believe what she was doing, outside, along the shoreline. Fishermen never came into the cove. No one ever did, but still the possibility that they might be spotted—

She truly did not care. Not when his hands were roaming over her as though every dip and curve had not been touched before. Not when she was straddling his hips and could see his cock jutting so proudly, straining . . . straining for the pleasure that she could provide.

After scooting farther down, she lowered herself to that beauti-ful part of him that could bring her such pleasure, that would see to children growing within her. And lapped at it as she had an ice concoction she'd eaten in the village last summer. With a harsh curse, he arched toward her as he burrowed his hands in her hair and dug his fingers into her scalp.

"Do you like that?" she asked innocently before lifting her gaze to his, surprised that the fire burning hotter than the sun in his didn't ignite her on the spot. Never taking her eyes from his, she kissed the head, licked the dew that had gathered there.

Then she closed her mouth over him, and his feral growl echoed around her, as he jerked and his breathing grew harsher. So she could drive him as mad as he did her. With a long wet stroke of her tongue and a suckle, and a low moan to affirm that she liked what she was tasting. And a wicked smile.

"Christ, Kathryn." Reaching for her, he brought her nearer. "You're going to make me spill my seed, and I want to be buried deep within you when that happens."

"Don't leave me this time."

He gripped her hips. "I won't. Never again will I leave you."

Lifting her up, he guided her down the length of his shaft, stretching and filling her. She dropped her head back, saw the top of the cliff, and wished she'd have a lifetime of looking up at it with him. But she would have the memory of now, rocking against him, moving in rhythm to the pace he set, languid at first, matching the cadence of the waves rolling in and out.

Sensations rippled through her. She touched him everywhere that she could reach. She loved the strength of him, the defined muscles, the dips, and shallows. The manner in which his arms bunched as he held her. The way he looked at her, as though she was the sun and the moon and the stars.

When pleasure cascaded through her, she cried out his name, and it echoed around them, quickly joined by his guttural howl that was her name, the sounds weaving together as their lives would. Bending forward, sated and content, she rested on top of him, savoring the feel of his arms folding around her, holding her close.

For several minutes, she simply absorbed the warmth and comfort of him. She wouldn't need her dances on the beach any longer. She had him. "When shall we wed?"

"As soon as possible."

"Perhaps we could get married in the church in the village."

"We'll get married wherever you like."

It was early in July. She had a few more weeks to gather memories here, memories with him. "Afterward, although I know you'll need to be in London each day to see to your business, as it's not such an awful distance, perhaps I could stay here and you could join me each day until the middle of August."

"You can stay here as long as you wish, visit whenever it suits."

Silly man. He hadn't yet recovered enough from making love to her to think clearly. "It goes to my cousin the day after my birthday," she reminded him.

"Actually, Kathryn, he's giving it to you as a birthday present, to celebrate you reaching a quarter of a century."

Sitting up abruptly, she stared down at him. "I beg your pardon?"

He grinned with such satisfaction and so much love in his eyes, that she thought she might melt on the spot. "He has decided he has no use for it and would prefer to see it in your hands."

"Why would he do that?"

"Because he has secrets to be kept."

She threw a hand over her mouth, striving to decide if she should be horrified or thrilled. "You threatened to reveal his secrets?"

"Took me nearly a week to discover them. Then we had to have a discussion about them. Otherwise, I'd have come to you sooner."

"You scoundrel. If he weren't so odious, I might feel badly for him." With a laugh, she hugged Griff as hard as she could in their prone positions. "But I've no doubt he deserved a visit from you. I love you so much, Griff." Then she sat back up. "Why didn't you tell me sooner?"

"Because I didn't want you to feel that you owed me—before I asked you to marry me."

"You were planning to ask me to marry you?"

"Mmm. But I prefer the way it happened."

So did she, but still she liked knowing he would have asked if she hadn't. "Acquiring the cottage must have been done at great inconvenience to yourself."

"Indeed, it was. Although, this time I won't ask for anything in trade because you've already given me the only thing of importance I could ever want: you."

ON A SUNNY Saturday morning, they were married at the village church, with only close friends and family in attendance. She had little doubt that the curious would have filled Westminster if they'd married there, but she had no interest in putting on a display for anyone who had ever shown him even a teaspoon of unkindness.

Her parents weren't particularly pleased, didn't understand her giving up a duke for a rapscallion, but they did give their blessing to the union, and her father walked her down the aisle. Althea and her husband were there, but Marcus was noticeably absent, and while Griff didn't give any outward indication, she knew he was worried about his brother and the fact that he'd heard nothing from him since that night by the Thames.

After the ceremony, everyone strolled down to the shoreline for a picnic that Mrs. McHenry had prepared. Simple fare along with champagne and wine.

Laughter and conversation floated on the wind. The sun glinted off smiles. As a couple of gents from the village played a tune on their violins, her husband waltzed with her over the sand.

"Happy?" he asked.

"Very. Today is perfect. Absolutely perfect."

"Wait until we get rid of this lot"—grinning, he jerked his head to the side, encompassing all the Trewloves and their spouses, Wilhelmina, and Kathryn's parents—"and I can have my way with you. I'll show you perfection."

She eased closer to him, her bosom brushing against his chest. "What do you have in mind?"

"Making love to you until dawn." His brow furrowed as he stilled. "Who is that?"

He turned her so they were both looking toward the path. A woman in a very proper dark blue frock was cautiously making her way down it. "I don't know. I don't think she's anyone from the village. We should probably let her know this is a private affair."

Holding on to Griff's arm as he escorted her, she strolled over to the woman who appeared to be only slightly older than herself. "Hello. May we help you?"

The stranger gave her a very serious study from her bare feet— she'd removed her shoes as soon as she reached the sand—to the top of her head. "Mrs. Griffith Stanwick?"

Kathryn smiled. "What gave me away?"

"The white silk and lace gown and the veil brushed back from your face," she responded with such seriousness that Kathryn wondered if she should bother to explain the question had been rhetorical. But before she could say anything else—

"I'm Miss Pettypeace, secretary to the Duke of Kingsland. He asked that I have this delivered to you on your wedding day, and as it seemed incredibly important to him, I decided to see to the responsibility of placing it into your hands myself."

Kathryn took the envelope she'd extended toward her. "What is it?"

"Something he wished you to have."

It seemed Miss Pettypeace took everything quite literally. "I do hope the duke is well."

"Why would he not be?"

Well, obviously he wasn't suffering from a broken heart, which made her feel somewhat better.

"Good day to you, Mrs. Stanwick." She turned to go.

"Miss Pettypeace?"

The young woman glanced back at her.

"Would you care for some refreshments before you leave?"

"Thank you, but I haven't time for such frivolities. I must away to London and tend to some other important business for the duke."

"Safe travels, then."

With a quick nod, the duke's secretary headed back toward the path.

"Well, she's certainly an efficient sort," Kathryn mused.

"Are you going to open the letter?"

She tucked it inside Griff's jacket. "I think I'll read it later. At the moment, I have a waltz to finish."

And another and another. As the sun arced through the sky and the champagne flowed. As her friends and family shared in her happiness.

When the sun began sinking into the horizon, before they took their leave, the revelers gave them one last round of well-wishes. While Griff accompanied Althea and her husband to their coach for a few final words, Kathryn stood at the edge of the cliff and read the letter Kingsland had sent her.

My dear Mrs. Stanwick,

I debated the wisdom of sending you the enclosed and decided it was something that belonged with you.

I would wish you every happiness, but I find it pointless to wish for what one already possesses.

Yours,
Kingsland

She wasn't surprised his missive was short and to the point, rather suspected marriage to him would have been as exacting. Although, perhaps he'd known nothing that he could say would compare with the additional letter he'd enclosed.

My Lord Duke,

You have asked the ladies to explain why you should honor them by making them your duchess.

I would argue that you do not want a woman who believes it an honor to have your attention. Rather, you should seek out a lady who makes you realize it is an honor to have her attentiveness directed your way.

To that end, I suggest you select Lady Kathryn Lambert, sole daughter, only child, to the Earl of Ridgeway. Unfortunately, the lady does not have a tendency to recognize her own attributes that make her so stunningly appealing to a man, and I have little doubt her letter will put you to sleep before you have finished reading the first paragraph. Therefore, I have taken it upon myself to champion her cause for becoming the next Duchess of Kingsland.

As you no doubt noticed during our encounter at the park, she has a quick wit, a biting tongue, and a sharp mind. She is a keen conversationalist, and while you want quiet in a woman, I believe you would find it a mistake not to seek out her opinion on all matters, whether they relate to your home or your myriad businesses or the management of your various estates. Her thoughts are not muddled but are concise, and she can offer a viewpoint you might not have otherwise considered. I have never known her to be capricious or irritatingly insipid.

Her mere presence will cause a man to yearn to know the intimacy of her thoughts, her secret desires, her touch. Like the finest of wines, she is bold, full-bodied, and tantalizing. Never disappointing. Yet never the same, always offering another aspect to be discovered. A lifetime in her company will never be long enough. She is a complicated, complex creature worthy of any man's heart. I have little doubt that in time, you will willingly place yours into her keeping.

You would be a fool, Kingsland, to let her get away. Trust me on this: there is no woman in all of Christendom who would serve better as your duchess.

Respectfully,
Lord Griffith Stanwick

She clutched the letter to her breast, careful not to crush or crinkle it because she intended to keep it with her forever. Kingsland had the right of it. It did belong with her, as did the man who had written it.

"What did Kingsland have to say?"

Turning, she watched her husband take the final few steps toward her. Then his hands were on her hips, and he was drawing her in close.

"He gave me your letter."

He sighed deeply. "Ah, that poppycock."

With a smile, she draped one arm around his neck and flattened the other against his chest, right where his heart beat, beat for her. "A year ago, I might have believed that it was all lies, but now I know the truth of it. There is no man in all of Christendom who would serve better as my husband."

With a low growl, he claimed her mouth as he had claimed her heart, wildly and passionately.

As the sun bade its final farewell to the day, he lifted her into his arms and began carrying her toward the cottage, where memories to be made awaited and dreams would be seized.

EPILOGUE

Windswept Cottage
Some years later

STANDING AT THE cliff's edge, with the late morning sunlight bearing down on him, Griff watched as his wife and three young daughters, the eldest eight, waded about in the blue water—wearing naught but their undergarments. But there was no one to see.

His wife gave a little screech, raced back to shore, and the wind carried her laughter up to him. A series of squeals from the girls followed as they all rushed out of the water, lifted their arms to the sun, rose up on their tiny bare toes, and began swaying, like saplings caught in a high wind when a rainstorm was coming. Only no storm was on the horizon. The sun had chased away the morning haze and promised a bright day of reflection off the sparkling sea. As one, they took to twirling, a ritual during which they laughed, smiled, and sometimes sang.

He'd never known such peace or contentment. His angels were all without cares or worries, and he was glad of that. He would do anything to ensure it. For his daughters, he'd already set up trusts. At five and twenty, each would be independent. They could marry if they wished but wouldn't have to in order to have anything they desired. No conditions would be set upon them.

Even with the best of intentions, Kathryn's grandmother had nearly damned her to a loveless existence. No, not a loveless existence, merely a marriage. For she would have had his love, if not his name. Always she would have possessed his love. But now she had both.

Glancing up, she held a hand to her brow, shielding her eyes from the sun at his back, and waved. "Come join us!"

He hadn't needed the invitation, had planned to do so, but first he'd wanted a moment to simply enjoy what he now held, what he'd never hoped to attain.

After striding over to the well-worn path that led down to the sea, he made his way along it until he reached the shore. The girls rushed ahead of her to his side, grabbed his hands, not at all bothered by the scars, and smiled up at him with Kathryn's eyes and her hair, and more of her than of him in their features. He'd have not wanted it any other way.

"Papa, will you carry us into the deep?" the eldest asked, their term for the area where the water went to his waist, where they could splash about and create a ruckus while holding on to him.

"Please?" pleaded the middle.

"Pretty please?" asked the youngest.

"I will, but I need a word with your mother first."

"Kiss her, you mean." The eldest was a sharp one and not shy about voicing her opinion.

He grinned. "Well, that, too."

"Go on, girls," Kathryn said. "Work on your castle while I greet your father."

"Kiss him, you mean," the eldest said, then giggled, her sisters joining in, before they all dashed off.

His wife came into his arms and kissed him as though they hadn't made love just a few hours ago, as though he hadn't kissed her thoroughly then. Not that he minded as he pulled her in close.

If he lived to be a hundred, he'd never have enough of this, enough of her.

She drew back and searched his features. "So what was in the post?"

He'd received a letter that morning from Althea, had wanted to read it, and had delayed his coming to the shoreline with her and their girls. The postponement had given him a chance to watch them from afar. He enjoyed basking in the sight of them, to be reminded of how close he'd come to not having any of this. "She's invited us to join her and the family in Scotland for a couple of weeks."

"That will please the girls. They always have fun visiting with their cousins."

Lowering his head, he nibbled on that soft spot just below her ear. "Will it please you?"

"You please me."

"Do I?"

"Mmm. Are you pleased?"

Drawing away, he held her gaze. At that moment the shade of her eyes matched the sea. "How can I not be? For a man who was merely to be held in reserve, I think I've done quite well for myself." His club was an immense success. Over the years, he'd made investments that had paid off handsomely. "I have as a wife a woman that a duke had once wanted to wed."

She grinned. "Why would I prefer a duke to a scoundrel? Especially when that scoundrel is all I desire, the scoundrel of my heart." She braced her palms on either side of his jaw. "I love this cottage, but not more than I love you."

"You are everything to me, Kathryn. You and the girls."

He captured her mouth once more, knowing he had a long way to go to being deserving of her, but not being foolish enough to let her go. She completed him, made him whole.

As the breeze blew around him, the seagulls squawked, and the waves lapped at the shore, he lifted her into his arms and swung her around. Her laughter, the sweetest of sounds, echoed around him.

After he'd taken each of his girls into the deep, he was going to take his wife back to the cottage she treasured and to the bed where he could show her how much he treasured her. With her, nothing about his birth or his past mattered. All that mattered was their love.

Author's Note

I<small>N THE EARLY</small> part of the nineteenth century, until at least the 1850s, *cock and hen* clubs existed throughout the less affluent sections of London, providing a place for unattached men and women to meet, pair up, go off somewhere, and spend an intimate evening together. A singles club, as it were. Eventually they began to fade away, the sexual aspect turning more toward a socializing bent, where people simply enjoyed music and other entertainments.

While it is unlikely that Griff would have found one to visit in his wild youth, literary license is a wonderful thing—and it's possible the rare one might have still been around to serve as inspiration for his club.

COMING SOON

The next book in the
Once Upon a Dukedom series.

The
Duchess Hunt

The Duke of Kingsland is still in need
of a duchess. But what if the perfect
woman for him is the one he can't have?